THE
DEVIL
INSIDE

SUSAN K. HAMILTON

This is a work of fiction. Names, characters, organizations, places, events, and incidents are either products of the author's imagination or are used fictitiously.

Copyright © 2020 Susan K. Hamilton
All rights reserved.

No part of this book may be reproduced, or stored in a retrieval system, or transmitted in any form or by any means, electronic, mechanical, photocopying, recording, or otherwise, without express written permission of the publisher.

Published by Inkshares, Inc., Oakland, California
www.inkshares.com

Edited by Lizette Clarke
Cover design by Charlene Maguire
Interior design by Kevin G. Summers

ISBN: 9781950301201
e-ISBN: 9781950301195
Library of Congress Control Number: 2021935526

First edition

Printed in the United States of America

*"We are all searching for someone
whose demons play well with ours."*
—*Unknown*

This book is dedicated to all of the wonderful readers out there—especially those who took a leap of faith and supported *The Devil Inside* during Launch Pad 2016, as well as those who have waited so patiently to read the "real thing."

CHAPTER 1

SHAKING THE RAIN off her shoulders, Mara Dullahan hustled into Bruisers Sports Bar, her favorite restaurant in all of Hollis City. Located at 45 Joyal Street, the bar—much like Hollis City itself—looked rather average on the outside. Inside, however, it was expansive and inviting, with a large dining area and massive U-shaped bar. Dozens of TV sets broadcast nearly every available sports competition, and since it was within walking distance from several hotels and the Hollis City Convention Center, Bruisers was often frequented by travelers, but it was a popular and well-known haunt for regulars as well.

Mara was one of those regulars.

The bar was only about half-full, but Mara knew that as soon as the convention center disgorged its contents, many of the jaded and restless businesspeople would find their way to Bruisers in short order for burgers, beer, and whatever else tickled their fancies. She slid into one of the seats, put her phone on the bar, and then tied back her thick dark hair. The sleek length fell over her shoulder.

"Hey there, Mara." Joe Louis Jones, Bruisers's owner and head bartender, held a glass up to the light, wiped it once more, and put it on the rack. Joe was short and stocky, and his hair was thinning at the top.

"Hi, Joe. What's up?"

"Same shit, different day," he answered with a chuckle.

"Oh, believe me, I know," Mara said with a sigh.

"Drink before dinner?"

"Jameson on the rocks."

"That means it was a tough day at the office." Ice clinked as Joe poured the rich dark liquid with a flourish. She took a sip and relaxed back into her chair.

"Had a prospect get cold feet about a deal we've been working on," Mara told him. She swirled the alcohol in her glass.

"He back out of it?"

A calculated smile curled the corners of her mouth. "Oh hell no. He's just going to need a little more encouragement than I expected. Nothing I can't handle." Mara was not about to lose that deal, not with year-end so close. *That little weasel is not going to screw up my winning streak*, she thought.

In response to her confidence, a chuckle rumbled out of Joe's chest. He excused himself to wait on another customer, and Mara took the opportunity to look around. The bar was a rich hunting ground for prospective clients—there was always some dissatisfied soul, a man who thought he could do better or a woman who thought she'd been wronged. And while she had an extensive list of solid prospects, unexpected gems could often be unearthed in a place like Bruisers.

Taking another sip of her whiskey, Mara savored the smoky flavor and slow burn as she glanced across the bar. One of her coworkers, a man with pockmarked cheeks and slicked-back blond hair, was slouched over a beer. He looked up and gave Mara a nod, his sullen eyes telling her he'd had a really bad day. She returned the gesture. Frankie was one of a handful of coworkers who Mara was friendly with. But as far as she was concerned, it was the end of the week, and she didn't feel like hanging out with anyone from her office. Even someone who she was on good terms with. As Mara finished her drink and flagged Joe down for a second, other patrons started trickling into the bar.

A rather beleaguered-looking middle-aged man dumped his waterlogged coat over the back of the chair next to Mara's, flopped into the seat, and barked for a beer.

"Having a rough day?" Mara asked.

He looked over and raised an eyebrow, clearly trying to puzzle out why Mara was attempting to start a conversation with him, and she elected to ignore the fact that his eyes immediately dropped from her face to her breasts and then stayed there.

He slouched over the bar. "Yeah. I'm in for the convention. My flight from Duluth was delayed, and I missed part of an important customer meeting. So Tony took the lead. Now everyone wants to listen to the new golden boy, and screw the guy with experience."

As annoyed as she was, Mara could smell the waves of discontent rolling off him. She shifted just enough to make the middle button on her shirt strain. It did the trick. The businessman's eyes bulged.

"Well, that sucks. My name's Mara."

"Donald," he answered, still fixated on her button. Mara noticed he never glanced at his wedding ring.

"Nice to meet you, Donald. So, what's this Golden Boy doing?"

"Tony? Bastard." Downing his first beer in a few gulps, Donald called for a second, then scowled and offered Mara a litany of Golden Boy's transgressions and the ineptness of his coworkers, who couldn't see the truth. "I'm due for that damn promotion. I *earned* it, and it's just going to go right to Tony now."

"So, what are you going to do about it?"

"'Do about it'? Get drunk. Try to forget. Maybe have a little fun for a change." Donald grunted as he finally raised his eyes from Mara's cleavage to her face and offered a lame attempt at a charming smile.

"You sound like my type of man."

When Donald's face lit up, her eyes glittered. He was almost on the hook. If she could come to an arrangement with him, she would be one step closer to closing her quarter with style.

"Let's have another drink and, you know, I bet we could come up with some fun ways to make Golden Boy's life miserable."

Mara waited, looking at him over the rim of her glass as she took a drink, letting Donald lose himself in whatever he thought he saw in her dark eyes.

"Maybe we could talk in my room?" Donald's offer was tentative and lacked confidence.

Before Mara could say another word, her phone began to vibrate and buzz like it had been set on fire. She picked it up and frowned at the Urgent Alert icon blinking on her screen. With a tap, she opened the message—*R. Nottingham/ DOA*—before shaking her head in disbelief.

"You've got to be friggin' kidding me. *Now?* What on earth have you done, you stupid SOB?"

"Trouble in paradise?"

Mara sighed. "Something like that. I'm so sorry, Donald, but that's my office and I have to go." She fished cash out of her purse and waved to Joe as she put it on the bar.

"Just my luck." Donald's shoulders slumped.

"Well, things have a way of turning out." Mara slid off the seat. She looked across the bar and caught Frankie's eye before she jerked her head toward Donald. His eyes widened in surprise—because of the many rivalries in the office, favors were typically few and far between. For a split second his eyes flamed red, but he didn't hesitate, and headed around the bar. Mara dawdled long enough for Frankie to pass close by her.

"Seriously? You're down with this?" Frankie whispered, and Mara could hear the disbelief in his voice. She didn't hold it against him. In their line of work, a kind gesture typically came with strings attached.

"For real. He's yours if you can land him," she answered.

"Thanks." There was a lingering trace of doubt in his voice.

"*De nada*. Don't say I never did you a solid, Frankie."

Outside, the night air was crisp and the rain had passed, leaving the pavement shiny under the glow of antique-style streetlamps. Mara hurried down the street for about two blocks. She glanced around, and then over her shoulders, to make sure no one was there before she ducked into a side alley between two older brick buildings. Silently, she moved in the shadows, heading deeper into the darkness.

She raised her hands and beckoned, her eyes glowing crimson. A satisfied smile crossed her face as the shadows responded to her call, peeling away from the brick, slithering and undulating down the walls and across the fractured pavement. Reaching her feet, the darkness eddied and churned, circling around her and rising higher, begging for her attention. Raising her arms, Mara drew the darkness up until it enfolded her, and she vanished into nothingness.

The front end of the magnificent black Maserati GranTurismo Sport was completely smashed into the trunk of a massive tree. The echoes of the crash had dissipated and the only sound left was the faint hiss of the radiator somewhere in the wreckage.

Mara folded her arms and tapped a foot. She didn't enjoy waiting. With an impatient sigh, she uncrossed her arms and looked at her fingernails. They were painted a beige color that had a gold shimmer in it, and she'd picked the color simply based on the name: "Tart with a Heart."

She glanced up when she heard a low, faint moan inside the car. She rolled her eyes and thought, *Oh, for the love of . . . Would you just die already, you stubborn bastard? I have better things to do than wait for you all night.* When an alert said DOA, she expected DOA. Mara made a mental note to have a word with the clerk who'd sent it.

Pacing around the car, Mara assessed the damage and offered a passing glance at the other body lying crumpled on the grass. Whoever the dying blond woman was, she wasn't Mara's problem. Behind her, Mara heard the whisper of wings. She looked over her shoulder as an angel softly touched down on the springy turf. He folded his wings back, tamping down their luminescence.

"Hey, Yehudiah. Been a while," Mara said cheerfully as the angel offered her a polite nod. She eyed his suit, glad that she'd taken the opportunity to transform her own outfit, from the stuffy corporate blouse and suit she'd been wearing at Bruisers to something more comfortable, more "her." Being able to change appearance while moving through shadows was one of the perks of moving up the ranks in Hell.

Compared to the angel, they were a study in contrasts. Yehudiah, with his salt-and-pepper hair, was dressed in a well-fitted gray suit with a solid-blue tie. Mara was now decked out in slim jeans and over-the-knee black boots that had chains and jewels strapped around the ankles. Her tank top was black, and spelled out across her chest in red crystals was The Devil Made Me Do It. Her dark hair, replete with red highlights, fell past her shoulders, and something feral and dangerous smoldered in her dark eyes.

"Where's Azrael? He got too much on his plate? Or is collecting collateral damage too far below an archangel's pay grade?"

"Show a little respect," scolded the angel, before giving her a suspicious look. "Why are you here?"

"Give me some credit, Yehudiah. I'm no poacher. The idiot behind the wheel with the nose full of coke? My deal's with him."

Whatever else she or Yehudiah may have wanted to say vanished as a low hum glided through the air, the vibration making the hair on Mara's arms stand up. She knew exactly what that feeling meant: a soul had slipped from its earthly bonds, ready to leave the mortal world for the Immortal Planes. Near the angel, the air thickened and clouded, light flickering inside the translucence, and a woman's form shimmered into existence. Young and blond, she wore a curve-hugging cocktail dress and obscenely high stiletto heels.

"Paula Winslow?" Yehudiah said her name gently, as if he were talking to a child.

"What? Oh . . ." Paula's eyes widened as she looked at them both. She started shaking.

"Who are you? What happened? Where's Ricky? Goddamn it, what's going on?"

The angel winced slightly at the blasphemy.

"Oh, Ricky will be along momentarily. Don't worry your pretty little head over that," Mara said.

Paula spun and stared at the car. "Ricky! You have to help him! Oh God! He's still in there!"

"No one can help Ricky," said Yehudiah, but the Angel of Death's words didn't seem to register. Paula just stared at the mangled chassis of the Maserati.

"We left Ja'Nay's party and were going up to the overlook in Thompson Park. I don't remember any of this. How did I get out of the car . . . ?"

Before Yehudiah could answer, Mara interrupted. "Technically, you didn't 'get out' of the car. You were thrown out."

"Must you do that? This is difficult enough," snapped Yehudiah.

"She deserves the truth. You angels sugarcoat death too much."

"Sugarcoat what? Wait just a damn minute. *Death?* I'm not . . . I can't be . . ." Paula shook her head stubbornly.

"Not what? Not dead? Hate to break it to you, sweetie, but yes, you are. Want to come around here and look at your pretty little corpse?" Mara waved toward the passenger side of the car. Unwilling to look but unable to stop herself, Paula took a few steps and stopped short. On the ground next to the tree was her body. Glass from the car's windshield was embedded in her face, and her blood-soaked cocktail dress was torn. One of her legs was bent entirely in the wrong direction, and her glassy eyes stared up at the sky: empty, blank, and utterly dead.

"See what happens when you don't wear a seat belt?" Mara asked.

Paula wailed in despair.

The mournful sound sent a sharp, swift, and very unexpected stab of regret lancing through Mara, and she flinched. With a quick roll of her shoulders, she dismissed the emotion, but to her dismay, the echoes of it lingered.

CHAPTER 2

WHILE YEHUDIAH TRIED to calm Paula, another hum rippled through the air, a sigh of relief from the universe as another suffering soul crossed between the Planes. The same fuzzy texture clouded the air as a new figure appeared. Mara looked him up and down. He was handsome, she'd give him that: great hair, intense blue eyes, square jaw with a tiny cleft in the middle of it. He had the ready-made looks of a movie star.

"Ricky, you stupid son of a bitch."

Still confused from his transition, Ricky offered Mara a blink and a blank stare. A moment later he seemed to finally recognize her, and he angrily blurted out, "Mara? What the fuck are you doing here?"

"Charming as always, I see."

Ignoring the sarcasm, Ricky whirled to stare at the mangled, leaking wreck that used to be his Maserati. "My car! I just bought the goddamn thing. Son of a bitch, it's totaled."

"Well, you're a quick one today, aren't you? Car's not the only thing totaled there, Einstein."

"Ricky! We're dead. We died in the crash," sobbed Paula, who'd managed to regain a modicum of self-control.

"Dead? I can't be dead. That's complete bullshit. We had a *deal*, Mara. A deal!" Ricky took an aggressive step toward her, and Mara's eyebrows went up sharply.

"Slow that roll, Sparky," she warned.

"A deal? What are you talking about?" Paula interrupted.

Mara sighed. "Paula. Sweetie. Yehudiah's explained to you what he is, yes? So, if he's an angel, logic would dictate that I'm what? Give it your best guess."

Paula's eyes doubled in size. "Oh my God. Are you the Devil?"

Mara threw her head back and laughed before she answered, "Am I the . . . ? Oh, sweetie, no. I'm not *the* Devil. Just *a* devil will do."

Standing straighter, Mara relaxed the iron control she used to conceal her true nature and allowed just a hint of it to shine through. Her eyes turned from deep brown to crimson, flames dancing inside them, while the red highlights in her hair grew more pronounced. Shadows curled and licked around her ankles, begging for her attention, but when she felt the discomfort between her shoulder blades—her wings thirsting to be released—Mara imposed her will again. She couldn't free her wings. Not in front of an angel. Not in front of any immortal.

"We had a deal," Ricky insisted again, but his voice faded and he stepped back as Mara turned toward him, her eyes still flaming.

"We *do* have a deal, but you didn't really pay attention when we made it, did you?"

"I did! You said I could have ten years of being the most famous movie star in the world, and get all the things that go with that. Fame, money, cars, houses, women . . ."

"And then what?" asked Mara.

"After the ten years, you'd come for something."

"'Something'?" Mara prodded.

"Yeah, you said 'something.' I figured it would be money and I'd have plenty of that," Ricky said dismissively.

Mara laughed. "Money? I don't need money. When we sealed our deal, you never made me define what the price was for my help. The 'something' was you, you moron. YOU."

"But it hasn't been ten years—it's only been three," Ricky countered quickly, a whiff of desperation clinging to his words.

"Do you remember what else I said, right before we sealed our deal? I told you that the deal didn't make you invincible. That if you did something completely stupid—like standing in front of an oncoming train and letting it hit you—that you forfeited your unused years? That I wasn't going to miraculously bring you back to life just so you could have the balance of your time?"

"I remember. And I wasn't doing anything stupid!"

"You're kidding, right?" That question came from Yehudiah, and Mara stifled a laugh.

"Ricky," she said, "you hit a buck twenty in your Maserati while you were completely coked out. I don't know, call me old-fashioned, but I think that qualifies as pretty fucking stupid." Mara looked over at Yehudiah, and although she suspected that he agreed with her, the angel refrained from additional commentary.

"And even better for me, you took poor little Paula with you. It wasn't her time to die, you know. She just had the bad luck to agree to give you a blowjob in your brand-new toy," Mara continued. Paula gasped and blushed, and Yehudiah looked decidedly uncomfortable.

"What? C'mon, what's with everyone?" Mara rolled her eyes. "You are so uptight. There's absolutely nothing wrong with being able to give great head."

"It wasn't my time to die?" Paula's voice was barely a squeak.

Yehudiah's voice was soothing and deep: "No, it wasn't—not really. All mortals have a day and a time when they are supposed to die, but it doesn't always happen that way. Sometimes the choices you make cause the plan to go awry."

"You're probably better off," Mara said.

"'Better off'? But what about the life I was supposed to have?" Paula sounded defeated.

"It wasn't going to be the life you dreamed of. Yehudiah, we should tell her what she would have been in for if this accident never happened. What her life would have been like with Mr. Movie Star here."

"That won't do anyone any good, Mara," said the angel. He looked at Paula. "We should go."

"Might make her feel better about being dead," Mara insisted.

Paula wrung her hands, her apprehension ratcheting up again, and the angel glared at Mara. Anxious, regretful souls were much harder to transition.

"You're. Not. Helping." The angel bit out each word.

"Depends on your perspective," the devil replied.

"Tell me," Paula demanded.

Mara came over to stand close to Paula, her flames diminishing and her eyes turning back to the deep brown they were before she let the flames shine through. Her voice softened with a touch of empathy: "Ricky here is—well, he *was*—bad news. If you'd made it to the overlook, you'd have gone down on him like you promised, and it would have been great. He would have kept you around for a little while. But he would have gotten you into the coke too. And when you got too strung out and turned into a liability, he would have cut you loose and found his next sweet young thing. You would have ended up on the street doing disgusting things for your next hit, and your family back in Ohio would have spent their days waiting for a call from LAPD telling them you'd overdosed or been murdered."

"You don't know that," Paula whispered, horrified.

"I *do* know that." Mara's voice was a little sad. "Go with Yehudiah, Paula. He'll take care of you—you really are going to a better place. A lot better than where Ricky's going."

Mara glanced up in time to see surprise flash across the Angel of Death's face, and she thought, *Are you really surprised? I'm a devil, Yehudiah, not a monster.*

Sirens wailed in the distance. Mara told Yehudiah, "You should go. She's seen enough."

"On that, we are agreed."

Yehudiah moved to stand next to Paula, but then paused. He cocked his head slightly and looked at Mara thoughtfully, as if he were weighing a serious decision, then said, "Peace be with you, Mara."

"Not easy in my line of work, but I'll try," Mara answered.

Yehudiah unfurled his magnificent white wings. Each feather was touched with a silvery-golden light, and he stretched the wings out to gather Paula closer to him. Enveloped by warmth and light, her face moved from terrified and angry to awestruck to calm.

"I'm not angry with him anymore," Paula said to the Angel of Death, her voice tinted with wonder.

"That's part of the process," he answered.

"There was a lot more I wanted to do," Paula said.

"I know," Yehudiah said. "Are you ready to go?"

"I am." There was resignation in her whispered reply.

Mara raised her arm to shield her eyes as Yehudiah's aura swelled until he and Paula were both lost inside it. In an instant the glow vanished and they were both gone. The serenity of the moment was ruined by slow sarcastic applause from Ricky.

"Well, that was lovely. Hope Heaven knows what they're getting with that little slut. Is this the part where you drag me down to Hell?"

Mara's fingernails dug into her palms. "Not quite yet. We still have a little time here."

Ricky lit up. "Ha! You can't take me, can you? Maybe I'm still alive in the wreck. Maybe they're going to save my ass!"

Any empathy that Paula may have stirred within Mara vanished, and with a feral growl, Mara's hand shot out. She grabbed Ricky by the ear. He screamed and clawed at her arm as she yanked him toward the wreckage.

"There! Take a good look at yourself. Does that look like you have any hope for resuscitation?" she shouted.

Ricky stared at his own body. Strapped in the driver's seat, it was twisted and broken, his face battered from the air bag. Blood soaked his fancy white shirt, trickling down from his neck where a piece of metal from the Maserati's windshield wiper had punctured it. He was stone-cold dead, and as Ricky grappled with his new reality, three police officers and two paramedics rushed onto the scene. It didn't take long for them to assess the situation and pronounce both Ricky and Paula dead.

"Tell you what," Mara said, "I'm in no real rush. Why don't we hang out for a bit, so you can watch them pry your body out of the car?"

A California state trooper walked by Ricky without so much as a passing glance. Ricky started to huff about the trooper's rudeness and then paused. Mara waited for him to work it out, but it seemed he refused to understand.

"Why doesn't he see me?"

"You're a ghost, dumbass, a disembodied soul. No one can see you now. Well, that's not entirely true: A real psychic might be able to see you, but the average Joe? Nope. We're actually in the Null."

"The Null?"

"The Null Plane. The universe is made up of two major planes of existence: the Mortal Plane, where you used to live before your little incident here, and the Immortal Plane. That's made up of Heaven and Hell. The Null Plane is where the two overlap. Right now we're standing at the edge of the Null Plane, so we can see what's going on in the Mortal Plane, but they can't see us. Essentially, we're invisible."

"Souls just wander around this Null place?" Ricky asked.

"A few that slip through the cracks do—that's how psychics can talk to the dead sometimes. But we keep a pretty close eye on the place. Any soul who dies without a contract comes here first to be processed and judged, and then they get sent to Heaven or Hell. But when someone has a contract—like you—we get to skip right to the main event."

As Mara talked, the paparazzi circled the scene, drawn by the scent of carrion and headlines, while Ricky watched, horrified, as one paramedic removed his lower leg—which had been completely severed—from the car and dropped it on a plastic mat. He swallowed hard and Mara smiled at him smugly.

"You're enjoying this too much," he whined.

"You have no idea. Come on. As much as I'd like to let you watch them pry the rest of you out of the car, that's going to take too long. Time for us to go."

Mara held her hand up, palm out, and a red glow materialized around her hand. The light intensified as she spread her fingers and flames filled her eyes again. A wind no one else seemed to feel swirled her hair as the red energy flowed out from her hand. About thirty feet away, the energy took on a life of its own. Crackling and snapping, it latched on, digging into whatever it had found, creating a flaming rectangular outline. The flames spread to fill the interior, and in a single flash the firestorm disappeared, leaving behind an utterly plain and ordinary white kitchen door in the middle of the grass.

Ricky looked skeptical. "That's the door to Hell?"

"You were expecting some cavernous, gaping maw spewing sulfur and brimstone?"

A door hinge squeaked ominously, and the door expelled a wave of hot air that rolled over them. Ricky swallowed hard and licked his lips, his eyes darting furtively from side to side. He backed up a step. Mara watched with amusement.

"Going somewhere?" she asked.

"I . . . I want to renegotiate," Ricky said to her.

Mara offered him an unladylike snort. "Renegotiate? With what? You don't have anything else that I want, and you're dead. We have a deal, Ricky, and you can't break it."

"I won't go," Ricky blustered.

"Seriously?" Mara's amusement deteriorated quickly.

"You can't make me."

"I can't 'make you'? What are you, a fucking four-year-old?" Mara snapped her fingers, and instantly two bulky demons stepped through the doorway. While they had somewhat human features, they possessed pitch-black eyes and disconcertingly sharp white teeth that showed when they smiled. They were the muscle in Hell, the blue-collar workers.

"You paged us?" one asked, his voice rough and guttural.

"Time to earn your paychecks, boys. Little Ricky here thinks he can tell me no."

They grinned again. Sometimes the demons didn't play well with devils, who they considered corporate lackeys, but Mara knew they'd help her because she always treated them fairly. The two seized Ricky by the arms and dragged him over to Mara as if he weighed almost nothing. He struggled anyway, and Mara just shook her head. She was perfectly capable of dragging Ricky through the door, but that's what demons were for. In Hell, they were mostly the muscle, the labor—although a few had worked their way into lower-level management jobs. And as a reward from time to time, demons were allowed to run amok on the Mortal Plane. Whenever they did, local churches were inundated with calls about possessions and other immortal mischief.

"Bring him," Mara ordered tersely.

The two demons followed Mara, dragging a thrashing Ricky between them. There was an ominous boom when the door shut, and Ricky went limp. The demons continued to drag him in Mara's wake down a long austere office hallway. On one side, offices with mostly closed doors. On the other side, a seemingly eternal field of identical high-walled beige cubicles with soul-sucking fluorescent lights hanging from the ceiling. With a nod from Mara, the two escorts dropped Ricky and he crumpled to the floor.

"Now, are you going to walk like a grown-up, or do we still need to help you along?" asked Mara.

"I'll walk."

Mara dismissed the two demons with a flick of her hand. Ricky slowly climbed to his feet and glanced from side to side. Different demons and devils came in and out of the cubes and offices that lined the hallways, bustling around with files and laptops. The devils looked very human, aside from their leathery wings. Many of the demons, however, also sported horns, claws, and fangs.

Shouting erupted from one office and Ricky whipped his head around, startled. Inside, a large demon dressed in a crisp white polo shirt lunged across the desk at a smaller one. The larger demon opened a gaping maw, dislocating his jaw, and clamped down on his coworker and then jerked his head back, swallowing his flailing victim whole in two gulps. Now twice the size he'd been, the big demon's polo shirt strained to hold in his engorged belly, and a tremendous juicy belch erupted out of him.

"What the . . ." Ricky gasped.

"Not surprising." Mara sighed. "Wayne was on his last warning. He knew what would happen if he got called down to HR again."

"Called down to HR? I thought you were taking me to Hell?"

"Oh, you're in Hell, sweetie. This is just a very small part of it. People assume Hell is just one fiery pit of horrors. There's plenty of that, don't get me wrong—all stereotypes start from a kernel of truth, right? But this is the business end of Hell, and where we start. Paperwork and all that."

"Hell's a . . . corporation?"

"No, Hell's just a division. Heaven and Hell make up one big company—Immortal Planes Incorporated, fondly referred to by the rank and file as IPI. Lucifer is the managing director of Hell, and Archangel Michael is the managing director of Heaven. Devils report to Lucifer, angels to Michael and the other archangels, and they all report directly to God—our fearless leader, the chairman and CEO."

They continued walking, taking lefts and rights until they finally stopped in front of an office door. The heavy brass sign in the center said Treasurers. Inside, the office was ornate, with a dark paneling on the walls and thick luxurious Persian rugs on the floor. Along the wall opposite the door were two windows covered with heavy velvet drapes, and in front of each window was an enormous mahogany desk. The legs of each desk were magnificently carved into twisted tableaus of debauchery, decadence, and sin: naked satyrs entangled with men and women, corrupt souls gorging on wine, and sinners debasing themselves for piles of gold.

Astaroth, the devil behind the first desk, was gaunt, with the stern countenance of an older man, save for his soulless coal-black eyes. His desk was pristine: files neatly stacked, all the same type of pen in the cup holder, and not a speck of dust to be seen. He wore a dark suit with a narrow tie and tapped away at his computer with thin, elegant fingers.

The other desk had several files stacked up and askew to one side of the computer. On the other side sat an antique scale with two brass dishes to hold whatever was being weighed. The demon seated at this desk was a hulking beast, with fangs that protruded up from a jutting lower jaw, the face all the more terrifying for the jagged scar that ran down his left cheek. His small, piggish eyes glittered, and his fingernails looked more like pointed claws.

With Ricky in tow, Mara waltzed up to the first desk. "Hello, Astaroth."

One of the Grand Dukes of Hell—and Mara's direct supervisor—Astaroth finished his entry on the computer and looked down his nose at her.

"Who have you brought us, Mara?"

"I have one Richard 'Ricky' Nottingham."

Astaroth clicked a few times with his mouse, and his frown grew more pronounced. "Nottingham, you say? He's not expected for some years yet. Why is he out of order?"

"He got stupid and cocky. Fast car, cocaine, pretty girl who promised to go down on him. Drove his car straight into a tree."

An annoyed sigh hissed out of Astaroth's nose and he lanced Ricky with a disapproving glare. Finally, after sweat beaded on Ricky's forehead, the skeletal devil said, "Very well. There is space for him?"

"Of course there is. I'm insulted you think I'd be unprepared." Mara smiled under the Grand Duke's icy, dead stare until he grunted and looked back at his screen.

"Fine. Get him weighed and make sure you update the database promptly. I don't want any loose ends once we close the quarter. I will be very unhappy if anyone from my team is on the delinquent list this time." He handed Mara a file, and dismissed them with a wave of his fingers.

"What does he mean, 'weigh me'?"

Mara ignored Ricky's question as she tugged his elbow, pulling him along to the other desk. She smiled up at Melchom as the bulky demon loomed over her. She'd always been fond of him, and as his fetid, dank breath enveloped them, Ricky made an odd noise.

"Do *not* throw up," she warned him.

"Hello, pretty Mara," said Melchom in his deep, booming voice.

"Hello, Melchom."

"Do you have it?" the enormous devil asked.

"I will in a minute." She turned to Ricky with a savage smile. "I've really been looking forward to this. Man up, Ricky, because it's going to hurt like a bitch."

"Looking forward to wha—AAAAAAGGGGHHHH!"

Ricky screamed in agony as Mara thrust her hand into his torso and started digging around his insides. Melchom leered down, reveling in Ricky's suffering, knowing that each time Mara moved her hand, Ricky felt as if razors were stripping him from the inside out. Mara bit her lip and leaned in, feeling her way around Ricky's innards.

"He held it down before, but I bet if you poke his heart, he will throw up," Melchom said.

"That seems excessive, doesn't it?" asked Mara, and Melchom pouted.

As she twisted her hand again, coming shockingly close to Ricky's heart anyway, she smiled as she found something solid and warm. Slowly, Mara withdrew her fist and Ricky watched—stunned—as the gaping hole in his chest simply closed and the bloodstains on his shirt vanished.

"What the *fuck*?" he screamed.

Melchom's response bordered on gleeful. "You're a disembodied soul now. You can feel pain, you can even bleed, but you won't ever die, no matter how bad it gets."

"What did you do to me?" Ricky asked as he ran his hands over his chest.

Mara opened her fist. Resting in her hand was a black coin about the size of her palm, and it glittered as the light hit it as if a million gold flecks were frozen inside. Bouncing the coin, Mara tested the weight and then handed it up to Melchom, who took it between two thick fingers. Placing the coin on one side of the scale, he added some square weights to the other before carefully watching the dial and registering a weight.

"Very nice, Mara. This one made the most of his time," said Melchom. "A shame he's here now. The tarnish would have been twice as heavy if he'd been smarter." He lifted the coin again and carved a circular piece out of the very center with one of his claws. He dropped the now donut-shaped coin into his coffer, smiling when he heard it clink heavily against the others, and tossed the central nugget back to Mara.

Catching it, Mara gave Ricky a grin. "Cheers," she said as she popped the section of black coin into her mouth and swallowed.

For a moment there was nothing. Then Mara closed her eyes as she felt the coin burn all the way down her throat, and when it reached her stomach, the familiar, invigorating warmth of the tarnish radiated out through the rest of her body. The sigh that escaped her was sated and happy.

"What was that?" Ricky demanded. "What did you take out of me?"

"That was all the tarnish on your soul," Mara answered. "All souls have power, and that power has value. The more awful things you do in your life, the more tarnish collects on your soul. When I close a deal, and the contract comes to an end, I then bring the soul to Astaroth and Melchom. When I pull all the tarnish out of you, it becomes that shiny black coin. They judge my success by how heavy the coin is—the heavier the coin, the more valuable it is, and I get a percentage of that power."

"So you . . . benefit from our deal?"

"Well, duh. Of course I benefit. That's what making a deal is all about. Both sides benefit. Why would I make a deal that didn't have something in it for me?"

"This one. He is not very smart," Melchom observed.

"No, he's not," Mara agreed. "This one is eye candy. I wasn't interested in his brains when I made his deal."

The big demon chuckled, while Mara took Ricky by the arm and escorted him out of the treasurers' office and down another hall. Finally she took a right and stopped at a medium-sized office. Her name was on the plaque outside the door.

"You have an office?" Ricky still sounded utterly confounded.

"I do. I'm in sales and acquisitions for Hell. You seem a bit overwhelmed, so let me refresh you: Hell's a division of IPI—that stands for Immortal Planes Incorporated, to be precise. I spend a lot of my time on the Mortal Plane—that's where you used to live—but I do get stuck down here doing paperwork every now and then, so I got the office." Mara left Ricky in the hall for a split second while she threw the file that Astaroth had given her onto her desk.

"However," she continued, "Hell has layers upon layers. Dante was on the right track with his circles of Hell idea. But it is so much more than that. There's plenty of fire, pain, and torture, but that's the funny thing about torment and torture—it's different for everyone. What is hell for you may not be hell for someone else."

Out in the hall, Ricky was staring at the opposite wall, where there was a shimmering black void. Mara let him gape for a second before she gestured for Ricky to precede her. He swallowed hard and took a step back, looking fearfully at the swirling, inky darkness.

"Don't make me call my minions again. You won't like what they do this time," she warned. Ricky took a mincing, reluctant step forward and Mara rolled her eyes in disgust.

"Sack up," she told him. "The first step's a bitch."

Ricky screamed when Mara put both her hands between his shoulder blades and shoved, sending him sprawling through the darkness and into nothingness. He plummeted down, images flashing in front of him. Some were scenes of souls suffering horrible tortures and torments. Others were phantasmagoria of his life: all the times he'd lied and cheated, all the times he'd been a ruthless bastard to get what he wanted. Even worse, he could feel the emotions of the people he had screwed over, each one slashing him with a razor's edge. He slammed hard and face-first into something, the impact making him see stars. A moment later Mara landed lightly next to him, as if she'd just stepped off a porch.

"That sucked," Ricky moaned.

"Like I said, first step's a bitch. Come on, superstar, we're almost there."

Defeated, Ricky followed Mara into another long hallway lined with what seemed like an eternity of identical closed doors on either side. Each had a small window in the middle of the door and a brass nameplate just below it.

"Another hallway?" Ricky asked.

"Not just another hallway. This is my hallway. This is where I keep every soul I made a deal with, once their contract has come due and I've collected them."

They reached one particular door, and he saw that the brass nameplate was engraved with his own name. Ricky moaned.

"No one forced you into this deal, Ricky," Mara reminded him.

His shoulders slumped. "I know. So, what's my eternal hell? Flames? Sulfur and brimstone? Ugly women and bad wine?" His attempt at flippant bravado was weak.

"Oh no, nothing like that. Do you remember when we first met? I asked you what you really wanted, even beyond fame and money. What did you tell me?"

"I wanted to be the greatest actor ever."

"True, that was the outcome you wanted, but what—deep down—did you *really* want?" Mara cocked her head slightly.

"Just that . . ."

Based on Ricky's perplexed look, Mara knew the question was beyond his grasp, so she opened the door and ushered Ricky into a room that looked like nothing but a gray box.

"Being an actor was the vehicle you chose, but what you wanted—what you *truly desired*—was to be extraordinary, to stand out from the crowd. You were so afraid of being overlooked and marginalized. Terrified of blending into the background the way you always did when you were a kid. You wanted to make sure you were never invisible again."

"I suppose." Ricky's words were simple, but the tone told Mara her own words had hit quite deeply.

"You were so desperate to avoid that fate, you were willing to trade your soul away for just a taste of it. So, here's your damnation, Ricky." Mara waved her arm in an arc and suddenly the gray walls were replaced with the hustle and bustle of Hollywood. The sidewalks were filled with celebrities and tourists.

Ricky laughed. "This? *This* is my Hell? Hollywood? I'm king of this town!" He sauntered down the sidewalk, glancing at the stars beneath his feet emblazoned with the names of all his idols.

From the doorway, Mara said, "Not in *this* Hollywood, you're not. Here, you're nothing. No one knows your name. No one even notices you or cares what happens to you. You're going to be invisible here, Ricky, working menial jobs, completely beneath the notice of your beloved glitterati. You're a nobody, and you're going to remain a nobody—forever."

She watched him try to get the attention of some people who passed by him. "Hey! I'm Ricky Nottingham! Don't you recognize me?" People averted their eyes and stepped away from him.

Ricky spun to face Mara, eyes wide and chest heaving. "You can't do this to me!"

"Ah yeah, I can. Enjoy eternity." She gave him a jaunty wave and slammed the door, the resounding thud of the bolt lock echoing down the long hall. And while she couldn't hear him, Mara knew that on the other side of the door, Ricky was pounding on it with his fists and screaming. She whistled a merry tune as she continued walking. On the way, she peeked in on a few of her other deals to see how they were faring with their own punishments.

Chastity LeGrasse, the former homecoming queen who lied to get whatever she wanted, wasn't Mara's most valuable contract, but Mara had been amazed at how shortsighted the woman had been. Chastity had bartered away her soul to be, as she so quaintly put it, "the queen bee of my hive." So she spent her time dominating her husband and children, and viciously lying about anyone who challenged or threatened her spot as leader of the PTA. Now, locked away in her hellish prison cell, Chastity woke up every day to new situations that compelled her to lie, and each time a falsehood left her mouth, it was followed by a spewing fountain of vomit.

As Mara shut the observation window, she shook her head. "You could have been anything, Chastity. Anything. But you settled for queen bee."

In the room next to Chastity, a corrupt sheriff from Wichita, who died in 1873, was spending his eternal torment in a more traditional way: pulled apart on a rack, day after day after day. Mara didn't bother looking in on the sheriff—she wasn't interested in seeing torn flesh and broken bones, at least not today. Instead she crossed the hall and peeked into one other window.

To fund his own extravagant lifestyle, Edward Boch had stolen millions of dollars from his company's pension fund and gotten away with it, leaving the miners it was supposed help with almost no retirement funds. Inside his room, Edward swung his sledgehammer and smashed it into stone. He paused, his arms trembling with exhaustion, until a supervisor chewed him out for being lazy. Crying, Edward struggled to lift the hammer again. Satisfied with his misery, Mara closed the window and walked away.

Eventually she came to the end of the hall, where a black iron gate barred her way. Beyond the gate was the "real" Hell, or at least what most mortals thought Hell would be like. Jagged cliffs rose higher than the eye could see, all pockmarked with caves filled with fire, pain, and suffering, while demons and imps crawled or flew between the levels. Some of the older devils insisted on these kinds of traditional torturous punishments. They were Hell's OGs and did things with their own special flair, but Mara preferred a more creative take on how to best give a sinner their just desserts.

Sometimes Mara found it refreshing to walk the cliffs, but decided to skip her stroll today. Instead she headed back to her office, glancing once at Ricky's locked door. She loathed the extra paperwork that came with a premature soul delivery. *But Astaroth will be up my ass with a microscope if I don't update the database.*

Mara hated close of quarter, especially at the end of the year. Everyone got uptight and bitchy about the numbers— everyone's bonus was riding on them, and if anyone screwed up, there was hell to pay. And an angry phone call from Astaroth was something she very much wanted to avoid.

It took her an hour to get all of Ricky's files updated and by the time she was done, she was tired of her drab little office and wanted to get back to Hollis City. As she stepped out of her office, Mara nearly collided with Kemm, her biggest rival in the sales and acquisitions group. They'd spent years climbing the ranks together, often butting heads and fighting for the same souls. The fact that they detested each other was common knowledge, and a quarter rarely went by without the two mixing it up over something.

"Mara, you bitch," he growled. "He was mine!"

Mara smiled at his furious expression. The week before, she'd managed to swoop in and steal a client Kemm had been working to close. This corrupt judge was a feeder for a network of for-profit prisons and was getting kickbacks for handing out maximum sentences for minor crimes. "Seriously? You're still pissed off about that judge?"

"That was my deal, my soul!"

"Your deal? Then you should've done a better job closing it. You know the rules—everything's fair game until a deal is sealed, and handshakes don't count," Mara said. "You snooze, you lose."

"You knew I was coming back to close him." Fire began to blaze in Kemm's eyes.

"You not paying attention isn't my fucking problem." Mara shrugged. "I'm not losing my number-one status to a hack like you—not this quarter. Plus, the judge thought my ass was a lot nicer than yours."

"You owe me, bitch. We'll see how nice your ass is when I'm through with it. Your office will do just fine. Let's see how much you like getting fucked, Mara." The threat in his voice was obvious and Kemm's eyes turned completely red.

In an instant Mara's irises went from dark to crimson. She channeled her dark power into her hands and crouched, waiting for him to attack. Mara was so intent on anticipating Kemm's strike, she didn't see Melchom lumbering down the hall until he dropped his meaty, clawed hand onto her rival's head and squeezed. Under the viselike grip, blood trickled down Kemm's head and face.

"You will not speak to Mara that way, fool," Melchom growled.

"I could have taken care of this," Mara said, relaxing slightly. The swirling black-and-red balls of demon-fire in her palms dissipated, but her eyes continued to flame.

Melchom's toothy smile was crooked. "I know. But I do not like it when people are rude to you. Do you understand that, Kemm? You will not be rude to my Mara."

The other devil squealed in pain and tried to nod. Finally the treasurer let go and Kemm staggered away, listing to one side, finger marks clearly dented into his cranium.

"Doesn't matter," Kemm hissed as he looked back, his face a mask of unadulterated malice. "I'm ahead of you in numbers this quarter. Wrecking your chance at the record will be plenty of payback. For now."

Mara blew him a kiss, then turned to hide her frown. She was acutely aware that Kemm was ahead of her on the sales leaderboard right now—and that was a problem.

"You are very pretty with your flames, Mara. You should let them out, wear them down more often," Melchom observed, his rough voice surprisingly soft.

"Outside of Hell, most people don't feel that way. And here, it brings attention I don't necessarily want—but thank you for the compliment."

"Then you should spend more time here," Melchom said gruffly. "Here with us."

"If I did that, I wouldn't bring more shiny black coins for your coffers. But I'll come back soon; you have my word."

Melchom laughed loudly and it made the walls shake. "A devil's promise? You are very funny, Mara. You make me laugh." He gave her a remarkably gentle pat on the head and stomped down the hallway.

Mara watched him go and then sat back down inside her office. She let out a sigh and put her head on the desk. The average devil's quota was around fifty signed contracts for the year, but for a top performer like Mara, the number was much higher; this year, it was one hundred. She still needed five more, and the clock was ticking. She sat up and rubbed her face with her hands.

"All right, Mara," she said to herself. "Get a grip. Focus on the positive. All you need is a few more souls, and you hit quota, and you're not on The List."

The List was a report given to all the Grand Dukes about which members of their teams didn't meet quota. No one liked being on The List, as it usually meant far too much personal "coaching" from the senior leadership team. Mara didn't even want to contemplate it, and her manager—Astaroth—was one of the more reasonable Grand Dukes. Her eyes darted to a sticky note on her monitor with a big 625 written on it. That was her real goal.

"That's the ticket," she muttered to herself. "Six hundred and twenty-five consecutive quarters of being *el número uno* in acquisitions. That would put me one quarter ahead of Grand Duke Baliel's best, making me one of the top two sales and acquisition agents of all time. After that, I only have to catch Lucifer to be the best ever."

She took a deep breath. Aside from bragging rights, the number-one sales person on each team was awarded an extra glittering black coin of tarnish, the equivalent of one thousand souls. Obtaining that coin—and adding all that extra concentrated power to her own—would make her virtually untouchable.

"I have to make my quarterly quota. But after that, I just have to be one ahead of Kemm. He's the only thing standing between me and that record." Mara rubbed the bridge of her nose. "I need a goddamn drink."

CHAPTER 3

TIME ON THE Mortal Plane moved a little differently than it did in Heaven and Hell, so when Mara finished with Ricky, she'd been away from Hollis City for nearly three days. She materialized in a back alley not far from her apartment at 42B Joyal Street, which just happened to be across the street from Bruisers and upstairs from Justa Cuppa, a funky little gourmet coffee shop. With a thought, her clothes transformed from her jeans and sequined top into a navy silk shirt and tan pencil skirt with sensible navy heels.

She sighed. The outfit was excruciatingly dull, but leather and sequins didn't exactly scream "business consultant," and there were bound to be a few lonely souls at Bruisers tonight. She only had until the end of December, and that quota wasn't going to fill itself.

Mara considered going up to her apartment first, but decided to go right to Bruisers. She took a quick look up and down the street, and after a green Mazda buzzed by, she trotted across the road and went inside. It was a Monday night, so the place was starting to fill up for the football game. The Hollis City Hornets were the NFL's newest franchise, and they were the featured game of the week to kick off the season. Townies were rabid supporters of their new team, and hopes were high for this year. The bar was half-full and most of the dining tables were taken.

Mara took a quick look around, taking an inventory of the clientele. She loved Hollis City. Back in the day, when it was just a little town named Hollis, Joyal Street and Main Street met in the exact center of town, which was exactly two blocks west of where Bruisers was located. Crossroads were very special places. They were where decisions were made: Go east or west? Press on or go home? Propose or break up? Sign the deal or lose your chance? The energy generated by all those decisions—great and small—attracted humans, even though they didn't know why. And where there were humans making choices, there were angels and devils.

Another quick scan of the bar told Mara that several angels and devils were mixed in and among the mortals. She recognized Frankie, and then scowled when she noticed Kemm in a far corner of the room. Two other devils were there but she didn't know their names. When they glanced up, a momentary flash of red glinted in their eyes—not unlike the glowing quality of a cat's eyes—and betrayed their immortal nature to her. Humans couldn't detect that reflective sheen, and Mara wondered what they'd think if they realized who they were really drinking with.

A few seats down from Frankie, Mara noticed a blond man nursing a tequila on the rocks. He glanced toward the door, a split-second sheen of gold in his eyes, then frowned and went back to his drink.

That is one bummed-out angel. I wonder who peed in his cereal this morning, Mara thought.

"Hey, Mara." Joe put a coaster in front of her and offered a wide smile.

"Hi, Joe. How's your day been?"

"Usual stuff, can't complain. What can I get you? Your usual?"

"Shot and a beer," she agreed with a nod.

"Absolutely." He took the glasses off the shelf behind him. "Where you been? Haven't seen you for a couple of days."

"Just got back from a little work trip out to Cali."

"How was it?" Joe asked as he poured the shot of Jameson.

"Fine. Not much time to enjoy the weather, though. Had a client who was a little difficult, but it worked out. He got exactly what he signed up for in his contract." She shrugged.

"Didn't like his deal?" The bartender put the drinks in front of her.

"People never do when it comes down to the brass tacks." Mara knocked back the shot. "They never read the fine print, and then they get pissed at me because they were lazy."

"They do say the devil's in the details," Joe said with a confident nod.

"Indeed, they do." Mara couldn't help but smile at his comment. Joe would have a cow if he knew what she really was and realized how many of his clients were immortal beings.

"But speaking of raw deals . . ." Joe gestured up at the TV, which was showing an abbreviated report of the terrible car accident that had taken the life of actor Ricky Nottingham and his companion earlier in the week. "That Ricky guy got shafted, didn't he? Just when his career was taking off with those action movies. He sure had the world by the balls."

"He sure did. I bet he would have had quite the career. But your luck tends to run out when you put too much of the snowflake up your nose."

"Cokehead? Huh."

"I don't know personally, but that's the rumor out there," Mara said.

"That's what happens when you don't raise your kids right, and let 'em do whatever they want. Bet your parents weren't like that," grumbled Joe, half to himself and half to Mara.

"I guess." Mara kept her answer noncommittal—the last thing she wanted to talk about were parents, especially hers.

"Want anything to eat tonight?"

"Yes, I'm starving! Plus, Monday is your bacon cheeseburger and cheese fries special, Joe. How could I not have that?" Her mouth watered just thinking about it.

"You're going to need to watch your cholesterol," Joe warned. "You won't be young forever, you know."

"We'll see about that. I have some pretty good genes in my family. You might be surprised by our longevity." Despite the laugh she forced into her voice, Mara felt her shoulders tense as she referenced her family. She had enough stress with her job right now.

It had been a long, crappy day and Duncan DeMarco was only interested in drowning himself in a few drinks and watching the game at Bruisers. He should be happy, elated even. It wasn't every day that he got the chance to save a despondent teenager from killing herself. But he knew she wasn't out of the woods yet. Duncan downed the rest of his tequila and waved at Joe. When he got the bartender's attention, he gestured to his empty glass, and a moment later another appeared in front of him. He took a sip and tried to not think about anything.

Across the bar, the front door opened and, for some inexplicable reason, Duncan looked up from the tequila on the rocks that he was nursing. The woman who walked into the bar was nothing short of mesmerizing, and he felt his entire chest constrict. She had a smooth walk that reminded him of a jungle cat, dark burnished hair with red highlights, and her tan skirt curved around her hips in just the right way. She looked around the bar and Duncan dropped his eyes, not wanting to be caught staring. Taking a seat, she started a conversation with the bartender while he gave her a shot and a beer, and Duncan grinned when she downed the shot in a single gulp.

My kind of woman, he thought. *I wonder if she has panties on under that skirt.* He flinched and tried to convince himself that was the tequila talking. Lustful thoughts like that would get him in big trouble, and he really didn't need any more. But a minute later he was covertly glancing up again.

He took a big swallow of the tequila as he debated with himself. Half of his brain told him to just stay in his seat and ignore the captivating woman across the bar, while the other half simply screamed, *Go for it, you idiot!*

"Ah fuck it. My career's in the shitter as it is. Why not have a little fun?" Duncan said to the empty tequila glass. He knew he'd get dinged for cursing out loud, but at this point, he didn't really care. Duncan walked around the bar to the open chair next to her, and as he sat down, he caught a whiff of something—a hint of cinnamon and . . . sweet smoke, like birch wood in the fireplace.

Cinnamon and smoke? His eyes widened. *Holy mother of God—she's a devil?*

Mara hardly noticed the blond angel get up with his drink, but knew the instant he sat down next to her because the faint smell of sandalwood with a few notes of myrrh drifted by. She frowned—Angel-Boy was going to totally cramp her style and her plans.

She turned in her chair, fully prepared to shoo him away, but the words never left her mouth as she found herself staring into a pair of blue eyes so deep, she couldn't believe they were real. After gawking for a few seconds too long, Mara blinked rapidly, collected herself, and gave the angel a more appraising look. Tall and slender, he had broad shoulders and a swimmer's lean waist. His hair was dark blond, and his face was angular without being too severe. He offered her a wide, welcoming smile and the skin at the corners of his eyes crinkled slightly. He was utterly delicious.

"And what's your name, Angel-Boy?" Mara asked. "Paul? John? Peter? Or something silly with an –iel at the end of it?"

"Actually, it's Duncan. Duncan DeMarco. And who are you?" he asked with a small grin as one of her eyebrows arched, the only indication that his name had surprised her.

"I'm Mara Dullahan."

He held out a hand. "Nice to meet you, Mara. This a regular haunt for you? I saw you chatting up the bartender."

A pang of fear hit Mara's gut as she shook his hand. "You're not here for Joe, are you?"

"No. I'm not in collections. Just chasing my monthly quota of saves," Duncan told her.

"Grinder like me, then." Mara didn't quite know why, but she immediately liked Duncan, and it wasn't just because she thought he was ridiculously hot.

"So, tell me, Angel-Boy, why are you looking so down in the dumps?" Even when he'd smiled so charmingly at her, the worry and sadness had still been evident. Duncan took another sip of his tequila.

"I saved someone today."

"Kinda the point for you, isn't it?"

"Guess so." Duncan finished his drink and gestured to Joe. "Another tequila, please. And something for my new friend here."

Once they'd tucked into the new round of drinks, Mara asked, "Why are you upset over saving someone?"

The angel sighed. "I was on my Midwest circuit and found her by accident. Janelle Loomis. Poor kid's seventeen years old and she'd swallowed a bunch of pills because some shit of a boy has been bullying her and spreading rumors because she wouldn't sleep with him. I found her on a park bench, near a playground she used to go to as a kid . . ."

Duncan sat down on the park bench. For a moment the girl didn't notice, her senses starting to dull from the pills she'd swallowed in a desperate attempt to make all the pain go away. He allowed his energy to show through and she looked up, startled.

"Who are you?"

"I'm Duncan. Who are you?"

"Janelle Loomis. Are you an angel? I wasn't expecting an angel."

"Why not?"

"Because I came here to kill myself and God will hate me if I commit suicide." She looked down, ashamed of herself.

"Sweetheart, God doesn't hate you, but I know He doesn't want you to do this."

"I'm scared."

"I know." Duncan let his wings surround Janelle. The angel-fire that was part of his being infused her, warming her just a little and temporarily softening the effects of the narcotics. God had given all humans free will—if Janelle was determined to die, Duncan couldn't stop her. He could, however, use his power to keep her warm, reassure her, slow the drugs enough to talk with her, and maybe—just maybe—make a difference.

"Why do you want to do this, Janelle?"

"I don't want to, but what else can I do?" She went on to tell Duncan a sordid tale about a boy she liked in school who wanted to sleep with Janelle even though he had a girlfriend. And when she said no, Ethan spread all sorts of savage rumors about her.

It hurt the angel's heart to think that people could be so cruel to one another, but it was the way of the universe. God had set up rules, but it was up to humans to do the right thing.

"I just couldn't believe he'd flat-out lie. And now when people at school look at me, I can tell they're judging me. Some of the guys look at me and give me smiles and looks, like they're hoping I'll do them. Some of them look at me like I'm disgusting and unclean. One even said he was going to nominate me for the girl most likely to be a porn star in the yearbook. And Ethan's girlfriend believes him, not me, and won't stop slut-shaming me." Janelle started to cry again. *"I hate my life."*

It broke Duncan's heart. "I'm not going to lie to you, Janelle. People do cruel things, they do bad things. Sometimes they do them for good reasons and sometimes for the wrong ones, and sometimes, like Ethan, they do them because they want to tear down people just out of spite. But you know what? I'm proud of you for telling him no."

"You have to say that," said Janelle. "You're an angel. You don't want me having sex before I'm married."

"It isn't just that. Do I think you should wait? Yes. Is it likely you will? I don't know. That's up to you. But you shouldn't do anything before you're ready to. That's why I'm proud of you—you could have just let him pressure you. There are a lot of girls who would have said yes because they were afraid to say no."

"Tell me what to do, Duncan." The plea in her voice was torturous.

"I can't tell you what to do, Janelle. It's up to you. But I can give you an opinion. I think the first thing you need to do is choose to live. Then I think you should go tell Ethan to his face that he's a fucking liar."

Janelle gasped. "Angels can swear?"

"We're not supposed to, but yes, we can swear. I'll get in trouble for it, but that's how I feel."

"Even if I told him off, I'm just a big disappointment to every-one around me. What do I have to live for?" Janelle sighed. Her eyelids drooped and Duncan made sure he jostled her gently with his wings to wake her up a little.

"I bet there are a lot of things. What do you love? What would you miss?"

She thought for a minute. *"I'd miss my family. I do love them. I'd miss Barry, my brother, even though he can be a jerk. I'd miss Kylie. She never believed the things Ethan said. We always have fun together."*

"They'd miss you too."

Janelle's head drooped and she whispered, *"No, they wouldn't. No one's even noticed how sad I've been. They just think I'm a moody teenager. I doubt they even noticed that I'm gone."*

"That's not true. Kylie's looking for you now," Duncan said.

"She is?"

"Yes. And so are your parents. Barry too. Kylie saw the message you left and got worried. She went and got your folks."

"They'll be so angry with me," Janelle sobbed.

"No, sweetie. They won't be angry, I promise. They're scared right now, scared out of their wits, but all they really want is for you to be safe and happy."

Leaning up against him, Janelle sighed and suddenly felt solid, and Duncan's heart lightened. Even if she hadn't said it out loud, Janelle had decided she wanted to live. She cried harder.

"I want to go home. Taking those pills was a stupid idea. I don't want to die. I want my mom . . ." Duncan tightened his wings around her protectively. He saw flashing lights across the park and could hear voices calling for Janelle. Blue cruiser lights and red ambulance lights flashed.

"Can you stand and walk?" As much as Duncan wanted to carry her to the ambulance himself, it was against the rules. If

Janelle wanted to live, she had to do the work. She tried to stand up but collapsed back down.

"My legs feel all rubbery," she whispered. More tears streamed down her cheeks.

"They'll be here in a minute. Just hang on."

He might not be able to carry her, but he could point the rescue team in the right direction. Duncan let his angelic energy flare for a fraction of a second, a golden-white beacon in the darkness.

"They got her to the hospital in time," Duncan told Mara. "But I'm afraid of what will happen once she goes back to school."

"Why?"

"Ethan. I know he's going to continue being relentless, and the fact that Janelle tried to kill herself is just going to encourage his lying, manipulative behavior. I don't know if she'd make it through a second attempt." Duncan's shoulders slumped.

For some reason, his suffering touched Mara. "Have you tried to set him straight?"

"As best I could, and he ignored me. But you know the rules—angels and devils can't act directly. We can only guide and suggest, maybe cajole, but I can't give Ethan the ass-whupping he deserves."

Mara gave the angel a thoughtful look. He was so conflicted over the obnoxious boy.

"I'll tell you what," Mara said. "This little weasel, Ethan, sounds like he might be too cocky to fear God at this point in his life, but I bet I could put the fear of the Devil into him. Although my definition of 'cajole' is probably different from yours."

Duncan glanced to the side. "That would be interfering, wouldn't it?"

"I'd consider it checking out a potential candidate for my future prospects list."

"And I'd be neck-deep in shit if I asked you to do something like that," Duncan said.

Mara offered an innocent bat of her eyelashes. "I'm just following up on something I overheard. You know, you can get great leads when you eavesdrop on angels who are half in the bag."

Duncan chuckled and finished the last of his tequila. He looked up at the ceiling as if he were just sharing his thoughts with the universe. "Well, the Loomis family in Milwaukee sure was lucky there was an angel around last night."

"Cheers," Mara said as she took a swig of beer. With the information Duncan had given her, it would be easy enough to find Janelle, and then her school, and then Ethan.

Silence stretched between them for a moment before Duncan blurted out, "You're really pretty."

Mara laughed, surprisingly flattered by the compliment. She gave Duncan a sly look. He was really good-looking and she indulged herself imaging what he might look like naked . . . *What am I thinking? Me and an angel? No way,* she told herself.

A buzzing noise interrupted anything else Duncan was going to say, and he pulled his phone out of his pocket.

"I recognize that look," Mara said.

"I really hate to say this, but I have to fly—no pun intended. Crisis of faith to deal with."

"How disappointing. If it doesn't work out, have your client call me," Mara said. Her eyes flashed as she laughed.

"Unlikely. You're not Sister Theresa's cup of tea."

"You never know unless you try."

Duncan stood up, but lingered for a moment. "Maybe I'll see you here again sometime."

"Then I'll see you around, Angel-Boy."

Duncan's saucy wink as he turned for the door delighted her. Mara tilted her head, admiring how his pants hugged his backside, and bit her lower lip.

"You look like you'd rather eat *him* for dinner," said Joe as he put her burger and fries down.

Mara chuckled. "You have *no* idea. He been in before?"

"Couple times, but not a regular like you. Seems nice enough. Quiet, for the most part. Get you anything else?"

"Just some water, thanks." Mara picked up a fry that was loaded with cheese and shut her eyes as she ate it, savoring the flavor. Food was something she loved about the Mortal Plane, and Joe put a touch of hot sauce in the cheese. Not enough to burn but just enough for a little kick. It was one of Mara's all-time favorite meals.

Despite what people thought, both angels and devils needed to eat, drink, and sleep when they coexisted with humans. Not nearly as much as the humans, but it was still a necessity from time to time, and to make herself less conspicuous, Mara followed the human routine of eating and sleeping regularly. After a large bite of her cheeseburger, a happy sigh slipped out of Mara, but her appetite soured a moment later when Kemm thumped down in the chair Duncan had been sitting in.

"I'm eating."

"Those cheese fries look good," said Kemm. His hand inched forward.

"I will stab you with my fork if that hand moves another inch," Mara warned him.

"You are such a bitch," he muttered.

"Something you want, Kemm?"

"Looking a little cozy with that angel."

"What, I can't entertain myself? You can have a pretty funny conversation with a tipsy angel. But you'd need a sense of humor to know that."

"You'd be just the type to go soft hanging out with an angel." There was a predatory gleam in Kemm's eyes that Mara didn't like.

"Whatever. You're still going to lose out at the end of the year." Mara took another bite of cheeseburger and ignored Kemm until he got up, glowered at her, and stomped off.

Two bites later Mara finished her dinner and leaned back in the chair. Kemm was breathing down her neck this quarter; it had been a while since they'd been in such close competition. She needed to close, and close big, if she was going to shut him up once and for all. And it wasn't going to be easy.

CHAPTER 4

FOR THE FOURTH time in a half hour, Mara looked over when she heard the door at Bruisers open, and for the fourth time, she was disappointed. A family clearly on vacation came in, followed by three random business colleagues all still wearing convention credentials. Then an elderly gentleman came in. Two young women holding hands followed about ten minutes later. None were Angel-Boy.

Probably just as well, she thought as an icy edge of anxiety slid down her spine. It would be a truckload of trouble if management found any devil fooling around with an angel. A veritable shitstorm of epic proportions. She sighed, knowing the trouble would also be a lot of fun.

"Looking for someone in particular?" Joe asked.

"Maybe." Mara didn't make eye contact and Joe just laughed at her as he finished a round of drinks for the after-work crowd at the end of the bar.

Finally Mara's patience was rewarded. Duncan was dressed casually in jeans and a sweater—quite a change from the suit she'd seen him in before. He scanned the bar quickly and she watched his eyebrows go up. She'd done the same when she arrived. For once, no other bar patrons had the telltale eye sheen of an immortal being.

"This seat taken?" Duncan asked.

"Nope."

"Good. Are you hungry?" He slid into the seat, ordered a Sam Adams, and opened the menu.

"I am." What she wanted, however, wasn't on the menu.

"Then let's try a few appetizers. What's good?"

"Definitely get the fried ravioli," Mara said, pushing her hair back over her shoulder.

Joe put a beer down in front of Duncan. "Anything to eat tonight?"

"Please. The fried ravioli and the chicken quesadilla. We'll need two small plates," Duncan said.

"Coming right up."

There was a moment of awkward silence as Mara and Duncan glanced at each other over their drinks. Mara looked up once to find Duncan watching her, and was a little shocked when she felt her cheeks color. She looked back down but couldn't hide the smile.

"How was your day?" Duncan finally asked.

Mara shrugged. "Same shit, you know the story."

"Then here's to living the dream." Duncan raised his glass.

They toasted and laughed, both downing nearly half of their drinks.

"I did add a new prospect to my list." Mara's voice was casual.

"Oh?"

"Yeah, a snot-nosed teenager in Milwaukee. Kid named Ethan. He's too young and unpredictable for a contract yet, but he's definitely worth keeping an eye on."

"Anything else interesting in Milwaukee?"

"Not much. There was a girl who Ethan was hassling, but I'm pretty sure he won't give her a problem again." Her smile was smug and satisfied.

"Well, she's lucky then," mused Duncan.

Mara kept her own smile to a minimum, knowing that Duncan was making a supreme effort not to gloat about the fact Ethan was going to get what was coming to him. They chatted about her quota, and she told him a little about her chance to beat Baliel's record as they waited for the food to arrive. Finally Mara had a chance to ask Duncan about his job.

"So, who do you report to?"

"Michael."

She raised an eyebrow. "Really? What's he like to work for? I've heard some stories and they all pretty much say he's a real uptight prick."

Duncan smothered a snort of laughter. "If you work for him, you'd better like being in the military. You don't question the chain of command no matter what, and every little infraction goes on your record—and he holds it against you. Fortunately, I don't have to deal with him every day, usually only if he has a hair across his ass about something and he calls a staff meeting. But he can be, let's say . . . demanding. That's a good word."

"So diplomatic," Mara said. "What about the others?"

"Gabriel is supposed to be great to work for, and Raphael, too, although Raph does run a tight ship. But he doesn't have Michael's reputation—"

"—for being a major-league dick?" Mara interrupted.

"Your words, not mine." Duncan finished his beer. "What about Lucifer? Working for the Big Kahuna can't be a walk in the park."

At the mention of the King of Hell, Mara stiffened and looked away for a moment, but she masked her reaction quickly, hoping Duncan hadn't noticed. "I haven't seen Lucifer for quite a while. He's got bigger fish to fry than a devil like me. Mostly I deal with the Grand Dukes. I have the privilege, if you'd call it that, of reporting to Grand Duke Astaroth, one of the treasurers."

"What's he like?"

"Not horrible. He's uptight in his own way and you don't want to be on the receiving end when he disapproves of something you've done, but we seem to have figured out how to work together. I've known him for a really long time."

"So, you're not a bigwig in Hell?" Duncan leaned a little closer to Mara.

For a fraction of a second, Mara hesitated. "Bigwig? Nah." Her smile widened. "Angels and devils like us? We're all just peons in the system—as long as you make your quotas, no one pays much attention, but if you miss your number? Shit. There's hell to pay."

They talked a little longer about life in the trenches for IPI, and then Joe brought the appetizers out. Both plates were heaped high and steaming, and they smelled delicious.

"Get you both refills?" Joe gestured at their empty glasses.

"Yes for me," Duncan said. "Refill for you, Mara?"

"Please, another Goose Bay Ale if you would."

"You've got it. Another Sam for you?" Joe asked Duncan.

"Please."

Duncan picked up one of the fried ravioli and dipped it into the spicy marinara sauce before popping it into his mouth. His eyes almost rolled back in his head as he chewed. Mara watched him with a smile before she took a bite of quesadilla.

"What do you think?"

"They're great. The sauce really makes it something else." He ate two more in quick succession before trying the quesadilla.

Mara wiped a little marinara from the corner of her mouth, dropped the napkin back in her lap, and threw Duncan a covert glance. The first time she'd met him, he'd been half in the bag and really torn up over the whole Janelle situation. Today he was much more relaxed. He smiled more, and she found herself looking for opportunities to enjoy that warm grin.

"Do you like your job?" she asked.

"Do I like it?" Duncan repeated the question thoughtfully.

"I mean, I can tell you don't really dig your manager, but the job itself. Saving people. Do you enjoy it?"

"Yes, absolutely. I don't think there's anything more rewarding than pulling someone out of despair, giving them hope." Duncan got a faraway look in his eye.

"Is there a 'but' in there?"

He shook his head. "Not really a 'but.' More of a 'wish.' I just wish I had the chance to do more meaningful saves. Lately it seems that most of what I do is more busywork. And it doesn't help that you spend a lot of time on the road. It can get pretty lonely sometimes."

"Very true," Mara said. It was truer than she was willing to let on. At least Duncan had angel friends, maybe even mortal ones that he could hang out with. Devils were different. They didn't so much have friends as they did allies. That's one reason Mara liked Joe so much—he might be the closest thing she'd ever had to a real friend.

Duncan paused and gave Mara a charming smile. "You're very easy to talk with, you know."

Avoiding eye contact, Mara reached out for more ravioli and accidentally brushed Duncan's hand. She let it linger, soaking in the feel of his warm skin, and then looked up with a smile, dark brown eyes meeting deep blue. They stared at each other for a moment, neither quite sure what to say, and Mara's eyes widened as Duncan's hand covered hers and he rubbed his thumb gently along the back of her hand. A thrill ran through her, but Mara pulled her hand back.

"I'm sorry," Duncan said.

"That's okay," Mara answered.

"I'd like to—"

"Me too, but it would be . . . complicated," Mara interrupted before he could finish his thought, knowing that "complicated" was a colossal understatement.

"Yeah." Duncan half laughed. "It would, wouldn't it?"

Another long moment of silence engulfed them before Duncan finally said, "What about you? Do you like your job?"

Mara sighed, grateful for the turn in conversation. "I love my job. You find satisfaction in bringing comfort. I find it in dishing out just desserts to really rotten people."

"Don't you ever feel bad for them? I mean, not all of them are evil. Some are just misguided."

Mara leaned back in her chair and gave Duncan an appraising look. The angel shifted a little under her scrutiny.

Eventually she said, "Not really. Anyone I do a contract with is already on the path to being reprehensible at best, and at worst, flat-out evil. But I just open doors. They have to choose to walk through them, and if they choose to be evil, they don't really get much sympathy from me."

She glanced away for a moment, hoping Duncan wouldn't notice that she was lying. A white lie maybe, but a lie nonetheless. Mara had felt sorry for Paula and for Janelle, but had convinced herself they were nothing more than collateral damage—but the fact that she cared about them at all made her vulnerable, and she wasn't going to let anyone see that.

"I suppose if you're evil, you get what you deserve. Speaking of getting what we deserve . . . will you be at the Annual Employee Conference?" Duncan asked.

After the close of each fiscal year, Immortal Planes Incorporated held a big company-wide meeting to review year-end numbers, hand out awards and bonuses, and set the tone for the upcoming year. It was really the only time that all the devils in Hell and the angels in Heaven got together, and it was always a bit of an adventure.

"Oh, I'll be there. If all goes according to my plan, I'll get to watch Grand Duke Baliel choke on his pride when he has to acknowledge that I've beaten his record. I'm not going to miss that for anything. Plus, Astaroth's a bit of a stickler for attendance at company events. What about you?"

"Normally I try to get out of it, but if you'll be there, maybe it's worth going. Will you wave to me from the podium when you get your big award?"

Mara laughed. "Oh, they'd love that!"

They chatted and laughed for another two hours, taking full advantage of the lack of prying immortal eyes. Eventually Duncan looked at his watch and made a face.

"Don't tell me you have to go?" As they'd been talking, Mara had found it impossible to ignore the chemistry between them. A fling might do them both some good.

"I'm sorry, but I do. Staff meeting. You know the drill."

"All too familiar with it," she said, clearly disappointed.

Duncan waved Joe over and handed him some cash. "I have to go, so I'd like to take care of the bill, please."

"You don't have to do that," Mara said.

"This is on me," Duncan insisted. "You can pick up the tab next time."

"Next time?" She looked him up and down.

"That is, if you want a next time."

"Oh, trust me, I want it." Mara was tantalizingly close when she whispered in his ear, and she felt the heat rise on his skin as his body responded to her cheeky comment. As he stood up, his hand brushed against her arm. The jolt of electricity when they touched startled them both.

"Then I'll see you soon?"

Mara smiled, and she was sincere when she said, "Yeah, I'd really like that."

For the next three days, Mara and Duncan met up at Bruisers, and each night the attraction between them grew exponentially. They managed to share drinks and food once, but the other two meetings were spent glancing at each other across the bar, because there were far too many other devils and angels around. Despite their best efforts, a few looks were noticed by other immortals.

Mara sighed when Kemm oozed into the seat next to her. He wore a severe suit and a narrow tie that had gone out of fashion in the 1980s. His thick dark hair was slicked back and his sparse goatee made his pointed chin look like dirt was smudged on it.

"You look at the leaderboard today? Closed two more deals—you're definitely in my rearview mirror. You're going down this time."

"Whatever," Mara replied. His snotty tone annoyed her, and she wondered how he'd managed to close two more deals so soon.

"Then you can slink around with your tail between your legs." He snickered.

"Hell really will freeze over before that happens. Keep yapping, Kemm. Only thing that matters is the numbers on the final day. Remember last quarter? You were ahead of me for two straight months, and what happened?"

Kemm's pinched frown was the only answer Mara got.

"That's right. I kicked your ass—like I do every quarter—with better pipeline numbers and higher closing rates."

Kemm changed the subject: "Noticed you getting all googly-eyed over your drunken angel. You really are setting your sights on some angel ass, aren't you? You'll have to use the extra-small strap-on when you bend him over. I hear angels have quite the puckered butts."

"Well, if anyone would know about puckered butts, it would be you." Mara turned in her chair to stare at him.

"You actually going to try making him fall? That would be a ballsy move. Or are you just slumming?"

The gleam in Kemm's eyes made it abundantly clear that he didn't think she could make an angel fall, and that anything damaging Mara's reputation or success would delight him. She ground her teeth and looked away. There was no way she was making Duncan—or any other angel—fall. She couldn't do it. Wouldn't. She'd promised.

She turned her sarcasm on Kemm: "Why bother? It isn't like we get anything for it. In fact, it would probably just piss off Astaroth and Lucifer. We work for the same company, so undermining an angel just takes our focus off the mortal souls we're supposed to be collecting."

"You really are a sorry excuse for a devil. 'Why'? For the fucking thrill of it! I mean, come on, Mara. Any of us would kill for the kind of street cred that comes with an angel fall." Kemm snorted in disgust. "But you're not a *real* devil anyway. Wingless freak."

Mara knew he was just trying to get under her skin, and she'd had centuries of practice ignoring digs about her wings. Nearly all devils had wings. The size and shape varied, but they could grow as a devil's power grew, and could be a tremendous source of pride and status among the denizens of Hell. She narrowed her eyes. One day Kemm was going to see her wings and it would blow his mind.

She buried her anger and waved a hand dismissively. "Whatever blows your skirt up."

"Probably what you want to do to that angel," Kemm said. "But all bullshit aside, Mara: get your rocks off with him quick if that's what you want, but don't get tangled up. You do know what happened to the last devil who shacked up with an angel full-time?"

Mara had heard plenty of stories over the years, none of them pleasant, and despite her lack of response, Kemm continued with his narration. "I heard that Lucifer literally ripped his wings out of their sockets and then yanked his rocks off and used them as paperweights—and followed that up by dragging him over coals until his skin blistered and peeled like a roasted pepper."

"So kind of you to look out for my well-being, but I'm doing just fine. Worry about me breathing down your neck this quarter."

Kemm scowled at her. "When you get fucked over, don't say I didn't warn you."

Mara ignored him as he left, and finished the last of her drink. She put some money on the bar and Joe came over to collect it.

"You okay?" His typically gruff voice was softened with concern, and he gave Mara's hand an affectionate pat.

"I'm fine. Just became really clear to me how damn complicated everything is. Shouldn't it be easier?"

"Yep. Should be. But it isn't. Life's complicated shit," Joe told her. "But if you want something, you gotta fight for it."

Mara nodded. Joe was absolutely right. If it was worth the price, it was worth the fight, and if nothing else, she was a fighter.

CHAPTER 5

AFTER HER ANNOYING encounter with Kemm, Mara
went home and slept. Then promptly the next morning she
cloaked herself in shadows and vanished, rematerializing on the
West Coast to check up on some of her investments. Most were
progressing nicely, adding quality tarnish to their souls. That
kind of development should have made her happy, but Mara
found herself sinking deeper into a rather pissy mood, and the
unexpected call she was on with the Accounting Department
wasn't helping.

"No, I'm not in the office today," she snapped into the
phone. "Loretta, I'm out in the field doing a quality assessment
and I won't be back until—"

"Invoices are due on the fifteenth of the month," Loretta
said. "We need time to close everything out."

Mara shut her eyes and wished she could incinerate the irri-
tating little cube rat barking at her. She kept her voice neutral
when she answered, "When I get back, I'll reconcile everything
and bring it to your desk myself—"

"They were due yesterday. All delinquent invoices have
been elevated to Astaroth."

"What?! What do you mean they've been 'elevated' to
Astaroth?" It took all of Mara's willpower not to scream, but

she was in the middle of a busy department store and causing a scene would scare away her prospect.

"It's procedure. Everyone on the sales force was notified ahead of time. You should check your email more carefully."

Mara mastered her temper, and once she was confident that she could speak at a normal volume, she sweetly said, "Oh yes. Don't you worry, Loretta. I'll be sure to take care of *everything* when I get back."

Loretta hesitated before she thanked Mara, and Mara had a moment of satisfaction knowing Loretta understood that she was included in the "everything" that would be taken care of.

Once she hung up, Mara turned her attention to the woman behind the perfume counter. Probably in her twenties, the woman wore her best plastic smile as she made small talk with a customer. After the stout woman with coiffed gray hair left the counter, Mara browsed until, after a moment to herself, the young woman approached her.

"Good afternoon, madam. I'm Evelyn. May I help you find something?"

"I was actually looking for you. You're Evelyn Rousseau, yes? The author of the *Plume de Parfum* blog?"

Evelyn lit up. "You've read my blog?"

"I have. You have some very interesting insights on scent combinations."

"Oh, thank you! That's so kind!"

Evelyn's boss, a grumpy man with a pinched frown, came around to the cash register and peered at Evelyn over his glasses. She sighed in aggravation.

"I'm very sorry, but I'll get in trouble if I talk about my blog with customers. I'm supposed to be selling."

"I understand completely. Do you have a break soon? Maybe we could have coffee? My name is Mara." She held out her hand. "It's really nice to meet you."

Twenty minutes later Evelyn met Mara in the food court. They started toward one table until Mara caught the momentary gold glint of immortal eyes. The last thing she wanted was to try closing a deal with two angels at the next table, so Mara steered Evelyn toward a table partially hidden by a huge planter. They talked for a few minutes about what had sparked Evelyn's interest in perfume.

"Have you thought about going to school for perfume?" Mara asked, knowing the answer.

"Have I? Like, every single day. But the good schools are impossible to get into." Evelyn heaved a sigh and rested her chin in her hand. "I want to have my own perfume empire. I'd do anything to get into the Givaudan Perfumery School outside Paris. But to do that you have to work for Givaudan. I've put in a ton of applications, but I've only gotten rejections back."

"You'd do anything? That's a pretty bold statement."

"I'm not kidding," said Evelyn, her face turning hard and calculating. "I'd pretty much do anything."

"Well, it just so happens I have some contacts at Givaudan. I can get you in the door, and into the school, but your own empire? You'll have to be pretty ruthless to do that."

"I have no problem with ruthless," breathed Evelyn, her eyes intense.

"No, I don't believe you do. So, here's what I'm proposing: I'll make sure you get a job with Givaudan and get into the school, but then you need to do whatever it takes to succeed, to build that empire. I can open the door, but you've got to seize the opportunity."

"You'd do that for me? Why?" Evelyn was nearly shaking with anticipation.

"Why? I like seeing people get what they want, what they really *deserve*, but make no mistake, I'm not doing it for free.

I facilitate business arrangements. Beneficial business arrangements," Mara told her.

"Do you want me to do something illegal?"

"I never said anything about illegal, but if you're worried about that, maybe I underestimated how much you wanted in at Givaudan. I'm sorry to have wasted your time, but I think your break is probably done. Have a good day working for Mr. Stick Up His Ass."

Mara stood up, put her notebook back in her bag, and only managed one step before Evelyn grabbed her arm. Her voice was desperate.

"No! I'm not working a retail counter for the rest of my life. I'm better than that. I deserve better than that. What do I have to do?"

Mara leaned in and locked eyes with Evelyn like a snake staring down its prey. "Your perfume empire, more success than you can imagine . . . in exchange for your soul." Mara's eyes flared red.

"Oh God . . ." Evelyn whispered. But she didn't turn away.

"Clock's ticking," Mara pulled a pen and set of papers out of her bag and put them on the table in front of Evelyn.

Evelyn eyed the stack of papers. "All that was in your bag? What else do you have in there?"

"Whatever I need when I'm working. Now, let's just review what we've discussed." Mara went on to walk Evelyn through the basics of the contract. Then she gave Evelyn a moment to flip through the pages again. The young woman gnawed on her lower lip as she stared at the signature line.

"You get the next thirty years," Mara continued. "Your dream school. The fame. The money. The power. I'll check in on you from time to time to see how you're doing. At the end of the thirty, I get to claim your soul whenever I see fit."

"But what if I don't get all that? What if I'm never CEO of my own perfume company?"

Mara offered a reassuring smile. "Sweetie, I see all the requisite skills in you to be a CEO. If you try your hardest with everything at your disposal and you don't get your empire, then I'll void your contract myself. It's right there in the voids clause. But it also says that if you just phone it in, and don't make an effort, then I can decide your time is up and claim your soul then and there."

"My own perfume company?"

"Your very own successful perfume *empire*," Mara replied.

Evelyn chewed on her lip more, flipped through the pages of the contract, and clicked the point of the pen in and out about thirty times. The sound made Mara crazy.

"Ticktock. Do we have a deal?"

Clicking the pen one more time, Evelyn signed her name with a dramatic flourish. "We have a deal."

"Excellent." The smell of charred paper wafted by as Evelyn's and Mara's signatures burned themselves into the document. Mara shook the ash off and tucked the papers into her bag, and then started tapping away on her phone. A swoosh heralded the email's release into the universe as Mara stood to leave.

"What happens now?" Evelyn asked.

"Now you go back to work. In about a week, watch your mail," Mara told her. "You'll be getting a letter from Didier Francoeur about a mistake that was made on your last application to Givaudan. By this time next month, you'll be in Paris at your new job, and then shortly after that, school starts."

Evelyn's eyes were glowing with anticipation. "Thank you."

"No, thank *you*." Mara leaned down and kissed Evelyn on the lips, the last step needed to make the contract official. Mara left the clearly flustered Evelyn sitting in the food court, found her way out of the store, and wandered down the street. Her argument over the invoices with Loretta and the appointment with Evelyn had distracted her from Kemm's snide comments about Duncan.

Now that was all she could think about—that and how she felt about the handsome blond angel. It was more than just lustful thoughts. She really did like Duncan, and she wasn't quite sure what to do with that realization. Fraternization between angels and devils wasn't explicitly forbidden in the Immortal Planes, but it wasn't encouraged. In fact, it was common knowledge in the rank and file that Lucifer frowned upon it, and that knowledge alone kept the Grand Dukes on alert. Mara was under no illusions about how a dalliance with Duncan would be received—she'd once seen Grand Duke Valafar poke the eyes out of a devil who was staring lustfully at an angel during a company-wide meeting.

Mara's last stop of the day was in Yuma, and when she finished up, she found she was still thinking about her angel. Uncertain about what she should do, Mara decided to get an unbiased perspective on the situation. Strolling through the front doors of Desert Ridge Church, she sat down in a pew in the second row. The décor was distinctly southwestern, with stucco walls and shades of brown, burnt orange, and dark red throughout the building. The slim windows had stained-glass inlays and let in a surprising amount of light, and the altar in front of her had a large cross hanging above it made of the bones of an old saguaro cactus. It was rustic and Mara liked it very much.

"Can I help you, miss?" The pastor came in from a side room carrying two Bibles, which he tucked into the slots in the back of the first pew before he sat down in front of Mara. He was short, perhaps only five foot seven, and portly around the middle, but he had a welcoming smile and friendly eyes.

"I was just thinking," she answered.

"Based on your expression, it seems like they're pretty serious thoughts. I'm Jim Montoya, the pastor here. Maybe I can help?"

Mara paused, momentarily reconsidering her decision to seek advice from a pastor. But she was already here and decided she may as well take the plunge.

"I met someone, and now I'm confused."

"About what?"

"I've never met anyone like him before. He's special; I knew that right from the moment I met him. I think about him all the time now, about how much I would like to . . ." Mara realized what she was about to say and stopped, a hint of pink touching her cheeks. "Well, the particulars of what I'd like to do with him aren't germane to our conversation."

Jim laughed. "I understand. I'm human just like you are, you know."

Oh, you are so wrong on that count, Mara thought as she sighed and folded her arms.

"You were saying?" Jim prompted.

"Being together would be complicated on a lot of levels, but I'm honestly not sure I really care about that. I'm used to it. Everything connected to me is complicated."

"You say that like there's something wrong with you."

"Oh, Pastor Jim—"

"Just Jim is fine. Please, go on."

She acquiesced: "Jim, then. Well, Jim, I'm not what you'd call a good woman. I've made my living by understanding all the awful things that motivate people and taking advantage of them. I'm really good at my job—*really* good—and frankly, I love it. But here's the thing—some of my coworkers would manipulate this relationship to their advantage if they knew about it, maybe even try to bring this good man down. And they'd certainly use him as a pawn against me."

"Why would you work for people like that?"

"Call it a family business."

"Does he know about this family business and what you do?"

"Yes, and he's in a similar situation—we're competitors." It wasn't exactly the truth, but Mara had no interest in explaining Immortal Planes Inc. to him.

"Hmm." Jim just nodded.

"I shouldn't care if they want to ruin him, but I do. I care a lot and I don't know what to do with that," Mara finally said. "I have no interest in seeing him ruined, or seeing him lose everything. And the higher-ups in the organization would lose their shit over this." The thought of her own eyeball stuck on Valafar's thumbnails left a pit in her stomach.

"How do you feel about him, honestly?"

"I like him. I like him a lot. Given some time, it could be much more than that. And it isn't just physical, although he's quite fine. I like being around him. I like how he makes me feel. He's someone I can trust, and believe me, trust is a very rare commodity in my world. I don't quite know what to do with that."

"Does he feel the same about you?"

"I think so."

"Sometimes in the darkness we find a surprising ray of light that changes our whole perspective. Could this relationship be a new road for both of you?"

"I don't know about a new path, Jim, but as I'm talking to you, maybe this relationship would be worth the risk. I'll just have to make sure no one else finds out about it." Mara stood up, and Jim followed.

"Be careful," the pastor warned. "Starting a relationship based on deception won't end well. It's not good for your soul or your spiritual well-being. The lie will eat away at you. How can you have a full and fulfilling relationship if it is based on deceit? If you're not giving this man your true self?"

"Jim, Jim, Jim. Sweetie. My entire existence is swaddled in misdirection and lies. He might be the only one who ever gets to see my true self." Knowing that rankled Mara.

The powers that be in Hell had no sense of humor when it came to devils showing their true nature, except in a few rare instances like closing a deal or collecting a soul. Otherwise, it raised too many questions. Mara was so damn tired of hiding who she was—who she *really* was.

Abruptly she said, "Screw 'em if they can't take a joke."

"I beg your pardon?" Jim said.

Mara's eyes flamed crimson and she allowed her inner fire to spread just enough to highlight around her eyes. Pastor Jim's hand flew to the small gold crucifix around his neck.

"Jesus, Mary, and Joseph!" the pastor cried. "You're a devil!"

"Indeed, I am." Mara's hair floated a little, caught in a breeze of her own making.

"You're in my church!" He sputtered a little, alarmed. "How can you be in my church? You *can't* be in my church!"

"Why not? All that stuff you see in the movies about holy ground? Utter malarkey. There's no supernatural barrier that keeps devils out of churches or holy places. There's also no reason an angel can't walk straight into a den of iniquity."

For the moment Jim was speechless, so Mara continued. She gestured grandly at the church and said, "Isn't this where I should go to seek guidance? Where I should go to unburden my soul, to confess? I am, after all, the very definition of a sinner."

"Then are you here to confess, or are you here to tempt me?"

Mara looked him up and down with a critical eye. "Honestly, there's so little tarnish on your soul right now that I normally wouldn't bother, but if you're open to a deal, I'm game. I get a pretty hefty bonus for any souls who are clergy members, and it *is* the end of the quarter."

Jim looked flabbergasted. Mara let him gape for a moment as he contemplated reality of actually being able to make a deal with a devil, before she continued, "Don't go completely crackers on me, Jim. I know you're not interested in a deal, although some of your clerical brothers are more interested in their own fortunes than the souls of their flock." She thought for a moment about one of her contracts in Texas, a reverend who had lost sight of God a long time ago. She was going to have to check in on the good Reverend Gideon.

"You want to know why I came here, to your church? For exactly the reason I told you—for advice. I've met a man who challenges and confounds me. Someone who won't be accepted by my . . . family. Someone I'm so deeply attracted to, it scares me a little. Can you even wrap your mind around what it takes to actually scare *me?*"

Mara walked toward the door of the church and was half-way down the aisle when Jim boldly asked, "So perhaps instead of corrupting someone, you yourself are being saved?"

Mara's shoulders tensed as his words sank in, and she turned back, her eyes narrow. Jim kept his hand firmly closed around the cross at his throat.

"Now, that would be something, wouldn't it, Jim?" she laughed, brushing off what he had said, and calling the shadows from where they lurked beneath the pews and in the shaded corners of the church. They curled around her until only Mara's red eyes could be seen inside the maelstrom of shadow and darkness. In an instant she vanished, leaving Jim to pray in her wake.

CHAPTER 6

ON HER WAY back from Yuma, Mara made one stop in Hell before heading home to Hollis City. Other devils scurried out of her way as she stormed down the hallway in Accounting, into the cube marked "Loretta," and slammed down some forms. The edges were singed from the power in her hands. Under Mara's angry stare, Loretta shrank back in her chair, her toad-like eyes blinking rapidly.

"Here's the paperwork. I've been a little busy with my sales quota—glad I had to take time away from that to take care of this."

"We have to balance the books." Loretta barely managed to get the sentence out.

"Whatever. You would have had plenty of time to do that. Don't ever make the mistake of ratting me out to Astaroth again," Mara snarled.

"But, but . . . procedure!" Loretta croaked. "We have to follow procedure!"

"You do *not* want to hear what I think about your procedures." Mara stalked back down the hall.

In Hollis City, the run-up to Halloween was in full swing. While it wasn't as crazy in the city as it could be in the suburbs, with all the fake ghosts in trees and inflatable grim reapers in front yards, there was plenty of décor. Mara was still huffy from having to deal with Loretta, and when she reached her block, she realized she was in no mood to cook for herself, but she hesitated when she saw two people in costume head into Bruisers. She vacillated for a moment. Joe always hosted a Halloween party, but she really didn't feel like watching the costumed mortals parading around. In fact, she found it a bit insulting—mortals had no clue what it was like to be a real devil.

The lure of one of Joe's cheeseburgers, however, was too much for her to resist, and since it was a little early, Mara managed to find a place at the bar. It was a Friday night, and the flashes of gold and red eye sheen told her there were a lot of immortals mixed in with the human crowd. Frankie was there, hanging out with two of his coworkers. At one of the tables, Kemm was sitting with another devil who looked exactly like him except he had no goatee.

"Christ on a raft," she muttered to herself. "I forgot Kemm had a twin brother. Just what I need—two of them."

On the other side of the bar, sitting in his favorite seat, was Duncan. He was flanked by two other angels—one lanky with red hair, the other shorter but also slender, with dark hair—and based on the way they were laughing, Mara guessed they were friends of his. Duncan saw her and tossed her a wink and a grin. Before long, another angel came in, wearing a magenta headband that was a sharp contrast to her curly black hair. Mara was slightly surprised to see her wave to one of the devils sitting with Frankie, who waved back. She threaded her way around the bar and gave the devil a quick hug. They clearly hadn't seen each other in a while.

Friendships between angels and devils weren't common but they did happen, especially among immortals who interacted with one another every day on the Null Plane, the place where unclaimed souls went to be processed, and where any business between the two divisions of Immortal Planes Inc. was transacted.

Joe was running around like crazy, so Joanie, one of his senior waitresses, took Mara's order and brought her a burger and a glass of wine. The bar filled with patrons, and with five hundred dollars being offered as first prize in the costume contest, most of them were dressed up. A human woman glided by in a clingy black dress with a plunging neckline. Her makeup was pale, and she had a wig of long, straight black hair. Mara grudgingly admitted the woman looked great as Morticia Addams. The other costumes were, as far as she was concerned, the usual assortment of pirates, cops, hookers, gypsies, ghosts, and vampires, and no more than pedestrian at best.

"I can't stand it when they dress up like angels." Duncan's warm voice drifted over her shoulder, and Mara flinched. She hadn't seen him leave his seat, and a glance told her that his companions, who were still across the bar, were as surprised as she was.

"You need a bell," she said, turning in her chair.

"Sorry," he said with a grin that said the opposite. He leaned past her and caught Joanie's eye. "Three Goose Bay Ales when you have a sec."

"Why don't you like the angel costumes?" Mara sipped her wine.

"When was the last time you saw an angel with an actual halo? Or dressed in those white robes? I mean, seriously."

"I don't know, I think you could pull off the robe. Very bohemian, if you ask me."

"Whatever." He laughed.

"I know what you mean, though. Look at that girl over there—little red horns, forked tail coming out of her skirt? Such an uninspired approach to what a devil looks like. And in a Catholic school uniform? Ugh."

Duncan looked at the miniskirt and then back at Mara. "Well, you'd probably look okay in that miniskirt."

"'Okay'? You think I'd 'probably look okay'? Please. You know I'd rock that outfit. It would just be a question of whether to wear stiletto heels or thigh-high boots," Mara said.

The boots. Oh dear God, please let her pick the boots, he thought.

At the bar, Joe suddenly appeared, looking frantic. "Hey, can the two of you help me out?"

"What's up?" Mara asked.

"Two of my judges bailed on me. Food poisoning from that goddamn sushi place in the mall last night. So I don't have enough judges for the damn contest. Since I'm one of the sponsors, I can't do it. The staff has narrowed the contestants down to the top ten. Can you both just sit through the parade and help pick someone?"

"Sure, sounds like fun. You game, Mara?"

For a second Duncan thought she was going to say no, but then she shrugged and said, "What the hell. Let's do this!"

Duncan picked up the beers that Joanie had just brought over. "Let me take these to my friends, and then I'll be right back."

"You're a saint. Thanks," said Joe, and Duncan chuckled.

Duncan managed to not spill any of the beer as he worked his way back to their seats. His friends Raymond and Basil watched him closely.

"You could have just ordered those from here," Basil said.

"Scenery is better over there."

"Nothing good would come of that," Basil replied when Duncan didn't elaborate.

"Of what?"

"That woman you were talking with . . . You know she's a devil, right?"

"I know. But c'mon, Basil, you have to admit, she's pretty easy on the eyes." Duncan couldn't help but look over at Mara again.

"That's one hot devil." Raymond guffawed at his own joke, and Duncan grinned.

Basil studied Mara for a second. "I suppose. I prefer blonds."

"Dude, you'd prefer any woman who showed an ounce of interest in you, blond or not," snorted Raymond. "If that devil had any interest in me, oh man . . ."

For a split second Duncan tensed—the thought of someone else putting their hands on Mara went right up his spine the wrong way—but then he laughed out loud. "You're a big talker, Raymond. That one would eat you for lunch."

"Maybe. But what a way to go!"

Mara had already selected her seat when Duncan joined her on the little raised stage along with the third judge, a local DJ named Donovan. Joe ushered the finalists onto the stage. Mara thought the first few—cheerleader, zombie, and 1920s flapper—were average at best. The next two were better—a woman with a funky unicorn headpiece, and a Chester Cheetah.

"The Chester isn't bad," Mara whispered to Duncan.

A sexy nurse paraded across the stage next. She flirted outrageously with Duncan, and Mara frowned when the angel checked out her ass as she left the stage.

"Average and no imagination," she whispered.

"Jealous?"

"No."

"Liar."

The last four contestants were excellent. Morticia Addams made the cut, as did a Mad Hatter. Charlie Chaplin's ghost crossed the stage, his face done in marvelous, luminous white makeup, followed by a woman in a green bodysuit and an elaborate cape of felt feathers. Her face was painted to look like a parrot and she wore a wig made of feathers too. After a ten-minute conference, the three judges awarded the five-hundred-dollar prize to Charlie Chaplin. Parrot Woman was second and Morticia Addams was third.

As the winners walked off the stage to applause, Joe shook hands with the three judges, thanking them profusely. Having Duncan so close to her but not being able to touch him was torture for Mara, and as she turned, she managed to brush against him briefly. But out in the audience, there were at least fifteen angels and devils, including Kemm, who stared at her maliciously. Annoyed she couldn't continue her conversation with Duncan, Mara hurried off the stage without so much as a glance at him.

Mara had another glass of wine, and once she was finished, there was no reason to stay. She glanced across the bar, looking for Duncan, and spotted him in the corner with several other angels. He glanced up and met her eyes, then offered a tiny, discouraged shrug. Mara gave him a wink and headed home, terribly disappointed to be going to bed alone.

CHAPTER 7

SHORTLY AFTER INKING her deal with Evelyn Rousseau, Mara closed two more souls: a gangbanger with a taste for the high life, and—through sheer luck—a midlevel banker who was fed up with his managers getting the bonuses while he did all the work. The last two did the trick, netting Mara her quota for the quarter. She celebrated with a round of drinks for everyone at Bruisers, and refocused her attention on catching Kemm on the leaderboard.

But after November 1, she hit a bit of a dry spell, and utter monotony was about the only way she could describe her week. She'd made several trips to Hell to deliver souls whose contracts were due, but none of them had the cachet of Ricky Nottingham. They were pedestrian sinners at best, the kind Mara wouldn't normally even glance at, but when a quota needed to be made, sometimes corners got cut. Many demons and devils made great careers for themselves, even moving into middle management, by delivering a passel of mediocre souls. But that was quantity over quality, and Mara had no interest in that—unlike Kemm, who, as far as she was concerned, had no standards at all.

Sitting in her office, Mara clicked the latest email with updated acquisition numbers, and it didn't improve her mood at all. She had made her base quota, but somehow Kemm had managed to stay one acquisition ahead of her for the week. She ground her teeth together. *Of all the quarters for him to pull his head out of his ass, it has to be this quarter?* Now the entire year-end scenario changed. If Kemm had a higher overall total this quarter, it wouldn't matter if Mara met her quota. She'd lose her one-thousand-soul coin—not to mention it would blow her chance at beating Baliel's record.

And she was not interested in second-fucking-place: she was about to hit 625 consecutive quarters as the best sales and acquisitions devil Immortal Planes Inc. had seen in eons. It would put her just past Baliel's 624, and then it was on to shattering Lucifer's record.

Mara spent another hour combing through her prospects list and following up on leads she'd gotten from various sources, but eventually her mind wandered to more pleasant things, namely Duncan DeMarco. She unabashedly thought about how Duncan's backside looked in the jeans he'd been wearing the other day. Her daydream was interrupted when she heard a voice snickering outside her office: "Wingless freak." Mara's eyes sliced to the side, but she refused to rise to the bait. She just stored the comment away for the day when all of Hell got to see her wings—and then they'd regret every single snide comment.

Rather than dwell on the malicious commentary, she returned to her roster of closed deals. It was high time she checked in on a few of them. These contracts were investments. She'd given them some latitude in the years they had coming, but she knew that one day they'd truly show their value and be worth the wait. In addition to the NFL quarterback Markus Winston, Mara had her hooks in one of the preeminent CEOs in Silicon Valley, several politicians who each had a decent chance of leading their respective countries at some point, and her current pet favorite: Gideon Miller, the preacher of a megachurch based in Texas.

It never failed to amaze her how blinding the lust for power could be. Gideon convinced himself Mara was an angel sent to help him, and she did not disabuse him of that notion until he was solidly hooked. She filed her list away, promising herself she'd go over her prospects list that night in the comfort of her own living room, with a glass of wine and some fuzzy slippers on.

Out in the hall, there was no trace of the idiot who'd commented on her unseen wings, and Mara didn't waste time, heading for the nearest door back to the Mortal Plane. With little more than a thought, the shadows brought her back to a darkened area not far from her apartment. Mara checked the street carefully before she stepped out of the alley and walked the remaining block to her apartment on Joyal Street.

She unlocked the foyer door. It would be so much easier to just materialize in her apartment, but devils were competitive creatures, to say the least, and Mara—like all devils—had magical wards protecting her home. If anyone tried to come in through a portal from Hell, they were in for a rude and painful surprise. Unfortunately, this particular spell kept her out as well. She'd learned the hard way that lesser spells, ones that would allow just her to materialize in and out, were vulnerable to "supernatural hacking." This one was not. The only way anyone unwelcome was getting in without her permission was by picking the lock.

Inside, she fixed herself a light dinner before heading over to Bruisers in time to get a seat before the post-convention crowd spilled out from the hotels. The National Association of Manufacturers was in town this week, along with the American

Association of Petroleum Geologists. There were bound to be a few ambitious souls in the crowd looking for a way to get ahead. Some might be willing to make a deal tonight, and adding to her prospect pipeline was never a bad thing. Plus, she had her eye on sous chef Kenneth Takahashi. Mara figured that at this point, he was pretty fed up with cooking for convention participants. He should be good and ready to make his move from sous chef to iron chef, and Mara had a plan in place to make that happen.

What did the last prospect tell me? she wondered. *That's right: if it's worth fighting for, then it's damn well worth fighting dirty for. My kind of man.*

To her surprise, Joe wasn't behind the bar when she arrived and grabbed a seat. Joanie took her order and brought her a beer.

"Where's Joe tonight?" Mara asked as she adjusted the shoulder of her turquoise surplice shirt.

"Oh, he's over there, having a quick meeting. I'm just covering the bar for a few minutes." Joanie tossed her head to the side.

"You don't sound like you approve."

"I'm forty-something years old, and I usually know trouble when I see it," Joanie groused. "And this guy talking to Joe, well, I don't like the looks of him."

Mara couldn't help but smile at the protective tone in Joanie's voice. She knew the waitress was sweet on Joe and wouldn't appreciate anyone messing around with him. Mara scanned the room, expecting to see some young stud looking for a bartending job. Instead she sucked her breath in and stiffened, her entire body rigid with rage. Her fingernails hardened and pointed, digging divots into the edge of the bar. Mara squeezed her eyes shut so no one would see the ember-red irises that she knew were blazing. She gulped in a lungful of air, desperate to calm down before she did something stupid.

"You okay, sweetie?" Joanie's concerned voice pierced through the enraged haze in Mara's mind. She let her breath out and felt the fire subside.

"Yes, fine. Had a bitch of a headache all day," Mara answered with a dismissive wave.

"Okay, but if you need anything, you give a shout, okay?"

Mara nodded and turned her laser focus back to the table where Joe sat. Directly across from him, turning on his best charm, was Kemm. Her adversary flipped a few charts quickly and then pulled them back before the burly bartender could really look at the details. Mara knew that trick. She'd done it a thousand times herself.

Kemm was trying to broker a deal for Joe's soul.

Mara angled herself so she could watch them without being obvious. Kemm's smile was as greasy as his hair, but Mara knew from experience that the skinny devil could be quite charming and persuasive when he put his mind to it—and that worried her.

A thoughtful expression crossed Joe's face as he looked at some additional charts. Mara couldn't tell what they were about, but the graphics were big. She knew this ploy as well—flashy, colorful charts showed off enough to impress and entice, but left out the details.

You're a smart man, Joe. She willed him to hear her thoughts. *Don't trust a fucking thing Kemm says.*

When Joe nodded in agreement to whatever Kemm was saying, Mara felt acid burn up her throat. Joanie brought Mara her chili and chips, but despite how good the food smelled, Mara just picked at it. Her mind was racing: *Could I have underestimated Joe? Does he have some desire that I never sniffed out when I met him? Did I miss something?*

She casually took a drink of her beer and stared at Joe over the edge of the glass, then cleared her mind, letting her instincts search for his tarnish. It was there—she could sense it. Joe had made mistakes in his life, made wrong choices, but none of the tarnish indicated a penchant for wickedness, at least not the kind that would attract Mara's attention. But she knew that devils like Kemm didn't have her discerning taste in tarnish.

By the time Joe and Kemm stood and shook hands, Mara was nearly apoplectic. But she knew Joe's soul was safe for the moment, since contracts were always sealed with a kiss, not just a handshake. Until then, nothing was set in stone. Dark, murderous thoughts swirled in Mara's head as Kemm walked out the door.

Suddenly the faint odor of sandalwood grabbed her.

"Do you even know how beautiful you are?"

The sound of Duncan's whispered voice soft in her ear made Mara's blood race and everything inside her tighten with anticipation and desire. She leaned back slightly, hoping to feel the angel behind her, wanting nothing more than to touch him, but he had already slid into his own seat. A small groan of frustration escaped her.

"You could get yourself hurt, Angel-Boy, surprising a girl like that," she said, slamming her bravado up like a shield, a sharp edge in her voice.

"You inspire me to do reckless things. But your smile doesn't match your eyes tonight. What's wrong? Why are you so angry?"

"Did you see the man talking to Joe? He's a devil too, and he's trying to close a deal with Joe. I don't like it one friggin' bit."

"Why not? That is your business, after all—collecting corrupt souls?"

"Yes, but . . ."

"Ah. This other devil is an interloper. You're working on a deal with Joe yourself?"

"Yes. No! But . . ."

"But what?" Duncan pushed her.

"Joe's different. He's not corrupted, not in a way that has any real value for Hell." Mara's brow wrinkled.

"I'll ask you again—why is Joe different? Tarnish is tarnish."

"No, it isn't that simple and you know it. Sins aren't all equal. And Joe is . . . Joe . . ." Mara ground her teeth, annoyed that he was pushing her.

"Joe's your friend," Duncan said. "And you care about what happens to him, don't you?"

Mara knew Duncan could see the struggle play out across her face. She shouldn't care about Joe, but . . . "Yes, Joe's my friend. I care about what happens to him. He's not a bad man. Sure, he's made mistakes, but when he dies, he should go to Heaven, not Hell."

"Then why don't you step in?"

"I can't. Stupid rules. Until a deal is signed, I can poach it, but I can't just ruin it. If I interfere, then I *have to* do a deal with Joe. I can't just warn him away from Kemm."

"That's all I needed to know. I'll talk to him and see if I can convince him that this Kemm guy doesn't have his best interests at heart."

"You'd do that for me?" Mara gave him a suspicious look, her comment to Pastor Jim about trusting Duncan suddenly reemerging from her memory. It was stupid to trust him. Mara had learned a long time ago that trust would eventually result in an ass-kicking . . . and favors never—*never*—came without strings attached.

"Of course I would. I like you, Mara. Plus, I'm an angel. Helping people out of trouble is kinda my jam."

"No strings attached?"

"Only if you attach them. Well, you will need to take care of your buddy, though. Devils can be pesky and stubborn sometimes, and just because I talk to Joe, doesn't mean this Kemm won't run at him again."

"Oh, trust me. I'll deal with him."

Duncan was right: Kemm was as ambitious as they came, and if he thought there was a deal to be had—especially one that would screw Mara out of the number one spot—he wouldn't give up easily. Mara got out of her chair. As much as she wanted to hang around and flirt with Duncan, she needed to be far away if he was going to talk to Joe. She took a step and stopped right next to the angel. She leaned so she could whisper into his ear, so close that her lips almost touched him, and she made a decision then.

"I'll leave you to talk with Joe. I guess now I owe you a favor . . . Duncan."

CHAPTER 8

DUNCAN WAS NOT prepared in the slightest for the thrill that raced through him when Mara whispered his name. He twisted around and watched her walk, admiring the sway of her hips, the shape of her ass, and how her ponytail moved in rhythm with her steps. It was a body built to go all night . . . He slammed a door on the thought before it could reach its inevitable conclusion but willed her to turn around, to come back. She reached the door and looked over her shoulder. Their eyes met and she threw Duncan a saucy wink before she walked outside.

The angel turned around to find Joe leaning on the bar, staring at him.

"You'd better come clean about your intentions for my Mara."

"Your Mara?" asked Duncan, amused by the protective tone in Joe's voice.

"She's a regular, a friend," said Joe. "She's special."

"You have a crush on her."

"A crush? Ha! She's too young for an old bastard like me."

Duncan smiled and thought, *Liar. You've thought about a go with her more than once, but you're too much of a gentleman to do anything about it since you think she's young enough to be your daughter.*

"So, what are your intentions?" Joe folded his arms across his brawny chest.

"I'm not sure what my intentions are."

"Well, keep 'em on the up-and-up, or you answer to me."

"Roger that. Look, Joe, I don't know you all that well, but can I ask you a personal question?"

"Are you drinking?"

Duncan realized he hadn't ordered anything since he'd arrived at the bar. "Yes. Guinness."

Joe poured the beer from the tap, using the traditional two-part pour to give the stout its perfect head, and gave it to Duncan. "Now you can ask your question," he said with a laugh.

"I saw you talking to a guy earlier. Name's Kemm, right?"

"Yeah, I was. Why?"

"Well, I don't want to meddle, but I know of him and he's got a reputation for doing dirty deals. Things in the fine print that get people kinda screwed. I don't know if he's trying to get a deal done with you, but if he is, I'd think twice about it. At least about doing it with him."

Joe grunted and wiped the bar down. Duncan didn't think the gruff bartender was going to say anything, but he was wrong. "He was asking me about franchising. Said I could make a lot of money off the deal. I don't really need it myself, but my daughter has four kids and they'll all need to go to college. Neither of my sons have little ones yet, but I think they both will. That's a lot of money that needs to be put aside for school."

"Admirable that you'd give the money to them. But what would Kemm get out of the deal?"

"That's the thing. He was a little vague on that part," said Joe with a frown. "And I didn't like how he avoided the details. Doesn't quite sit right with me."

"I wouldn't dream of telling you what to do, Joe. This is your place, so any decision you make is up to you. But the advice I will give you is this: You've got good instincts. Don't ignore them."

"I won't," Joe said. "Enjoy the beer. And try the special tonight."

Duncan took Joe's advice and ordered the fried haddock sandwich, and while he waited for his meal to arrive, he thought of Joe's warning about Mara. Devils were usually bad news and most angels steered clear, although he'd heard stories here and there about some outrageous hookups—but those were one-night stands, and he hated the idea of just being one-and-done with Mara. He was interested in more than just a romp in the bedroom and the revelation startled him. Even if he wanted to "save" Mara, he wouldn't.

She likes her job. No, she loves it. Even if I wanted to save her, I . . . Shit, I don't want to change anything about her. She's perfect just the way she is right now.

CHAPTER 9

THREE DAYS LATER Mara and Duncan managed to meet at Bruisers with enough time to have dinner, even though it meant dinner sitting side by side at the bar as if they didn't really know each other. Mara's phone buzzed and she picked it up, accessing the screen with a swipe of her finger. She made a disgusted sound as she read the message, and Duncan glanced over.

"Bad news?" he asked, putting his napkin on the bar and pushing the plate away.

"Just more corporate bullshit. Mandatory training tomorrow. Who schedules training with six weeks left to close the year? So instead of making my numbers, I have to spend the day bonding with my hellish counterparts, talking about our code of conduct."

"Devils have a code of conduct?" Duncan put a twenty down on the bar to pay for his meal.

"Wiseass. You know we do."

As Duncan shrugged on his overcoat, his own phone buzzed. After opening the message, the angel tapped a link on the screen—then tapped it again, and a third time even harder.

"Goddamn it," he muttered.

"Demerits for that," Mara said.

Duncan held the phone out so she could see the dotted wheel caught in its eternal crash loop.

"Well, that sucks," she said.

"You'd think we'd get a communication network that really works," he replied. "I swear they program these emails to crash just to test our patience."

He held the power button down to reboot the phone, and waited for the screen to come back to life. Mara got up and pulled on her own coat.

"Leaving?" Duncan asked.

"I have some work to do. Drudge work I'd rather do on my sofa in my sweatpants."

"Maybe after your training we can get drinks somewhere . . . more private . . . than this?"

"I'm game if you are," Mara answered. She let her fingers graze his hand as she stood up. "Have a good night, Angel-Boy. Good luck with whatever that message is about."

Mara strolled out of the bar and took a deep breath of crisp air, the smell of coffee wafting across the street from Justa Cuppa. Behind her, the bar door opened and suddenly there was an arm around her waist. She spun around and Duncan kissed her. Shocked to the core, Mara froze for a moment, her lips unyielding, but then she softened, understanding deep down that this was more than just a kiss—it was a first kiss, and it was the first that ever truly meant something to her. Duncan stepped back, a roguish grin splashed across his face.

"Are you crazy?" Mara asked, but all she could think about was the roar inside her, the roar that demanded more of the reckless blond angel.

"Just wanted you to know how game I was," he said before he turned to walk down the street. "And that should give you something to think about in your training class, if you get bored."

The next day, despite being annoyed that she had to waste energy a day on this drivel, Mara made sure she was on time for the training class. Grand Dukes Astaroth and Baliel were running the meeting, and the last thing she wanted was a lecture from Astaroth on the value of punctuality.

The room was half-full and a few heads turned when Mara sauntered in. Her dark hair was down and loose, and she wore a cropped leather jacket over a black tank top. Her knee-high boots were laced up the back and she wore her favorite pair of skinny jeans. Mara strolled down to the front of the training room and dropped into a chair. Baliel—in his impeccably pressed suit—assessed her sourly, his dark gold-rimmed eyes oozing disapproval.

"A little casual for a corporate training session, Mara?" he asked, not bothering to hide the snark.

"If you wanted business attire, you should have been more specific in the meeting invitation." She glanced at her nails. They were a new shade of red she was trying called "Tasmanian Devil Made Me Do It." It was a little too orange for her taste, and she made a mental note to change it the next time she traveled through the shadows. A minute later a devil, his eyes also black with a ring of gold around the edge of his irises, sat down in the seat next to her and had the audacity to put his hand on her thigh.

"Maybe after the class we could meet to discuss . . . business," he said with a lascivious grin.

Clearly related to Baliel, he was handsome enough and, in another time and place, Mara might have considered hooking up with him for a bit of sport, but she didn't appreciate having anyone put their hands on her without permission. She slid her own hand over, letting it rest over the rising bulge in his pants, and her suitor's eyes lit up. Then Mara extended her nails, the sharp points pressing into his most sensitive areas, and his expression turned quickly to fear.

"You have until the count of three to take your hand off me." She didn't even make it to two before he hurried to another seat.

"Seth's not going to forget that," said Frankie from his seat three across and one row back from Mara.

"Good. Hopefully he'll be smart enough to not do it again. How you been, Frankie?"

"Same shit, you know the drill. Going to be a tough quarter for me, but I'll get by. Not crazy about cooling my heels in this all day long, though."

"You and me both. I've got some leads to follow up on, and I was supposed to be checking on a contract in Texas right now."

Mara looked casually around the room. Loretta from accounting was there, and she was avoiding eye contact with Mara at all costs. Kemm was also there, along with his brother, Kal. They were on the other side of the room, and Seth had settled into an empty seat near them. He saw Mara looking and gave her the finger. She laughed, unimpressed.

Astaroth walked down the center aisle between the seats, the faint, sickly sweet scent of a rotten apple tainting the air in his wake. He walked up to the lectern, spoke briefly with Baliel, and turned to face the room of about forty-five restless, fractious devils and high-potential demons.

"Sit down, all of you. Let's get this started," Astaroth barked. There was some shuffling behind Mara as the rest of the training class found a seat.

Baliel stepped up and smoothed back his perfect hair. "Every one hundred years we have to make sure you maggots understand what we expect out of all of you . . ." He droned on for at least fifteen minutes about the full corporate structure, mentioning at least twice that he commanded some of the Legions of Hell. A few impressed murmurs ran through the crowd, as well as one inappropriate fawning giggle.

Once he dived into his own impressive resume, Mara's attention wandered to more interesting things, namely Duncan and the kiss they'd shared the night before. A tremendous clap right in front of her startled Mara out of her very enjoyable daydream. Her cheeks scarlet, she looked up into Astaroth's cold eyes.

"Well, Mara, would you like to answer the question?"

"Not particularly, but run it by me again?"

The question was for Astaroth but Baliel interrupted, clearly annoyed with Mara. "The question was why we have this class."

"To remind us all what's expected of us and how to behave," she answered, bored.

"You expect us to raise hell," crowed a voice in the back. "Anything goes!"

A few other voices echoed the one that had shouted out, and she shook her head. Baliel was going to lose his shit over that. If there was one thing the urbane and sophisticated Baliel couldn't stand, it was stupid in any form, and she didn't have to wait long for the anticipated blowout.

"No, you bunch of fucking idiots!" Baliel raged. "Who put you out in the field if you can't answer a simple question? No wonder collections are in the shitter. You're here because you need to understand what we expect of you as well as a few ground rules for how you interact with one another!"

"Without rules, there would be chaos," said Astaroth calmly. "And we can't have that. So, what is the first rule? Anyone?" His expression got colder as no one answered. Finally a small voice to Mara's left piped up.

"No killing humans who don't go along with our deals?"

"Finally, a non-moron," Baliel snarled. "That's correct. If someone won't take your deal, you can't off them out of spite."

"Why not?" asked another demon.

Before Baliel could verbally abuse him, Astaroth stepped in: "A couple of reasons. First, with no contract, the soul goes to the Null Plane to be weighed and judged. If the soul is too heavy, it will go to Hell, but no one gets credit for it—"

"Second," Baliel interrupted him, "if you don't get the deal, then learn to be a better fucking salesman. Don't take your ineptitude out on someone else. And what happens if you're stupid enough to pull a bonehead move like that?"

Mara didn't want to listen to the painful silence so she answered, "Either hours on the racks or years cleaning the Hell Hound kennels."

"Correct," Astaroth said. "And if you are ever given that choice, opt for the rack. Trust me—no one wants to clean up Hell Hound crap. Next we're going to talk about annihilation. Now, many of you don't have to worry about this—yet. You're all too worthless and weak to annihilate a butterfly, let alone another devil. But the more tarnish you collect, the stronger you'll become. Eventually a select few of you will gather enough power to perform a full annihilation."

"How much do we need?" a chunky demon with teeth like a warthog asked.

"It depends. The more talented you are, the less you'll need," answered Astaroth. "Some of you will collect tarnish for thousands of years and not have enough to conduct an annihilation."

Baliel chimed in: "We know there are going to be squabbles over territories, even over specific deals. But you will not—I repeat, *not*—completely obliterate another devil. That's reserved for Lucifer himself."

"Or a Grand Duke with Lucifer's blessing," Astaroth added.

It was very difficult to truly kill a devil, or an angel, for that matter. Any physical injury would eventually heal, even ones that might be lethal to a human. But the act of obliterating a devil—breaking apart the very fragments of their existence—could only be done through sheer psychic power. Very few devils outside of Lucifer and the Grand Dukes had that ability.

"Mara," Astaroth said after a moment. "You were so bright as to answer the other questions, so here's another. What will Lucifer do if you are caught obliterating another devil?"

She kept her face impassive. "I can't answer that because no one knows. Lucifer will dole out punishment as he sees fit. I suppose it could be anything from working in accounting to your own annihilation. It probably depends on who you destroyed and how the Big Dog feels that day. I did hear once that Lucifer peeled the skin off the offender before deciding to annihilate him."

There was an uncomfortable murmur in the group at the thought.

"Teacher's fucking pet," whispered a voice.

Mara turned in her seat to look over her shoulder, and found Kemm staring at her. "Awww. You're jealous. That's so cute." Her voice dripped sweetness.

"I'm not jealous of a freak like you. Like anyone would have to worry about you annihilating them," snorted Kemm.

Overlapping his comment, Seth added, "Bitch got no wings . . ."

"I don't have to be able to annihilate you to beat your ass, Kemm, so I suggest you shut your mouth." She glared at him and he returned it with a snarl.

"Settle down," Baliel ordered.

There was shuffling and grumbling throughout the room and some murmured comments drifted out from the seats on the right side. Both Grand Dukes stared at the crowd and they all fell silent.

"Getting back to our program," Astaroth huffed. "Next on the list is sex."

A tittering giggle filtered through the room and Mara rolled her eyes. *Bunch of damn adolescents . . .* Her thought, however, trailed away as she remembered the night before again—Duncan's mouth covering hers, the kiss more sensual than any she could remember. Her cheeks flushed, but Astaroth's chilly voice brought her back to her senses.

"Fornicate all you like," he said. "I honestly don't care who you bugger as long as it isn't in front of me. But we will not tolerate long-term sexual relationships with humans—"

"A quick fuck in the back seat of a car is one thing. I mean, who hasn't enjoyed one of those?" interrupted Baliel with a licentious grin. "But no emotional entanglements. The angels are under this same dictate—no long-term shit with any humans. We don't want another incident like the Nephilim."

"What's a Nephilim?" croaked someone in the back.

"Seriously? We're really are breeding 'em stupid now, aren't we?" muttered Mara.

Astaroth gave her a sharp look before he addressed the question with a scorn-laden voice. "Clearly someone didn't pay attention in basic history. The Nephilim were the children of angels. These particular angels dropped in on the Mortal Plane and started sleeping with human women with the sole intent of impregnating them. The offspring were so rancid, they not only offended God but also tried to take over Hell. Impudent bastards. God put an end to them—and their idiocy—with the great flood. Then God informed Lucifer and Michael that any angel or devil who has relations with humans—with the express intent of creating offspring—will be locked away in isolation for eternity."

Across the aisle, a slender devil with skin that glittered like snake scales raised her hand. "What about fornicating with other devils?"

"That's another matter entirely," Baliel said smoothly. "As long as you don't miss your quotas, there're no issues. But I'd be happy to discuss the details with you outside of class if you'd like to come to my office."

"I'll make an appointment," she cooed while Mara rolled her eyes in disgust.

"How about angels?"

Mara flinched slightly when she heard Kemm's question, knowing he'd said it to get under her skin, but oddly grateful that someone had asked so she didn't have to.

"They don't have that in the rules," said Devil-Snake's neighbor. "Who would want to do one of those uptight fuckers, anyway?"

The room erupted in laughter, except for Mara, and she felt Astaroth's gaze settle on her. Mara turned her head slightly to stare into his black-abyss eyes, challenging him to ask a question. He watched her for another long moment and then addressed Kemm's question:

"That is a much trickier area, Kemm. Are you in a situation?"

Kemm sputtered. "Me? Shit, no. I'm asking for a friend."

"Well, tell your friend to get his head out of his ass," ordered Baliel, and before Astaroth could say anything else, the sleek Grand Duke went on: "When you're knocking uglies with an angel, you're exposing yourself to all that goody-two-shoes, do-the-right-thing, everyone's-got-some-good-in-them, namby-pamby, New Age bullshit. It gets all over you like bedbugs. You'll go soft. Start feeling things like . . . empathy. I need a shower just talking about it. And that's why Lucifer will shred your wings."

Janelle, Joe, and Paula flashed through Mara's mind, and she slowly dug her nails into the seat's armrests, tearing into the fabric.

"So, if any of you are thinking about getting all lovey-dovey with an angel, think again. What happens if you do? Come on, someone say something. What will Lucifer do to you, assuming I don't get to you first?" Baliel swept his gaze over the crowd.

"One devil got fed to the Hell Hounds," offered a voice.

"My cousin's cube-mate's sister-in-law said her nephew got his wings permanently severed," said Kal.

Behind Mara, Frankie chimed in: "I heard about one she-devil—I don't know her name—who had her wings mangled for doing an angel. Then she was stripped of all the tarnish earnings she'd collected over the centuries and left to wallow in one of the pits of pus and blood at the very bottom of Hell."

The group groaned collectively, offended less by swimming in pus and blood than by the prospect of being stripped of their power, or their wings being mangled.

That's beyond cruel. Lucifer wouldn't really cut off a devil's wings . . . would he? Mara wondered, her stomach clenching.

"Moving on," said Astaroth. "Our last topic for today is The Deal, and we have three areas to cover: poaching, collateral damage, and lying." He took a sip of water and let his eyes scan the room. "Anyone care to elaborate on any of these?"

Another she-devil finally spoke up after an uncomfortable silence: "Collateral damage means you can't worry about the chaff—and you also shouldn't be greedy."

"Very good. With each deal, there's probably going to be some collateral damage. Mortals who your contract hurts in some way. Unless you have a contract with them, a fully signed deal, they're not yours to hoard. This spillover of damaged souls is an excellent opportunity for junior members of the team to hone their own deal-making skills. So, embrace the collateral damage, but don't stockpile it."

Baliel shifted restlessly. Mara could tell by the crease between his eyes that he was getting impatient, being more interested in his private meeting with the Devil Snake than in the rest of the class. Astaroth gave his co-instructor a nasty look.

"Would you like to cover poaching, Baliel?" Astaroth asked.

"Not really. You're doing a bang-up job."

Astaroth's face didn't change, but Mara could see in his eyes that he was going to have a lot to say to Baliel after the class.

"Don't poach," Astaroth told the class. "Until a deal is sealed, we have fair-market competition and you are free to try to finagle it away from any other devil. But once the deal is done and sealed, you cannot go and renegotiate a contract that someone else made. Even if you got away with it to start, I would know when the soul came due on my roster, and any of you who try that shit will get turned over to Melchom, and I will enjoy watching him pick his teeth with your bones."

Mara had seen Melchom do that once and it was unpleasant. She wasn't worried. She was in the clear with Joe, at least—Kemm never sealed the deal before Angel-Boy wrecked that train.

Astaroth tossed an even nastier look at Baliel, who was gesturing for him to move it along. "And lastly, don't lie in a deal."

"But isn't Lucifer the Prince of Lies?" asked a demon.

"A very good point to bring up," Astaroth said.

"Gold fucking star for you," Baliel snorted.

Astaroth moved on as if the other Grand Duke wasn't even there. "Yes, that is one of his many titles, and none of us have any quibble with lying as a concept. We all lie all the time, really. However, in a deal, there must be no misrepresentation, no possibility of a loophole. Always represent your deals accurately—what the mortal will get, what they must give you in return, and when the payment is due. Also, load the contract up with clauses to account for the unnerving human capacity to fuck things up. Remember, the devil's in the details."

In the silence, forty-five pairs of eyes blinked back at Astaroth.

"Any last questions?" the Grand Duke finally inquired.

The chasm of blinking silence widened.

"Class dismissed!" Baliel yelled.

Mara slipped to the side entrance and disappeared, her head aching. She wanted a little peace and quiet to sort out what Baliel had said about angels, but there was no rest for the wicked. On the large ticker board over the sales area, her name was still in second place behind Kemm.

CHAPTER 10

REVEREND GIDEON MILLER was the pastor of one of the largest megachurches in Texas. His flock had been a paltry seventy-five before he met Mara and shared with her his burning desire to expand. She was the answer to his prayers, he had told her. Now, at his gleaming church that could seat eighteen thousand parishioners, Gideon routinely preached to a congregation that reached at least thirty thousand individuals, thanks to the wonders of the Internet.

Five years ago Gideon and his wife founded a private religious school just down the road from the Church of Our Blessed Savior, bringing the reverend even more attention. And as the congregation and his fame grew, so did the wealth. The good Reverend Miller and his wife adorned themselves in the finest designer clothes, drove luxury cars, and lived in a twelve-thousand-square-foot home with two pools and a four-car garage just outside of Houston.

Mara smiled with satisfaction as she looked up at the expansive mansion from outside the gates that kept the riffraff out. *I see your goal to live modestly is going well, and you clearly give to the poor. Excellent, excellent job, Gideon*, she thought.

The sun had set and the mansion was lit up in the dark, so Mara decided to take a closer look at her investment. She cloaked herself in darkness and shadows, slipped through the gate, and strolled up the driveway, pausing to admire the luxury E 350 Mercedes-Benz. The fact that the exterior of the car was an angelic white amused her, and Mara ran a finger along its sleek lines. At the house, she glanced into a few windows, but found nothing of interest—at least not until she reached the living room. Both of Mara's eyebrows went up.

Inside, Reverend Miller's wife, Vivian, was on her knees—completely naked—and the penis in her mouth did *not* belong to her husband. Mara pulled out her phone, took some terribly detailed photos, and hit the video-record button. These photos would certainly add a special something to the conversation she was going to have with Vivian the next morning.

After Vivian stopped sucking her lover's cock, he bent her over the end of the sofa. Based on the moans and cries, Mara guessed they were alone in the house, or didn't care who heard them. She kept the video rolling until she captured Vivian yelling, "Fuck me harder, Bobby!" as well as the rather odd face Bobby made when he finally came. Stepping back from the window and making sure she was hidden by the darkness, Mara let the shadows take her to the Church of Our Blessed Savior, twelve miles away.

Mara strolled down the main aisle of the cavernous megachurch and stopped. For a moment she considered wandering up to the altar, but she decided against it. While she had no plans to do anything untoward, some of the Archangels had major sticks up their asses about demons and devils messing with altars. And she really didn't need some prissy Archangel throwing a hissy fit and saying she'd defiled it. Heading toward the back offices, Mara finally heard voices, and she followed them to Gideon's private office.

"Reverend Miller, I'm not . . ."

"Elizabeth, you have nothing to be ashamed of. You should be proud of how God made you. You are a beautiful young woman, and I need your help to inspire my sermon tomorrow."

The young woman Miller was talking to couldn't have been much older than fourteen, and she was standing in front of Gideon in nothing but her simple white bra and a pleated blue school-uniform skirt. Mara wouldn't have been surprised to see Gideon having sex with a woman—or even another man—but the sight of him with a young girl shocked her to her core. When Miller reached up under Elizabeth's skirt and pulled her panties down, Mara felt like she was going to throw up.

"Reverend . . ." Elizabeth's voice shook a little.

"You want to help me do God's work, don't you?"

"I do. Of course, I do . . . but . . ."

"No 'buts,'" he replied as he slid his hand up the girl's thigh. "Remember, my dear, love in all of its different forms is a wonderful and beautiful thing."

Revulsion and disgust soured Mara's stomach as she watched. She pulled out her phone and with each picture and video she took, her rage burned hotter. When Gideon finished, it was all Mara could do not to shred him to pieces.

"I'll see you again next week, Elizabeth. We need to talk about making sure your scholarship to the school stays in place. I trust you'll be here?" There was no mistaking the threat in Gideon's voice.

Hurrying to button her shirt, Elizabeth's voice quivered as she said, "I'll be here."

"That's my good girl."

Elizabeth gathered her things and scurried out of the room, her cheeks red with shame and confusion, struggling with a self-loathing she didn't even understand. Back in the office, the reverend seemed pleased with himself as he organized his papers, never realizing that Mara was staring at him from the shadows with unrestrained malice.

Mara chewed her lower lip. Fornication, extortion, child abuse. Gideon was everything she could possibly want in a corrupt soul, and she didn't understand why she felt . . . Mara couldn't even come up with the words to explain the feelings churning in her gut when she looked at Gideon and his smug smile. She wondered how many more girls like Elizabeth were out there.

Repulsed and disturbed, Mara disappeared into the night.

Rather than go home to Hollis City, Mara found her way to a lovely little lake surrounded by pines, oaks, and a few rugged hawthorn trees. She kicked off her shoes and carried them as she waded out into the water until her ankles were covered. The sandy soil gave away a little under her feet. She wandered until she reached a large rock and climbed up to sit on it. Looking up at the moon, Mara let the sounds of the woods at night distract her.

"I hate feeling like this," she finally said out loud.

The deep, bold hoot of an owl answered her, and Mara chuckled.

I should be over the moon about Gideon, she thought. *He's a gold mine of sins! His tarnish could be worth twice—hell, quadruple!—what I thought when I signed his deal. But that little girl . . .* Acid crept up the back of her throat. *I can't let him keep doing this. It's . . . wrong.*

The owl hooted again.

Mara dropped her head into her hands. She started to wonder if her Angel-Boy was behind this, if spending time with him was making her soft, throwing her off her game. But even as she entertained the idea, she knew it was wrong. Duncan had never once tried to sway her away from collecting souls or making deals. Besides, she had been feeling sorry for souls before the angel had ever appeared in her life.

Glancing up, Mara watched the owl glide silently across the silver-white face of the moon and bank away, eventually disappearing into the night-cloaked woods. The soft silver light from the moon hit Mara right in the heart. This wasn't a fluke. This was all part of her mother's legacy. Tears brimmed in her eyes. It had been ages since her mother had died, so long that sometimes Mara struggled to remember her features.

"I shouldn't be surprised," Mara whispered to the moon. "I got your eyes—and your wings—getting your compassion was part of the deal. I'd give anything to talk to you about this. I miss you so much."

She pulled her knees up to her chest and let herself cry, the owl in the woods the only witness to her pain. Finally Mara stood up and dropped her guard. She didn't tap into her inner flame—instead she released her wings. Black and glossy, they spread out behind her, the feathers rippling in the breeze. With two large beats of her wings, she rose up into the air over the lake, drinking in the feeling of flying. But she knew it couldn't last. Even in these remote woods, there might be humans, and the last thing she needed was a fuzzy picture of her appearing in a tabloid paper.

Mara settled on the rock again, her wings disappearing as she folded them back, and the weight of her confusion settled over her, heavy and cold. She gazed at the moon again and pressed her lips together, forcing the tears away. "Daddy always said that devils who cry get their asses kicked, but you never cared," Mara said to the pale orb. "Duncan wouldn't care if I cried, either."

Sitting alone on her tiny island, Mara finally admitted to herself that she was so tired of being lonely—and alone. All she did was work, chasing the almighty sales goal, at the expense of everything else. She really didn't have any friends. As much as she wanted to believe Joe was her friend, she knew that if he discovered what she really was, he'd cut and run—and she wouldn't blame him.

She continued her one-sided conversation with the moon: "The closest thing I have to a friend in Hell is Frankie. How freakin' sad is that? Guess that's one reason I like Duncan so much—he doesn't judge me. I don't have to hide who I am around him. And maybe, just maybe, I could show him all of me?"

She thought of the taste of his lips on hers, of the passion that had flooded her in that moment they had shared. Then her shoulders slumped, the quicksilver hope dissolving as soon as it had appeared. Being with Duncan was a dream, a fantasy that was too good to be true. She held her head in her hands for a long time, the conflicting feelings pounding through her heart.

"You didn't get a happy ending, Mom. I'm not going to get one either." Mara called the shadows and vanished into the night.

The next afternoon, Mara—wearing a Prada suit, heels, and large Audrey Hepburn–style sunglasses—knocked on the door of the Millers' house. She smiled genially when Vivian opened the door.

"Can I help you?" Vivian asked.

"Yes, I believe you can." Mara smirked. "We have some business to take care of."

"No, I don't believe we do. I've never seen you before. Good day."

"Oh, we *do* have some business." Mara held up a large glossy print of Vivian naked on her sofa with Bobby's head between her legs. All the color drained from Vivian's face.

"Put that away and come in." Vivian stepped back and they went to the living room.

"Such a lovely home," cooed Mara.

"Have a seat." Vivian wrung her hands anxiously.

Mara tried not to laugh. "Honestly, after what I've seen, I'd prefer not to sit on any of the furniture in this room."

Vivian looked like she was going to pass out. "What do you want? Money? Access to my husband? What will it take for that photo to go away?"

"Do you love your husband? And be honest—I'll know if you're lying."

Vivian looked Mara up and down slowly before she answered. "Gideon and I haven't been in love for quite a long time. He has his flock, and I, well, now I have Bobby."

"Fair enough. You may not believe me, Viv, but I'm glad you have Bobby."

"Get to the point, please. Miss . . . ?"

"You can call me Mara."

"Well then, Mara. I'll ask again: What do you want?"

"I want a couple of things. First is your word. Your husband is heading for a fall, a spectacularly big fall from grace, and when it happens, I don't want you to play the loyal, steadfast wife. No standing by your man. I want your word, your vow, that you'll repudiate him in front of the whole world. If you do that for me, I'll make sure these photos disappear forever."

"What's going to happen to Gideon?"

"Nothing that will blow back on you so long as you keep your word. Consider it a surprise, and trust me, you won't have to wait for long."

Vivian looked skeptical, and Mara let her think for a few moments before she said, "I know being with Gideon got you all of this." She gestured around at the house, the paintings, and the luxurious furniture. "But once he's knocked from his pedestal, it's all yours—or, at least half is, right? I'm offering you a free get-out-of-an-unhappy-marriage card."

Vivian's response was faster than Mara had expected. "Fine, I promise."

"Delightful!"

"What else do you want?"

Mara's eyes flamed. "Your soul."

"Oh sweet Jesus!" Vivian gasped as she fanned herself.

"No, sorry. Wrong side." Mara waited for a second while Vivian hyperventilated. "Do I need to get you a paper bag?"

"No, I'm fine. This is because of my affair, isn't it? I have sinned. *Oh!* How I have sinned . . ." Vivian fanned herself again with her hand, the true stereotype of a Southern belle.

"Hey! Drama queen!" Mara snapped her fingers sharply three times. "Dial it back a little. You're not getting an Oscar for this. Technically, yes, you're a sinner, but you're really a small fish in a very big pond. Normally, you wouldn't even ping on my radar—I usually make deals with much more heinous people than you. But some other devil might get a whiff of your sins and try to manipulate you into a different deal, and that would complicate the first promise you just made me."

"What happens now?" Vivian wrapped her arms around herself.

"Normally, I would guarantee you something that you want in exchange for a claim on your soul when you die. In many cases, there's a time limit, too. You get a specific number of years to live. But, because you're doing me a favor, I won't cap your years—you can live your full natural life. When you do finally die, I'll collect your soul and bring it to Hell for your punishment."

"What will my punishment be?"

"That would depend on what else you do in your life. The more you sin, the worse the punishment is. It's a pretty direct equation. So, here's my proposal to you: I'll make sure that you and Bobby have a long life together, and all I want in return are two simple things: First, you keep your promise to repudiate Gideon. Second, I get the rights to claim your soul when you die."

"No other strings?" Vivian, rightfully, sounded doubtful.

"Aside from the standard nondisclosure amendment and noncompliance clauses, no strings from me. Other than your relationship with Bobby, I can't promise anything else. I can't promise when you'll die or what you'll die from. You could be fifty, you could be one hundred and five."

"After Gideon is gone, I can be with Bobby?"

"For the rest of your life, if that's what you want. I'll pave the way for a happy life, but you and Bobby need to make it work. I'm not going to wave some magic wand and promise you'll never have any issues," Mara said.

"And Gideon won't bother me?"

"No, he won't. I can guarantee that."

Vivian was silent for a long time, and Mara kept a close eye on her, unsure if the reverend's wife was going to faint or throw up. This was the most generous deal Mara had ever offered anyone. She kept silent because it had to be Vivian's choice, but Mara wanted to scream, *Vivian. Do NOT fuck this up.*

Finally, with a resigned sigh, Vivian said, "You have a deal, Mara."

"Outstanding."

"What's next?"

"First, we sign." Mara pulled a stack of papers out of her purse and dropped it on the coffee table. "Take all the time you need to read through this, and let me know if you have questions."

Vivian glanced over the wording and signed at the bottom. Mara added her signature as well and as soon as she did, the ink began to burn and made permanent marks on the paper. Mara tucked it into her seemingly bottomless purse.

Vivian asked, "Do we shake on it?"

"Shake? Oh, sweetie, not exactly . . ." Before Vivian could ask another question, Mara put her hands on each side of Vivian's face and French-kissed her. Hard. When she stepped away, the mixture of consternation and curiosity on Vivian's face was priceless.

"Deals always get sealed with at least a kiss. Look at it this way: How many people can say they got tongued by a devil?" Mara pulled the shadows in around her and as she vanished, she said, "Remember your promise, Vivian. When the time comes, disavow him!"

Mara managed to get photos of Gideon with five different girls, all under the age of sixteen. The day she left the state, an anonymous source sent a dozen photos and videos to *The New York Times*, *The Dallas Morning News*, *The Houston Chronicle*, and the *Fort Worth Star-Telegram*.

To Mara's tremendous satisfaction, Rev. Gideon Miller's world imploded.

CHAPTER 11

THE SCANDAL SURROUNDING Gideon Miller consumed the media's attention, and they savaged him. Leaving the reverend to flounder in the midst of the storm, Mara returned to Hollis City, knowing it wouldn't be long before she'd see him again. She stopped at the Hollis City Convention Center to do a little prospecting, and when she was done, she had added three more souls with great potential to follow up on in the future. Prospects were all well and good, but Mara still had that sales record—and Kemm—to contend with. She glanced across Joyal Street, where the lights coming out of Bruisers's windows seemed particularly inviting. Mara frowned. She really wanted to be around people she actually liked, but she was afraid to see Duncan—even though he was the person she wanted to see the most.

I can't run and hide forever. As much as I want to be up close and personal with Angel-Boy, it would just turn into a train wreck. Probably for both of us. Cutting this off now is best.

Inside the bar, Duncan was there, along with the two angels she saw him with most often, but Mara did her best to avoid eye contact. When the other two angels left, however, she knew it wouldn't be long before he came over. Fortunately, the only other devil there that night was Frankie. Mara slipped into the chair next to Frankie just as he put some money on the bar for his drinks.

"Hey, Frankie."

"Hey, Mara."

"Before you go: How'd it work out with that lead I gave you a while back?" she asked.

"Great. Never underestimate a pissed-off middle manager," Frankie answered. "I was going to mention it to you after training, but you blew out of there pretty fast."

"No rest for the wicked," she quipped.

"Ain't that the truth? Anyway, thanks for the solid, Mara. Without him, I wouldn't have hit my number for that month, so I owe you one."

She gave him a grin. "Yes, you do."

"And you'll be sure to collect, right?"

"You know it, Frankie. Have a good night. Happy hunting."

Shortly after Frankie left, Duncan slipped into the seat on Mara's right, and a few notes of sandalwood tickled her nose.

"Hey. Haven't seen you around."

"Crazy travel schedule. Year-end crunch, you know. It gets a little mental when it starts coming down to weeks and not months," Mara said, with a sarcastic roll of her eyes. "In fact, I'm heading out for an appointment in a minute."

"That is unfortunate. My night is appointment-less, and I was thinking maybe we could spend a little time together . . . alone."

A night alone with Duncan. That simple thought unleashed all the passion and want that had flooded through her the night Duncan had kissed her. It consumed her with a vengeance as Mara contemplated what that kiss could have turned into. A reminder chimed on Mara's phone, dousing her fantasy as if it had been ice water to the face.

"See you here when you get back?" Duncan asked. Her skin tingled as his hand brushed against hers on the bar. "Maybe we can finally get a little time for just us?"

"No, I can't. We can't." Each word cut Mara to the core.

"What?" Duncan was clearly caught off guard. "Why? What's wrong?"

"'What's wrong?'? You do understand what will happen if we do this and get caught?" Her thoughts were whirling: *My wings! If they saw my wings . . . If he saw my wings! I can't take that chance. I—*

"You don't get anything worthwhile by playing it safe," he countered. "I thought devils liked playing with fire."

Mara's jaw set in a stubborn line, but she didn't respond. She tilted her head and gave him a serious look. "I have to ask you a question. Are you trying to save me? Get me to go soft?"

"Save you? No . . ." Duncan sounded flustered.

"You wouldn't lie to me, would you?" Mara pressed.

"Lie to you? You know I don't lie. I've got that whole 'angel thing' going on, remember? How can you even ask me that?" Duncan's voice quickly went from startled to offended.

Mara knew he was telling the truth. Angels were subject to much stricter rules about lying than devils were. She wasn't entirely prepared when Duncan turned the questions back on her.

"Are you trying to make me fall? That would be quite the feather in your cap."

"Keep your voice down!" Mara hissed. "People are looking."

"Answer my question."

"No. No, I'm not." She didn't blame him for asking, but at the same time she resented it.

"Would you lie to me?"

"Christ on a raft, I'm a devil: of course I'd lie to you. But I'm not. Not about this."

Duncan smiled. "Okay, good. I'm glad we cleared that up. Then tell me, why aren't you trying to make me fall? Not cute enough?"

She knew he was trying to make her laugh, distract her from what she needed to say, but her brow knit and she struggled to answer. "Why? I . . . I promised someone once, someone important to me, that I would never do that to an angel." She looked away, clearly finished with that part of the conversation.

"I'm sorry. I was just trying to make you smile."

"Don't worry about it. It doesn't matter." Mara sounded bitter.

"It does matter. You matter. You matter to me."

Mara closed her eyes to hide their anguish. *All I want to do is be with you*, she thought. *And we can't—we just can't.*

"How about telling me, then, why we can't see each other again?"

"We just can't." Mara hesitated, falling over her own rationale, hating the bitter taste of the words. "We're better off staying away from each other. I love being around you, but I can't be distracted, not now."

"No, we're not better off," Duncan said. He sounded hurt and angry, and that only made Mara feel worse. "I like you, Mara. I really do. The thought of hanging out with you after work is the best part of my day."

"Duncan, I'm sorry. I can't. You have friends you can hang out with. You don't need me."

"You can have friends and still be lonely. And you know what, when I'm with you, I'm not lonely. I want more of that. I *need* more of that. It is the only color in my black-and-white world."

That one word—*lonely*—was a punch to the heart for Mara.

"No," she whispered, her eyes shiny. "We can't. Just, please don't do this . . ." Her phone chimed again, and she bolted out of her seat.

"Mara . . ."

"I have to go." Impulsively, she reached out and put a hand on Duncan's cheek. "I'm so sorry, Angel-Boy. I really am."

Mara fled the bar feeling worse than she'd ever felt in her very long life.

CHAPTER 12

DUNCAN STARED AT the bar, turning over the things Mara had said in his mind, wondering if it had been something he'd done that had made her flee. He ordered a double tequila and then chased it with another, but neither drink did anything to dull the pain. Finally he left, wandering the streets back to his apartment.

In the lobby, he ran into two other angels who lived there. He knew Andiel and Simon in passing, but they worked for Archangel Jophiel so he didn't typically see them at work. They said hello as they walked by and Duncan managed a nod and smile. In the elevator, he let his head fall back against the cool wall, and shut his eyes until the door opened on the seventh floor. He wandered down the hall until he got to apartment 724, and let himself in.

He tossed his keys on the narrow table near the door and left his coat on the floor where he dropped it. It was a small one-bedroom apartment with a combined living room and kitchen. The peninsula island in the kitchen served as the kitchen table and split the space into the two rooms. There were enough pictures on the walls to look like someone lived there, but not quite enough to make it feel like home. Duncan almost poured another drink, but then thought better of it and flopped down on the sofa instead. After a minute, his eyes went unwillingly to a framed picture on a shelf not far from the television set. It was the only personal image in the entire apartment.

In the photo, Basil and Raymond smiled and raised their beers at him in a toast. He'd taken it during the Halloween party at Bruisers, just around the time he'd been pulled into Mara's orbit. It was a great picture of his friends, but there was another reason this particular picture was the one Duncan had framed and put on display. In the background, just beyond his two friends, was Mara. She was laughing at something Joe was saying, and he loved how spontaneous it looked.

He wished she had been sitting closer, so he could see more details of her face, but there was no way he could keep a picture of her here. At least he had the chance to look at her every day, no matter what. Duncan felt a little guilty that the photo was up there just so he could see Mara. He should have one of Raymond and Basil for no other reason than being friends with them.

He looked around the apartment. It was quiet, austere, and empty. This was why he'd told Mara she was the color in his world: when she was around, things were brighter, more vibrant, more interesting. Duncan had friends, he knew that, but Basil and Raymond were really the only ones, and even they didn't understand what it was like to be him, to be under Michael's unrelenting scrutiny every single day. The Archangel had a very narrow view of what was acceptable behavior, and anyone who didn't fit that mold was subject to his wrath. Duncan had never fit that mold, so Michael had never passed up an opportunity to remind him of how disappointing he was. For a while he'd talked to Basil and Raymond about it, but then he stopped sharing, afraid they'd tire of his complaints.

But once he started doing that, Duncan found he felt lonelier, even when he was with angels who he knew were his friends.

"Goddamn it," he said to the empty room, his thoughts about his friends interrupted by a sudden memory of what Mara had said to him at the bar: *We're better off staying away from each other. I love being around you, but I can't be distracted, not now.* Resentment churned inside him. He'd never tried to distract her from her work. How could she even say that?

Even as the thought crossed his mind, he had his answer, because it was the same for him. Mara had never tried to interfere with his work, but time and time again, he found himself thinking about her when he should be focused on the task at hand. He let out a heavy sigh.

"I'm not going to play this game, Mara. You think we're better off apart? You think there's something about you or your family that's going to scare me off? Not a chance."

Duncan lay back on the sofa, putting his feet on the cushions, not caring that he hadn't taken his shoes off. He closed his eyes, hoping—in vain—that the tequila would make him sleep. Instead all he did was think of Mara—how her eyes flashed when she laughed, and the thoughtful look that would cross her face when she answered a serious question. The challenging smile when she'd have a shot of whiskey and dare him to keep up. Even the predatory gleam in her eye when she sensed a potential deal—he loved seeing that look she got when she took stock of the clientele at Bruisers.

Duncan looked over at the picture. "You aren't going to run me off that easily, Mara Dullahan. There isn't a snowball's chance in Hell that I'm letting you get away from me."

CHAPTER 13

THE MOTEL ROOM was dingy and small. Brackish water stains graced one corner of the ceiling, and no sane person would walk barefoot on the ancient rug. Gideon Miller sat alone in that dismal little chamber. He'd checked in that morning under an assumed name and asked for a spot on the third floor. The kid manning the front desk had been so engrossed in the video game on his phone that he barely made eye contact with Gideon. The disgraced reverend didn't mind. The death threats and abuse had started the moment the photos of him and the girls were released. The fact that his lawyer had been able to get him out on bail was a miracle, but no matter where he went, Gideon was the subject of unrelenting vitriol.

His plan to have a media conference to explain his side of the story had been dashed when Vivian had told him that he disgusted her, that she never wanted to see him again and that he was a monster. Then she'd gone to the media and disavowed him in public. He scanned through the online news headlines, hoping to find someone who supported him, someone who understood. It was an epic failure. With tears streaming down his face, Gideon opened his word-processing program and began typing. He emailed the document to Vivian but left it open on the computer and, with a heavy, resigned sigh, yanked the sheets from the bed. He methodically tore them into strips, which he then knotted into a single long length.

The balcony outside was contained with little more than a metal railing, and Gideon secured one end of his rope to the railing post. Then he knotted the other end around his neck. Swinging his legs over the railing, he leaned back, but too timid to jump, he watched a group of kids play in the pool, enjoying their afternoon. None of the children—or their parents—looked up. A pretty little girl with curly black hair caught his eye, and he watched her wistfully as she splashed in the shallow end of the water.

Ugly headlines barreled into him: *Pervert. Child Molester. Monster.*

Gideon leaned forward and then back, repeating his cycle of determination and hesitation several more times. The last time he leaned back, some of the old brick crumbled beneath his heel and he slipped off the balcony edge. Surprised, Gideon instinctively tried to break his fall but only managed to not break his neck.

The loop of cloth around his neck tightened as the weight of his body pulled him down, and Gideon started thrashing and clawing at his own throat. A woman at the pool heard the noise and looked up. Horrified, she pointed and screamed. Another motel guest called 911 while parents scrambled to shield their children from the gruesome spectacle. By the time someone reached Gideon's room and broke down the door, it was far too late to save him.

"Hello, Gideon." Mara leaned on the sliding door that led from Gideon's motel room to the balcony where his corpse was hanging.

Gideon's ghost turned around. "Mara."

"Time to go," she said sternly. She walked by him and peered over the railing. She stared at the carcass's purple-red face and bulging eyes. There were scratches on the cheeks where Gideon had clawed at his noose.

"That's a sucky way to die," she said after contemplating the scene for a moment.

"Shouldn't you be happier?"

"Probably, but you're repulsive, so just stop talking." Without any other conversation, Mara summoned a door to Hell, grabbed Gideon by the hair, and dragged him through as he wailed and cried. She flung him into the treasurers' office with such force that Gideon was sprawled on the floor. Melchom wiggled his fingers in an attempt at a dainty wave. Astaroth, as usual, glowered at her.

"The Rev. Gideon Miller," Mara announced.

Astaroth scrolled through his list and frowned again as he said, "Mara, he could have accrued so much more worth if you'd just given him an opportunity, offered him a way off the ledge."

"Didn't seem worth the risk of him being overwhelmed by guilt and repenting in earnest." It was a lie and she knew it—Gideon would have never repented when he didn't believe he was doing anything wrong.

"Mara, we need to talk about this." Astaroth's voice held a very stern warning, but she turned her back on him and brought Gideon to Melchom's desk.

Melchom waited silently as Mara jammed her hand into Gideon's stomach. He writhed and screamed as she spent several minutes digging around for the tarnished parts of his soul. The glittering black coin she pulled out was twice the size of Ricky's and so heavy that it took some effort for Mara to lift it up to Melchom.

The pig-eyed demon studied the scale. "Impressive. But Astaroth is right, Mara: his coin could have been double—triple—the weight with more depravity. And all the girls are food for the younger staff to practice on. You'll get a reputation if people think you interfere."

"I didn't interfere," Mara lied. Gideon opened his mouth to say something and Mara slapped him into silence. "Plus, I already have a reputation—as a badass."

Melchom grunted and handed Mara her chunk of the coin, which was about the size of a large chicken egg. "Here is your share, plus your clergy bonus."

Mara eyed the glittering black mass, reluctant to ingest it because of where it came from, but she could feel Astaroth's and Melchom's eyes on her, weighing her actions, judging her decisions. She'd already attracted way too much of the wrong kind of attention by stopping Gideon's pedophilia. Refusing to eat it would be noticed by the very highest levels of Hell, and she didn't want Astaroth or anyone else asking a lot of questions or sending her down to HR to talk about her job satisfaction. No one wanted to deal with that shit.

She opened her mouth and swallowed the egg whole. As much as she despised Gideon, she sighed as the warm sensation of power infused her, spreading from her stomach out through every part of her body. Almost giddy, Mara felt like she could conquer the world. Her eyes flared for a moment and Melchom chuckled at her.

"I'll see you soon." Mara gave Melchom a sassy wink before she grabbed Gideon by the elbow, dug a fingernail into the soft spot at the joint, and led him through the maze of cubicles until they reached the void across from her office, the one that led to Mara's hall of souls. Broken and pitiful, Gideon stood passively next to her.

"Are you going through or what?"

Cowering, Gideon stepped through the swirling void and stumbled into the other side. He stood back up and peered down the hall.

"You made deals with all these people?"

"I did." Mara's voice was a touch smug. She was proud of her collection of souls. She was, after all, a devil, and accumulating corrupt souls was her job. Other, older devils had longer halls, but she had a veritable who's who of debauchery and depravity.

"What's behind the doors?"

"Each door either leads to a self-contained Hell or down to one of its deeper levels. I get to design the punishments for each soul I bring in."

As they walked, Gideon slowed his pace and gawked while he read the nameplates on some of the doors. He read them out loud: "Ted Bundy . . . Jack the Ripper . . . Belle Gunness . . . Caligula . . . Ivan the Terrible . . . Ilse Koch . . ."

"Ah, Ilse." Mara smiled with satisfaction. "The infamous Bitch of Buchenwald. She and Ivan, real pieces of work." She stopped three doors later and let Gideon stare at his own name for a long time. He trembled, bit his lip, and tried not to cry as Mara opened the door and gestured for him to go inside.

"No . . ." His voice was barely audible.

"Are you going to man up and go in by yourself, or am I going to have to force you through the door?"

Mara hoped he'd panic and give her an excuse to pummel him one last time, but to her immense disappointment, Gideon scurried in like a whipped dog, shuddering as he crossed the threshold, as if something uncomfortable and unseemly had touched him. On the other side, they walked into a circular room with a central area cordoned off by clear walls, and a door on the opposite side of the room. Mara led him to the central area and put her hand on the plexiglass wall. An opening shimmered into existence. She ushered Gideon through.

"*This* is my Hell?" Gideon looked around. The circular area they were in was a little more than twelve feet across, with floor-to-ceiling walls of clear acrylic glass. Other than the void Mara had opened, it had no door. The outer walls of the room were a bland gray, interrupted only by the door they'd originally come through as well as one on the opposing wall. The second door opened and Gideon recoiled for a moment, expecting some horrible devil-spawn. Instead the outer part of the room started to fill with young girls, barely teenagers—all with jet-black eyes, and all dressed in the Church of Our Blessed Savior school uniform. Gideon licked his lips and swallowed hard.

One of the devilish temptations dropped some papers and made sure Gideon got a glimpse of her panties under her pleated skirt when she bent over. Another "accidentally" spilled water on her blouse, the material turning translucent. A few beads of sweat appeared on Gideon's forehead and he practically started panting. Mara's disgust blossomed as Gideon lost track of everything else around him, his attention solely focused on the girls just out of his reach.

"You're really something else, aren't you?" Mara's voice was heavy with sarcasm, and she made a face when Gideon turned to her, his erection blatantly obvious in his pants.

"They're so . . ."

"Tempting? Beautiful? Of course they are. And that's all you're going to see for the rest of eternity, Gideon. The thing you want most, young girls who just can't wait to offer themselves up to you, who will act out whatever fantasies are in that fucked-up little brain of yours. And they're *just* out of reach. You'll never put your hands on one of them again. No easy access like you had at the church."

"Let me in," interrupted the girl with the damp shirt. She pressed herself against the plexiglass. "I need some help with my homework."

"And no way in or out of your little room here, for you or them."

Gideon put one hand on the glass, and the girl pressed against the other side. The reverend moaned and his other hand moved to the front of his pants.

"Don't think you're getting off that easy—no pun intended, of course," chortled Mara. "You're in Hell, and the only pleasure here is mine. Go ahead, try to rub one out, see what happens."

Gideon hesitated for a second, but his perverse carnal desires overrode his fears. He put his hand on the bulge in his pants and started rubbing.

"On second thought, wait," Mara said.

Gideon's face twisted as his hand turned numb, a useless hunk of clay. He tried with the other hand and the same thing happened.

"What's happening to me?"

"Nothing, and that's the point. I really don't want to sit here and watch you get off on your nasty little predilection. So, for the moment you can get turned on, but if you try to jerk off, your hands will go numb—totally, utterly useless to you."

"Forever?" Gideon bleated.

"No, not forever, but trust me when I tell you, once you have your hands back, you're not going to find masturbating nearly as pleasurable. Not unless you're into acid shooting out of your Johnson. You're never going to get pleasure from little girls ever again."

A hint of what his eternal punishment would be like finally sank in, and Gideon dropped to his knees in front of Mara, clutching at her legs. "I'm sorry! I'm sorry! I shouldn't have done those things. What can I do to change this? I want to repent all of my sins!"

"You can't repent now. You have to do that—sincerely—*before* you die. You made your deal with me, Gideon. And now it's come due." Her voice was impassive as she used her foot to shove Gideon away from her.

Gideon struggled to his feet. "Mara! Please don't leave me here. For the love of God!"

Mara laughed. "'The love of God'? That's funny. You should have thought more about God when you were alive, Gideon. Oh, and before I go, I have one last little gift for you."

She snapped her fingers again and a TV screen materialized in the air.

"How did you do that?" Gideon asked.

"The TV? We all have the ability to make some things appear. It's easier in Hell," Mara said. "I couldn't materialize the TV on the Mortal Plane. When I'm there, I can pull a few things out of Hell if I need them, contracts and stuff like that, but it takes a lot more of my energy, so I don't do it often."

As Mara talked, the screen began to glow and then filled with snowy static. Mara tapped the side of the screen, and it flickered to life. The image became clearer: A naked woman straddled her lover, grinding up and down on him. Slick with sweat, they both moaned in ecstasy. The woman threw her head back as she came.

"Vivian?" Gideon's eyes widened as the man's head turned to the side. *"Bob?"*

"Just thought you ought to know. Your wife's been fucking the accountant."

Mara stepped through the portal in the plexiglass wall and sealed it up behind her. She walked out the door of Gideon's eternal damnation and slammed it shut. With a purposeful step, she headed down the hall. She ducked into her office and shut down her laptop, fully intent on getting back to the Mortal Plane as soon as possible. Then her phone rang, the deep bass notes of Van Halen's "Running with the Devil" telling her that it was Astaroth on the line before she even looked at the screen.

She let his call go to voicemail.

CHAPTER 14

KEMM WAS WEARING his best suit for his final meeting with Joe. He had been more than patient with him, even relenting when the bar owner postponed their second meeting for a little over a week. But tonight everything was going to be ticked and tied, and Kemm couldn't wait to shove it in Mara's face. Once they sat down at the table, Kemm leaned forward and smiled his wolfish smile.

"Terrific to see you again, Joe. Now that you've had some time to think about it, I know you understand how lucrative this deal will be for you."

"I have thought about it—" said Joe, but he couldn't finish before an eager Kemm interrupted him:

"I have the paperwork ready so that—"

"—and I'm going to have to pass," Joe finished firmly.

Kemm's smile vanished and his nostrils flared. "*No?* You're backing out? How can you pass up an opportunity like this?"

"It just isn't right for me, not now."

"You're leaving millions on the table!"

As Kemm blustered, Joe stood his ground. "Maybe so, but I'm not ready."

"We had a deal! We shook on it!" There was a snarl buried in Kemm's voice.

Joe's expression hardened. "No, you listen to me, son. That handshake was a courtesy. The only thing I agreed to do was think about your proposal, and to not make deals with anyone else until I'd given you an answer. And that's exactly what I've done. I thought about it for a long time, and my answer is no."

"Did someone offer you better terms? I'm sure we can salvage this," Kemm countered quickly, his tone turning conciliatory. "A deal in principle and then we can work out the details?"

"You see, that's the thing. I like details and you don't seem willing to give any. Like this: you've never said what you get out of the deal. There's got to be something in it for you. That don't sit right with me. A man doing business ought to be honest about it. And I got some good advice from a friend about trusting my gut, so again, the answer is no." Joe stood up from the table. "Thanks for coming in. If you're interested in dinner, the fried fish is excellent tonight."

Joe adjusted the polo shirt he wore with the Bruisers logo over the right breast and returned to his bar. Kemm stared daggers at his back and then his eyes slid to the side. On the other side of the bar, sitting next to Basil and Raymond, Duncan was waving at him. Kemm gave him a hateful stare.

"Friggin' goddamn angels," Kemm cursed. "I'll get that deal, screw his interference." The devil stormed out of the bar. From across the room, all three angels watched him leave.

"You mess up his deal, Duncan?" asked Basil. At no more than five foot two, Basil looked every inch the proper middle-aged businessman.

"I made a few suggestions to Joe," Duncan answered.

"Nice job. That should rack up a few points with the boss," said Raymond. With his red hair, freckles, and large blue eyes, he was Basil's complete opposite.

"Maybe."

"Why aren't you happier about it?" asked Basil. The shorter angel glanced over to where Mara normally sat. "Is this about that hottie devil who usually sits over there?"

"No," Duncan snapped quickly. Too quickly. "It's got nothing to do with her."

"Sure. Whatever you say," Basil said.

Four blocks away from Bruisers, Kemm still had his fists clenched as he fumed. He'd done everything right—Joe should have taken the deal. Now he was going to have to find another way to lay claim to Joe's soul, because no one said no to him. No one. He stalked past a dark alley and a soft voice followed him down the street.

"You're going to stay away from Bruisers and from Joe."

Kemm stopped and turned, incensed. "It's my deal; I've done the work. Screw you, Mara."

"I won't tell you again. If you go after Joe, we're going to have a problem." Mara's voice drifted out of the shadows in the alley. Kemm stepped into it and stopped, searching the darkness for some sign of her.

"I knew you had a soft spot for that stupid mortal. Your own little pet human. I cannot wait to tell Grand Duke Valafar that you fucked up my deal yet won't put your mark on Joe's soul either," Kemm snarled.

"I haven't said a word to Joe about you."

"You must have."

"Ask around, you'll see."

"Then who . . ." Kemm paused, suddenly realizing what had happened. "I don't fucking believe it. That angel you've been flirting with is making you soft. Have you let him do you yet? Because I'm going to have the best day ever when they skin you alive." He chortled like a hyena as he walked deeper into the alley.

Mara stepped out from the darkest of the shadows. "Who I do is none of your business. And I'm only going to tell you once more: stay away from Joe and Bruisers."

Kemm looked her up and down. She was almost too pretty to be a devil. "You don't scare me, Mara. You don't even have any wings. I don't know how you've gotten as far as you have, unless you're sleeping with one of the Grand Dukes. You and Astaroth got a little thing on the side? He did pick you off the trash heap when you were barely an imp. How long have you two . . . " He made an obscene gesture and leered at Mara, letting his human mask slip away. His gargoyle face was pock-marked and punctuated by two eyes that burned a dull orange. Thin lips pulled back in a macabre smile to show small pointed teeth.

Mara didn't flinch. "Just walk away," she warned him.

"Screw you. I'm going to do a deal with Joe and I'm going to make sure you know how much he's suffering. No wing-less she-devil freak is going to scare me away from my mark." Large leathery bat-like wings unfolded from Kemm's back and he cupped his hands, gathering his power as he prepared to assail Mara with demon-fire. "And just for spite, I'm going to take every single soul you care about at Bruisers and make deals with all of them. Joe. Joanie . . ."

He flung the ball of red-and-black demon-fire at Mara. She crossed her arms in front of her, her own power shielding her from the bulk of it, but as the flames dissipated, Kemm's voice cut through again.

". . . and once I'm done with them? Then I'm going to destroy the angel."

The instant Kemm threatened Duncan, Mara reacted. Her irises turned from deep brown to crimson in an instant, and red flame—touched here and there with a hint of blue—danced around her eyes, curling and flaring. The way the flames painted her face made Kemm gasp, and when her enormous black wings fanned out, he stared at her in horror and wonder.

"What kind of freak are you?"

The hesitation and the question cost Kemm as Mara slammed him back into the wall, chunks of brick showering down to the ground, her nails tearing and digging into his chest. Rivulets of blood stained Kemm's linen shirt as he squealed in pain.

"What the fuck are you? No normal devil has wings like those. And your eyes? There's only one devil whose eyes flame like that!"

He felt Mara's sharp nails cut him as she tore him from the wall. Mara flung him down the alley and Kemm crashed into a dumpster, denting it.

She stalked through the darkness toward him. "How very, very unfortunate for you that you've seen all this."

Her voice was silky and cold, and Kemm was suddenly very afraid. He hurled another crackling sphere of demon-fire at her. She deflected it with a casual flick of her wrist, and Kemm's insides turned to water when he saw what little effort she expended. He was out of his league and he knew it. Kemm turned away, starting to call the shadows so he could escape to the Immortal Plane, but an orb of black fire, hotter than he'd ever felt, slammed into his back.

He fell to the ground screaming, rolling in the grit and dirt of the alley as the fire ate into his flesh, dissolving the webbing in his wings. He shrieked in anguish and dragged himself along the ground. Bits of his shredded wings trailed behind him. He only made it a few yards and started to pant in terror as Mara's footsteps came inexorably closer. Twisting onto his back, he held up his hands in supplication.

"Stop!" he begged. "Stop!"

Mara loomed over him, another churning ball of black-and-red fire the size of a melon floating above her cupped palm.

"I won't go near Joe! I won't. Or the angel!" he screeched. The bones of one wing crumbled away as the last of the demon-fire on his back sputtered and went out. "And I won't tell anyone about you! About your wings!"

"You're right," growled Mara. "You're not going to tell a single bloody soul about them."

Kemm realized in that instant, as he looked at her utterly impassive face, that there would be no mercy. Mara raised her hand and slammed the ball of fire down on him. He screamed, the sound reaching a fever pitch. A second ball followed a moment later, drenching him in hissing, spitting black-and-red fire. His body entirely engulfed in flames, Kemm thrashed in agony, and then one of his charred clawed hands stretched out in a vain effort to drag himself down the alley. He made it about three feet before he finally collapsed.

The demon-fire continued to burn until Kemm was completely consumed and there was nothing left but an acrid pile of greasy black ash. Mara had annihilated him.

She stared at Kemm's remains. As her rage and fear subsided, she realized what she'd done, and she knew she was screwed if anyone found out. The irony of having just gone through a training on this very topic was not lost on Mara, but she was in no mood to find humor in in it. If anyone found out she'd crushed Kemm like this, Mara was going to get a royal ass-kicking. She thought about the last devil who had crossed that line. She hadn't seen it herself, but everyone said his skin had been peeled from his body by Lucifer over three long excruciating days.

I could argue self-defense, but the fact that I have the ability to do . . . this . . . raises more questions than I'm willing to answer, she thought as a wave of panic washed over her. Mara took a deep, steadying breath. This was no time to get hysterical. Panic made people—and devils—do stupid shit.

"You only get punished if you get caught—so I certainly can't leave this mess lying around," she whispered to herself.

"Kemm? Kemm! Where are you?"

Fear froze Mara's blood when she heard Kal's voice at the end of the alley, near the street.

"Kemm! You said you had something big to celebrate, bro. Where the fuck are you?"

Kal was too far away to see her, but Mara heard the crunch of his boots on the gravel and broke out in a cold sweat. If Kal found her there with the charred remains of his brother? Her heart pounding, Mara spread her wings and gave two tremendous flaps, churning up a cyclone of air that lifted Kemm's ashes and scattered them far and wide. It was the best she could do without Kal seeing her.

Mara called the shadows to her side. They wrapped around her, warm and comforting, and she dissolved back into the dark, leaving behind some greasy ash and the revolting smell of burned flesh.

CHAPTER 15

KAL STRODE DOWN the sidewalk. It had been a bad day, and he was angry with everyone. And not being able to find Kemm wasn't improving his mood at all. His twin had invited him for drinks at Bruisers—something about closing a special deal that he wanted to celebrate, but no one at Bruisers had seen him. The dark emotions radiated off him and people scrambled to get out of his way. Kal was tired of dead ends and was about to send Kemm a nasty message when he walked by a dingy alley. Abruptly, he stopped dead in his tracks. The man walking behind him on the sidewalk slammed into him.

"Jesus Christ, nice job, you . . ." The man began, but backpedaled quickly when Kal turned and glowered at him.

"You got a fucking problem?"

"No, no problem. My fault." The man gave Kal a wide berth and then hurried down the street.

The devil walked back to the alley and stared down into the dimness. His brother had been here, he could sense it. Kal marched into the dark, confident that nothing in that alley was more terrifying than he was. Dumpsters dotted the walls, and grit and glass crunched under his shoes. The hiss of pipes punctuated the gloom, and behind him, the rumble of a large truck on the road reached its apex and then faded away.

Kal crouched down and touched a small pile of ash with his finger. He inhaled deeply, the odor of charcoal and lighter fluid overwhelming him, and it felt like a punch to the gut. That was his brother's scent. An enraged roar bubbled up from deep inside, but Kal clenched his teeth, forbidding the grief and rage to explode out of him. There would be a time and a place for that, but it wasn't here.

He grabbed a discarded plastic produce bag lying on the ground near a dumpster. Carefully, he swept as much ash as he could into the bag, but before he sealed it, he held the pouch under his nostrils and inhaled again. It was definitely Kemm, but there was another scent too. It smelled oddly sweet, like wood from a fireplace, but it was the tang of another devil—the one who had destroyed his brother.

Kal racked his brain. He knew that other scent, he'd smelled it before. It reminded him of Louren, another devil he'd worked with, but it wasn't quite right. And Louren would never do something like this—he was too chicken-shit. Then his mouth sagged open. *It couldn't be, could it?* he wondered. *That devil Kemm was always butting heads with? What's her name? Marisa? Maura? Mara! That's it. Mara.*

"They hated each other," Kal said out loud. "But how could she have done this? She's deformed. There's no way." He put his nose over the bag and inhaled one more time. Mixed in with his brother's charcoal scent was sweet birch smoke. It had to be her—no other devil smelled sweet like that—and frankly, he found it disgusting.

Kal stuffed the bag in his pocket. "I'll get that little bitch for you, Kemm. I promise you that."

The hunt was on.

CHAPTER 16

IN THE DAYS following Kemm's untimely demise at her hands, Mara kept her head down and avoided nearly everyone. She cleaned up her paperwork and kept her eye on the sales numbers. With only about six weeks left until the quarter closed and the year ended, she still needed six more souls to beat Kemm for the number one spot, and she had to admit, it was a relief to know that he wouldn't be adding any more to his tally. But she still needed to be one better. It had been a long day and she was tired, but she didn't relish returning to the Mortal Plane, either, not when she knew Duncan might be at Bruisers. Not when he might be able to sense her fear and anxiety over what had happened with Kemm—and the consequences hanging over her head. The phone on her desk rang, and Mara reluctantly took the call.

"Astaroth?"

Her manager's voice, thin and annoyed, slid out of the speaker: "See me before you leave."

"But I was about to . . ."

"*Now*, Mara. No excuses."

Astaroth hung up before Mara could answer. She heaved a beleaguered sigh and headed toward her manager's office, away from the portal out of Hell.

"I'm here, Astaroth. What do you want?" Mara asked as she came into the office. She closed the door behind her so no passersby would overhear anything Astaroth said.

"You left before we could finish our discussion about Gideon Miller the other day, and you've been less than responsive to my voicemails." Astaroth stared down his beakish nose at her and came out from behind his grand mahogany desk. At his own desk, Melchom busied himself with paperwork.

The door to the office crashed open, cutting off anything else Astaroth was going to say to her, and Grand Duke Valafar stormed in, the grimace around his exposed skeletal teeth even more pronounced than usual. The light from the gothic chandelier overhead followed the twisted black horns that curved back from Valafar's head and around to his ears, making them look sleek, shiny, and sharp.

"Where is he?" the Grand Duke thundered. "This is the third meeting that little fuck has ignored, and I'm going to rip Kemm's puny little head off! Has he brought you any souls?"

At the mention of Kemm's name, Mara tried to conceal her flinch and avoided looking at Valafar.

"Not recently," Melchom said.

"Tell me what his turn-in schedule is, Astaroth! When is his next soul due?" Spittle sprayed out of Valafar's mouth, staining his already neglected shirt.

"I'm in the middle of something. I'll text you when I have a moment to look it up."

"There could be souls out there past their due dates!" shrieked Valafar.

"I'll look it up when I'm finished talking with Mara."

Valafar snorted derisively. "We could be losing income and you're fawning over the scum you picked up sifting through that garbage pile of orphans while looking for new blood."

Mara nearly exploded.

"I clearly have more of an eye for talent than you do. She may be lagging slightly in deals, but at least Mara isn't AWOL. Now, if you'll excuse us, Valafar, we have work to do." The tone of Astaroth's voice said the matter was closed, and after another few moments of bluster about all the things he was going to do to Kemm, Valafar stomped back out of the room. Astaroth's sigh of annoyance filled the sudden silence.

"Have you seen Kemm?" Astaroth asked her.

"What? Why?" Mara's answer was a touch too sharp. Astaroth raised an eyebrow, and she hustled to recover. "I mean 'why' as in, why would I see that little good-for-nothing hack? He can't stand me and the feeling is mutual."

"I see." Astaroth continued to study her and Mara made every effort to stand still and not fidget.

"What's your problem with Gideon?" she asked, hoping to move on to any subject other than Kemm.

"My problem? We need to talk about Gideon. I think you deliberately diminished the worth of your own contract, Mara," Astaroth said sternly.

Mara flinched. "Why would you think that?"

"I know you, Mara. Everyone knows I picked you out of that orphan pit. I mentored you. I know *all about* you. Must I remind you that I know your pre-orphan story as well? While no one has traced the photos back to you, the rumors are already out there that you either did it deliberately or you weren't paying enough attention." Astaroth pressed his lips into a thin, disapproving line.

"Paying enough attention?" Her voice went up slightly.

"You could have prevented the suicide if you'd really wanted to—you could talk a dog down off a meat wagon. You could have encouraged his debauchery or any number of things to add weight to his soul. But some out there are saying you're just getting sloppy."

That got under her skin. Mara snarled, "Screw them. You know me, and I am *not* sloppy."

"Perception becomes reality. You know what your peers call you already," said Astaroth. Mara's jaw set, as jibes like *freak*, *mutant*, *aberration*, and *mongrel* settled heavily on her shoulders, and the Grand Duke watched her closely.

"You're eventually going to need to disabuse them of those ideas, you know," Astaroth told her. "But in the meantime, don't let them add 'slacker' or 'sloppy' to the list. It reflects badly on you, and on me."

"They're just jealous. Their numbers can't compare to mine. They're not within a thousand miles of me." She raised her chin, defiant.

"Keep it that way. Kemm works for Valafar and if I have to listen to him lord over me how his boy kicked your ass . . ." He left the thought unfinished, but the implication was unmistakable. If Valafar made him miserable, he would make Mara doubly miserable.

"You can go." The dismissal was curt.

Mara set her jaw in a hard line and gave the Grand Duke a sullen glance before she slunk out. She hurried down the hall, bumping into an imp carrying an armful of file folders. They scattered on the floor, and she cursed at her, but Mara didn't even notice. She was too wrapped up in realizing how tired she was of hiding who she really was . . . and that all she really wanted was to go home and see Duncan.

It suddenly occurred to Mara that maybe she wasn't that different from Ricky and Gideon and all the others. She was suffering too. Suffering in her own hellish prison that she'd built out of her own lies and denial.

CHAPTER 17

MARA REMATERIALIZED ON the Mortal Plane a good half mile from her apartment. She wanted to walk for a few minutes, clear her head, and calm down. After her collision with the imp, she'd had the bad luck of crossing paths with Dagon—one of the more senior devils—who had ripped Mara a new one because she hadn't swayed Gideon away from suicide and capitalized on the preacher's predilection for underage girls. That was one of the drawbacks of being so close to a record. Mara knew every other demon and devil in Hell was interested in her business, and—like Dagon—many of them would be just as happy to see her fail.

It was one thing to have her ass handed to her in private by Astaroth, but Dagon's public assault was uncool, and Mara had fired back with just as much vitriol. Then, emboldened by Dagon's behavior, a lesser devil had mocked her for being soft. Mara had shredded him—literally—in front of his companions. It would take weeks, perhaps months, for all his damage to heal, and while it might not quell all the whispers about how she had handled Gideon, it would certainly slow them down.

It was nearly eleven at night when she rematerialized and stepped out of the shadows onto the crowded sidewalk in Hollis

City. She'd only made it a block when thunder rumbled, and despite the fact that it was dark, Mara looked up at the sky crossly. She was never going to make it home before it started to pour, and there were too many mortals around to use the shadows to transport her. Folding her arms angrily, she stalked down the sidewalk, barely noticing any of the people around her as they hurried along. Mara couldn't get Gideon out of her head—how revolted she was by him and the things he'd done.

Astaroth was right, and so was Dagon. Left alone, Gideon would have been much more valuable. Mara wondered what was wrong with her—she was a devil from the pit of Hell. She should have been thrilled that Gideon was so consumed by his lust and vice. But the only thing she *could* feel was sorry for the girls he'd hurt and angry about how manipulated and damaged they were . . . and how they'd be easy pickings for her brethren. She sighed heavily, wishing she could just blame her feelings on Duncan, but she knew she was lying to herself. He might be the only one who understood what she was feeling.

Two blocks from her apartment, the sky opened up. It didn't start as a sprinkle or a shower—it just came down in a cold, raw torrent, soaking Mara to the bone in a matter of moments. A woman sprinting for shelter nearly ran into her, but Mara didn't change her pace. She wasn't going to get less wet, and she was still preoccupied with her own thoughts. Maybe she needed to talk to her father. He'd always said that she was like her mother in so many ways. But going to him opened up so many more complications.

By the time she reached her apartment, the street was deserted. Mara glanced over at Bruisers. It looked warm and welcoming, and she wondered if Angel-Boy was there. But she was confused, angry, and wet, and the thought of seeing Duncan just made her heart ache more, so she turned away from Bruisers. She climbed the steps to the building's foyer, which led to the staircase that would bring her up to her place, and rummaged in her bag for her keys. There was a small overhang above the door, which gave her some respite from the rain. She put the key in the lock and stopped, her head snapping up at the hint of sandalwood. Angel-Boy!

"Terrible weather."

She closed her eyes when she heard Duncan's voice behind her. There was precious little room in the door's alcove and she felt giddy—even sitting next to him in the bar, Mara had never been this physically close to Duncan. There was an intimacy in their closeness that she wasn't prepared for. She turned and found herself staring up into his amazing blue eyes. He was soaked to the skin as well, his blond hair matted and stuck to the sides of his face. Drops of water fell from the tips of his hair, and one rolled down his nose before it fell.

"I told you to stay away," she whispered.

"You did, but I don't want to."

Every part of Duncan's being responded to her voice. Even drenched, Mara was the most amazingly beautiful creature he'd ever seen, and the fact that the wet silk shirt clung to every single curve on her body didn't hurt. He wanted her so badly, the sheer force of the emotion nearly overwhelmed him.

"I've missed you." He kept his voice low. "I was getting worried. You haven't been to the bar in a while."

"Work stuff," she answered softly. "Got my ass handed to me today."

"What? Who do I need to go rough up?"

Mara smiled at him. "That's okay. I gave better than I got."

"That's my she-devil." There was satisfaction in his voice as Duncan lowered his head a fraction of an inch. As Mara pressed up against him, all Duncan could think about was how much he wanted to kiss her. *But an angel and a devil? It couldn't happen, could it?* he wondered.

"I think about you all of the time," Mara confessed.

"Good. I think about you too. I dream about you." And, oh, those dreams . . . Duncan could feel her hesitation, her confusion. "Do you still want me to stay away?"

"No," she whispered. "I hate it when you're away."

Oh thank God! blazed through his mind.

"We're crazy to think about this. We could lose everything."

"I know," he said. Patience may have been a virtue, but Duncan wasn't certain how much longer he could be that close to Mara without kissing her.

"Our careers will be shot. And then there's my family. You have *no* idea what you'd be getting into."

"Screw my career." Duncan's voice was deep and husky. "It's on a fast track to nowhere, and I don't care about your family. I only care about you."

They stared at each other longingly for a few seconds that felt like an eternity. Duncan said, "Say my name."

"What?"

"Say my name. I want to hear you say it." He didn't know why, but he loved hearing Mara say his name out loud. She was so close, Duncan could practically taste her, and when she granted his wish, whispering his name, he couldn't stop the soft moan that escaped him. His hand cupped around the back of her neck, holding her close, the touch electric between them.

"Kiss me." He felt her draw back slightly, resisting his request. The grin on her face, one that managed to be sultry and mischievous all at once, only heightened his desire.

"You do see the irony of the situation? An angel tempting a devil?"

He laughed. The knowledge that he tempted her sent a thrill through him right to his core. It was followed immediately by an avalanche of fear over what this temptation could cost them.

"Duncan?"

"Damn the consequences," Duncan said as he pulled Mara into his embrace.

As his mouth covered Mara's, he thought he might die. He'd intended to start gently, softly, but he couldn't help himself. And when her mouth opened, inviting him to deepen the kiss, he was lost. He pulled her body closer to him and reveled in her arms wrapped around him, her fingers dug into him. Sliding a hand down her back until it reached her waist, Duncan held her tight as he pushed against her. With a tug, he pulled her hips even closer and as Mara leaned in, the swell of her breasts pressed against him. A primal moan escaped the back of Duncan's throat. Mara broke their kiss and nuzzled at Duncan's neck before she raised her head slightly so they were cheek to cheek.

"I said your name," she whispered, her lips grazing the edge of his ear. "Now I want to hear you screaming mine."

CHAPTER 18

IN A FLASH, Duncan grabbed Mara's wrists and pushed her back against the door. Her eyes flashed red for a moment, until the desire coursing through her took over. She thrust her head forward, her kiss both a challenge and an invitation, and he crushed his body up against hers. Letting go of her wrists, he dropped his hands to her waist. Her head fell back against the door as his lips nearly scorched her skin.

When Duncan lifted his head again, he whispered, "Take me upstairs."

She took his hand and led him up to her apartment. Inside, Mara kicked off her heels and used a small amount of her power to partly dry her hair. Physical changes were much less draining when she did them while using shadows to move between Planes, and if this evening was going where she thought, she didn't want to feel like a drowned rat. She turned back to Duncan in time to see him vigorously rub his hair, the excess water spraying around him.

"Sorry about the mess."

"Who cares? That is a very good look for you, Angel-Boy," she said, referring to his tousled hair.

He grinned and ignored the comment. "Come here."

Mara gave Duncan a coy look, but when he held out a hand for her, she found she had no interest in playing hard to get. She crossed the kitchen and took it. Duncan didn't yank, not with the ferocity he had on the front steps, but he pulled Mara in close to him, and she caught her breath when he slipped his arms around her. She ran her hands up his wet shirt and slid them around his neck.

"Kiss me again," she said. "Like you did before."

There was no hesitation as his head dropped down, and Mara allowed her fingers to wander over him, relishing how his body felt under her hands. Without a word, Mara led Duncan into the living room and when they reached the sofa, she pushed on his chest to make him sit down.

Duncan did as she asked and stared, unabashed, as she took her skirt and hiked it up with a few sensuous pulls until it barely covered her backside. Slowly, she put one knee on the sofa cushion next to him, and he pressed his palms against her thighs as Mara settled into his lap.

"I like the feel of you between my legs," she said, and laughed softly as his fingers tightened on her legs before sliding up to her waist. With a casual flick of her fingers, she undid the top button of her silk shirt. Duncan watched, mesmerized, as she unbuttoned the second, and then moved to the third, which was directly between her breasts. As the damp silk moved, he could see the edges of her bra and how they curved around the swell of her breasts. His breath stuttered in his throat. With a few quick tugs, she pulled the bottom of the shirt out from her skirt waist and undid the final two buttons, letting the sides of the shirt fall away.

"Holy mother of God . . . I didn't think it was possible to want you more . . ."

Duncan cupped her breasts and felt the sheer fabric of the bra slide under his hands. As he feathered his fingers across her nipples, they tightened under his touch, and Mara let her head fall, clearly reveling in the sensations coursing through her.

"Do that again," she said in a husky voice when he stopped.

Instead Duncan used his finger to pull down the edge of the bra, baring her, and took her into his mouth. She gasped as his tongue flicked across the sensitive skin. He looked up after a moment and smiled. She was flushed, and that thrilled him. Mara unknotted Duncan's tie and once it was loose, she unbuttoned the top of his shirt. Her fingers had just finished undoing the second button when the chime of a cell phone rudely interrupted.

"You've got to be fucking kidding me," Duncan said.

"Oh, I love it when an angel talks dirty." She laughed as he struggled to retrieve the phone from his pocket. Duncan nearly dropped it as she undid another button and ran a fingernail slowly from his throat to the middle of his chest.

"You're not helping." His voice was somewhere between laughing and pleading.

"Really? I think I'm being terribly helpful." She slipped her hand inside his shirt, exploring, and with his free hand Duncan tried grabbing hers so he could at least attempt to answer the phone without sounding like he was panting.

"Hello?"

Duncan tried to pay attention to his call as Mara peeled the wet silk shirt off her arms, dropped it, and let it puddle on the floor. She leaned forward and whispered in his other ear, "I want you, Duncan."

Just hearing her whisper his name nearly broke him. He closed his eyes and held his breath to master himself before he said anything else.

"Yes," he snapped. "I heard you, Malachai. Right now? I'm kind of in the middle of something. Okay, fine— Jeez . . . No, I was not about to take the Lord's name in vain. I'll be there." Duncan ground his teeth. Malachai was a mini-Michael, and he had no doubt that he'd get ratted out to the Archangel for nearly swearing.

He hung up the phone. "Jesus Christ," he cursed. "Michael runs the division with military precision. Nothing ever happens that isn't scheduled. Except today. We have an emergency staff meeting—right now. Un-fucking-believable."

"I can't believe you can get away with cursing like that," Mara said.

"Get away with it? Oh no, every curse that's said out loud will be duly noted and crammed right down my throat. Every year on my review I get reminded by Michael how my bad habits and lack of discipline hold me back," Duncan muttered, thoroughly pissed.

Mara shifted in his lap and tangled her fingers into Duncan's blond hair. Tightening her grip, she tilted his head up until their lips were nearly touching. He stared into her expressive dark brown eyes, intoxicated by the possibilities he saw there. He'd said it to himself before, and getting lost in her eyes just confirmed it: Mara was everything he'd ever wanted.

"You could blow off the meeting," she purred.

"Are you trying to tempt me?"

"Um, hello? Half-naked devil here."

He looked at her longingly. "Would that I could, you sexy thing. But Michael called the meeting, which means he's pissed about something. And if I blow off a meeting with an Archangel, it won't be a slap on the wrist or a demerit. I'll be riding a desk in some backwater office for the next thousand years."

Mara sighed and reluctantly got up from Duncan's lap, but didn't bother getting her shirt. She lounged on the sofa while he quickly buttoned up and attempted to adjust his tie, his hard-on still conspicuously visible through his pants.

"You're going to need to do something about that," she said, resisting the urge to rub her palm against it.

"Believe me, knowing I'm going to get reamed out by an Archangel will take care of that in short order. Better than a cold shower."

Mara got up, her movements feline and sensual, and she felt Duncan's eyes follow her as she went to the door, traveling up from her slender waist to the sheer black bra that he'd had his hands on moments before. Just as she reached the door, Duncan pulled her in for one more ardent kiss. Mara could feel every inch of him pressed up against her, and she in gasped in shock when the angel's hand slid under her skirt and cupped her between her legs.

She recovered in an instant, curving one of her legs around him. "All ready and waiting for you," she said as she tugged the button on his pants. "It would be so easy. We could do this right now, before your meeting."

"No." His whisper was hoarse and pained.

"No?"

"Oh, it isn't because I don't want to. Believe me, right now there is nothing I want to do more. But I won't have our first time be a quickie up against a door." Duncan tried to put a few inches of space in between them.

"Friggin' angels," Mara muttered, making sure Duncan heard the humor in her comment. She opened the front door to let him out, but just as he crossed the threshold, Duncan dragged her in for one last desperate, frustrated kiss.

"I'll see you at Joe's soon," he whispered. "Don't wear panties next time."

Mara's knees nearly buckled. When the door closed, she pressed her forehead against the cool wood, listening to the sound of Duncan's feet fade down the stairs, unfulfilled desire churning through her blood.

Before vanishing to join his angelic brethren at the staff meeting, Duncan stood on the dark street, taking a few deep breaths in a vain attempt to get ahold of himself. With the taste of Mara's lips still on his, it was next to impossible. Finally he took one longing glance up at Mara's window and then vanished into thin air, only to reappear at a hotel in Cleveland.

Cleveland? Couldn't do one of these in Cabo. No, that would put us at risk of a little fucking fun. Can't have that, he thought, sullen. Duncan stomped into the large meeting room, which was about three-quarters filled with other angels. Most were rank-and-file soldiers like he was, but there was a smattering of supervisors and even a few midlevel managers. Then, to his relief, Duncan saw Basil and Raymond looking trapped and uncomfortable as they stood by the coffee with Malachai, Michael's biggest fanboy. Duncan walked over to them, unwilling to abandon his friends to such a dismal fate.

Duncan poured himself a cup of coffee. Malachai was insufferable, but at least Basil and Raymond would help make the bullshit meeting bearable.

"Sugar?" asked Raymond.

Duncan shook his head. "Black, thanks."

Malachai, who admired Michael so much that he dressed like the Archangel and even cut his hair the same way, gave Duncan a squirrely look. Duncan stared back. He was in no mood for any of this.

"Spit it out, Malachai," Duncan said.

The prim angel sniffed and wrinkled his nose in distaste. "You have the smell of a woman on you. Of a woman's sex. I hope you washed your hands."

Duncan smiled salaciously, knowing it would stick in Malachai's throat. "No kidding. I told you I was in the middle of something when you called."

"Nice!" crowed Basil while Raymond's already large eyes popped out of his head.

"No wonder your career is in the toilet. You are so distracted by the mortals. You waste your energy fornicating, using foul language," Malachai sneered. "I *know* what you were going to say on the phone."

"Whatever," Duncan said. He deliberately turned his back on Malachai. "What's this meeting about, anyway?"

Basil tossed his coffee cup in the trash. "Who knows? I'm sure it's a shape-up-because-someone-screwed-up meeting. They never have meetings like this to tell us what a good job we're doing."

"Why bother with praise and all that stuff?" Raymond said. "We'll keep doing the work. It isn't like we can get a different job. And they've all got sticks up their butts with it being year-end."

"Michael does this to teach us. When he corrects us, we become better angels," Malachai said, inserting himself back into the conversation. All three other angels glared at him, but before Malachai could continue pontificating, Michael swept into the room.

"Hoo-freakin'-rah," muttered Duncan. He closed his eyes as he took a drink of coffee, giving himself license to think about Mara in that sheer black bra.

Malachai's overly cheerful voice ruined the fantasy. "I can't wait to hear what Michael has to say—he's always so inspiring! We'd better get to our seats." He hurried off without waiting for the others, eager to make sure Michael could see him in the first few rows.

"You know, I didn't think he could get his nose any further up Michael's ass," Duncan said. Raymond snickered, and Basil gasped at his audacity. It was one thing to curse out loud, but to do it in the middle of a meeting like this bordered on scandalous.

At the front of the room, Michael stood out from the crowd. The Archangel was probably six feet six inches tall, with broad shoulders and a square sculpted jaw. His tailored three-piece suit was impeccably pressed and had a pocket square to match his tie. Duncan wasn't even wearing a jacket—the sleeves of his wrinkled shirt were rolled up and his tie was loose and askew.

"Stop wasting time and sit down! We need to get started," bellowed the Archangel.

Duncan slouched into the back row and folded his arms in front of him, frustrated beyond belief. "This is not how I planned to spend my evening."

CHAPTER 19

"ARE YOU EVEN watching the game?" asked Basil, exasperated.

"What? Oh, sorry. What happened?" asked Duncan, tearing his eyes away from Mara. At the emergency staff meeting, Michael had tasked several angels—including Duncan, Basil, and Raymond—to track down old leads to make sure they were still on the straight and narrow. It was the type of grunt work that should have been assigned to an intern cherub, not midlevel angels. The drudgery, however, had given Duncan plenty of time to think about Mara, to wonder about their relationship.

Basil gave him an odd look and turned back to the TV. Duncan watched the baseball game for a few minutes and made sure to comment on one or two plays for Basil's benefit, but it didn't take long for him to glance at Mara again. She caught him looking this time and he glanced away, flustered.

"You're kidding, right? I thought you were done with that little fantasy."

"You can be a real downer, you know that?" Duncan said to Basil.

Basil finished his beer and put some money on the bar. "Come on, let's finish that stuff Michael assigned us. It's going to take a while to track down these old leads. Some of them are nearly fifty years old. You'd think they'd at least know if these souls were dead or alive."

Duncan tossed his phone onto the bar, the spinning wheel of death that signaled a system crash clear on the screen. "With our system, we're lucky we have any leads at all. I can never get a connection. Never."

"You and me both, brother," Raymond chimed in.

As they were talking, another group of three angels came in, laughing and joking. They made their way around the bar looking for seats, and Raymond waved them over.

"Hey, we're on our way out. You can have ours," he said.

"Thanks, brother. Appreciate it," said one angel. "I'm Laurence, but you can call me Larry. This is Lou and Deion."

"Nice to meet you. I'm Raymond. This is Basil and Duncan."

"You guys seem awful happy," said Basil. "Good day?"

"*Great* day! Gabriel gave us the afternoon off since we've been doing so much extra for year-end," Lou said, laughing.

Duncan looked at the ground, a wave of resentment toward Michael welling up from deep inside him.

"Extra time off?" Raymond gaped. "It must be so awesome to work for a manager who appreciates you."

"It is. Don't get me wrong, he doesn't put up with any BS, but he's always fair, and he always lets you know he appreciates you."

"That would be nice for a change," muttered Duncan as they stepped away and let the other angels take their seats.

"Come on," Basil said. "I don't want to get another nasty-gram telling me how awful I am at my job."

Duncan grabbed his phone and shoved it in his pocket. "Give me five. I'll catch up with you guys outside."

"Duncan . . ." There was a cautionary note in Basil's voice.

"What? I said five. How much trouble can I get into in five minutes?"

"Do you really want me answering that?" Basil asked.

"Not really."

CHAPTER 20

SITTING IN HER favorite seat at Bruisers, Mara swallowed her disappointment. Duncan wasn't there again, and she was starting to wonder if Michael really had found an excuse to assign him to some backwater post halfway across the universe. Angel-Boy was constantly in her thoughts, and she would wake up at night frustrated and aching for his touch. She looked around the bar for potential clients, but it was a halfhearted effort.

Only four days had passed since the last time she'd seen her angel, but it felt like a year. Mara thought back to the last time she'd seen him. Duncan and his friends had been on their way out, and he'd lingered long enough for them to leave the bar. Then he'd picked up their bill and walked it all the way around the bar—until he was right next to her—so that he could give it to Joanie, the waitress. Then he'd leaned close to her as he turned and whispered, "I hope you're not wearing panties." The chemistry between them had nearly boiled over when she'd told him he should check to find out.

Even though she knew he wasn't there, Mara glanced across the bar, hoping to see Duncan in his usual seat. Instead there was a bald middle-aged black man having a tremendous chuckle with his friend. They clinked their beer glasses together and roared at each other's jokes. She considered checking them out as prospects, but neither had that special something that typically grabbed her attention—unlike the stripper from Arkansas who Mara had landed the day before after she'd stabbed her sleazy manager with an ice pick. It certainly gave new meaning to the phrase "want to get away"—the stripper was now on her way to Oregon, where she could spend the next ten years in a June Cleaver life before Mara came to collect.

"I haven't seen him either," said Joe as he put a dish in front of her.

Surprised, Mara glanced down and saw Joe had brought her a large dish of ice cream with her favorite two toppings: hot caramel and red-hot cinnamon candies.

"I didn't order . . ."

"It's on the house, honey. I remember that same look on my daughter's face when a boy she liked wasn't noticing her very much. This Duncan guy. He didn't, uh, get the goods and then not call you again, did he? I'll whip his ass if he treated you bad." Joe gave her a very serious paternal stare.

Mara blinked and then laughed. "No, nothing like that. We were . . . out on a date, and some urgent thing at work interrupted him, and since then it has either been crap with my job or crap with his. But thank you for offering to rough him up for me. That's very sweet of you."

"You're a regular, Mara. Like family. No one messes with my family."

"I won't forget that." An unexpected feeling of warmth enveloped Mara, and for a moment she let herself indulge in the sentiment. But she couldn't ignore the nagging thought that came after: Would he think I was family if he knew what I really was?

Ignoring the sting of reality, Mara dug into the sweet treat, relishing the hot crunch of the candies mixed with the smooth, mellow vanilla and sweet caramel. It was a dessert to die for, as far as she was concerned. It didn't take long for her to finish the entire thing and lick the spoon clean.

Disappointed that Duncan hadn't shown up, she paid her tab and left, taking care to dodge the cars on Joyal Street as she crossed, and cursing another evening of rain. It had been a truly dismal fall and winter in Hollis City. Inside Justa Cuppa, there was a decent crowd and a few strains of music escaped out the café's front door. For a minute Mara considered going in, but without someone to enjoy the show with, she didn't really feel up to it.

As she opened the foyer door to her apartment building, a folded paper fluttered down from where it had been stuck in the door frame. Mara's name was written on the front, so she picked it up. A whiff of sandalwood drifted up: Duncan! Unfolding the paper, she apprehensively looked at the note, fearing it was a rejection. Instead, in his neat and rather elegant handwriting, it said: *I've missed you. Want some company tonight?* Mara's heart leaped into her throat and she glanced around, finally noticing Duncan across the street, partly hidden in the doorway of a closed shop. She felt the primal pull between them and made her decision: she retreated inside the foyer, leaving the door open behind her.

Upstairs, Mara took a quick glance around. Over the course of the week she had dusted everything, scrubbed the kitchen and bathroom, and made sure all the floors were clean. She had to admit that was one benefit of sexual frustration: her apartment was spotless.

Behind her, a floorboard squeaked.

"I don't care how hard it is to be together. Nothing's worse than being away from you."

Mara's breath caught as Duncan's deep, rich voice wrapped around her. Raw desire coursed through her and she pressed her fingers to her lips. The door lock clicked, and she finally looked at him. Duncan had come directly from a job, and the rain had all but ruined his charcoal dress pants.

"I'm sorry it took so long to come back—that stupid assignment from Michael has buried us in paperwork. I hated keeping you waiting," he said.

Her laugh was low, sexy. "I trust it will be worth it." She looked up at him and was completely beguiled by his blue eyes. This time, he didn't hesitate. He bent his head and captured her with a longing-filled kiss, and as she softened against him her lips parted, welcoming him.

"I haven't been able to think of anything but you," he said as her fingers traced over his back and chest.

"Good." A thrill of anticipation raced through her.

Mara's heels clicked on the kitchen tile as he turned her and backed her up until she bumped against the island. She reached for him but he pushed her hands back to the island's smooth butcher-block surface.

"Leave them there," he said.

A grin crooked her mouth at the command, and she did as he asked, gripping the edge as Duncan took the top button of her silk blouse and popped it open. Crowding closer, he pulled a little of the material back and kissed her neck, letting his lips linger on her skin. She sighed deeply and, unable to restrain herself, reached out for him again.

He smiled. "No. Let me unwrap you."

She dropped her hands while her eyes searched his face. Leaning forward, she put her lips to his ear and whispered, "Whatever you want, Duncan."

He caught a handful of her hair at the back of her head. His grip tightened and she gasped with pleasure as he pulled her head slowly back, exposing more of her throat. With his free hand, he unclasped another button and kissed the bare skin of Mara's throat and chest. Her breath quickened with every touch.

Letting go of her hair and quickly unfastening the last two buttons, he tugged the hem of Mara's shirt out of her skirt waist and threw the edges of the shirt to the side. Her lacy demi-bra was a deep teal color, barely covering her nipples, and he watched the rise and fall of her chest, mesmerized.

"You are beyond beautiful, Mara."

She shrugged and the shirt slid down. Mara had to shake her hands when the still-wet material caught on her wrists. It fell—forgotten—to the floor as Duncan, in a single fluid motion, crossed his arms and pulled his own shirt up and over his head. It landed partly on the island before it slid off the edge and into a heap on the kitchen floor. He caught her wrists and pinned her hands behind her, his lips hovering over hers.

"Please . . ." she said breathlessly.

"Please, what?" His voice was teasing.

"Let me touch you."

Duncan let go of her wrists and leaned forward, bracing his hands on the edge of the island, while Mara ran her fingers up his stomach to his chest, tracing them along the lines of his muscles. Every place she touched ignited. When she moved her hands to caress his back, she was close enough to kiss him, but hesitated deliberately—a delicious temptation that he failed to resist. He kissed her fiercely, possessively, and an instant later she feathered her thumb across one of his nipples, shocking him with the touch.

"I love your hands on me, but I'm not done yet." He gently took her wrists and pushed them back to the island again. She gave him a look but acquiesced, and he ran a finger underneath one of her bra straps. Pushing it to the side, he let it fall from her shoulder and kissed the newly revealed skin with a flick of his tongue. She gasped and laughed. He did the same with the other strap and then he brought his hands up to touch her breasts, rubbing his thumbs across the peaks of her nipples, just barely hidden beneath the lace.

"Duncan!"

He wasn't sure which was sexier—hearing Mara whisper his voice so intimately in his ear, or hearing the need that consumed her as she cried out when he touched her again. He spent a moment massaging her, the motion of his hands pushing the edge of the bra down and exposing her breasts. She reached around to unclasp the hook and flung the bra away just before he grabbed the zipper at the back of her skirt and yanked it down. With nothing left to hold it up, the skirt dropped from her waist. Duncan took a step back to drink her in. Other than her teal bikini briefs and her heels, she was naked. Mara ran her hands up her hips and her stomach and over her breasts as she stared at Duncan. Then she stepped forward.

"Your turn to be submissive." Her eyes were bright and she licked her lips, moved close to him, and nibbled on an earlobe for a moment. He savored the feel of her lips and then, to his utter astonishment, Mara took his hand and put it between her legs, on top of the panties. It was hot and wet, and Duncan felt himself get even harder.

"Holy Mother of God, do I want you . . ." he groaned.

"Good."

Mara already found a deep carnal satisfaction in the way Duncan was looking at her, but it wasn't nearly enough. And it wouldn't be until they were tangled up together in her bed.

She slid her fingers into the waistband of his pants and slowly, deliberately undid the buttons and pulled the zipper down, letting her hand graze along his erection as she did. She never took her eyes from his and nearly purred with pleasure when he responded to her touch. With a few tugs at the hips, Duncan's slacks dropped to his ankles, and it was Mara's turn to stare in lustful admiration at her angel in his dark red boxer briefs. She pressed the flat of her hand against the bulge of his cock.

"If that's not evidence that God is good, I don't know what is," Mara said.

Duncan's breath came out in labored gasps as Mara rubbed her palm along his hardness. She leaned in, kissing random places on his chest, flicking her tongue across his nipples as she worked her way down his abdomen. She knelt down and felt him tremble each time her fingers or lips touched him.

Mara dragged her fingernails down the front of his chest. Duncan locked his hands on top of his head, giving her full license to touch him wherever she wanted. She grinned wickedly as she hooked her fingers into the band of his boxer briefs. Slowly, inch by inch, she worked them down until they were free enough to slide down his legs.

Duncan just stared at Mara, his mouth slightly open as she gazed back up at him through her thick lashes. He made a strangled noise at the back of his throat as she slowly took him in her mouth, letting her tongue run across his most sensitive skin. Duncan was no prude. He'd been with other women—both human and angel—but not one of them had ever made him feel the longing he felt in that moment.

"Stop," he said, his voice hoarse. He put his hands gently on her head.

"What's wrong?"

He laughed as he helped her stand. "Wrong? Absolutely nothing. I just can't take any more of that. Not if I want this to last."

As he talked, Duncan kicked off his shoes, dragging the socks with them and shaking the pants from around his ankles.

He seized Mara, crushing her against him as he kissed her with abandon. They broke apart, both breathing heavily.

"Take me to bed," Mara said.

"Soon," he promised as he spun Mara to face the island and pressed against her from behind. With a soft cry, Mara widened her stance as he slid a palm inside her panties. He moved his fingers expertly, brushing, stroking, caressing, until Mara's head fell back against his shoulder. When he finally slid a finger inside her, Mara's knees nearly buckled.

CHAPTER 21

FOR HER PART, Mara couldn't even form a coherent thought as Duncan drove her relentlessly toward an orgasm. Somehow she managed to pull her own bikini panties down far enough that they fell to her knees and then to the floor as she writhed under the angel's hands. The feeling of being wound tighter and tighter consumed her, and she arched her back and whispered his name.

"Say my name again," he said softly in her ear.

"Duncan," she whispered, and then moaned as his fingers explored her most intimate places. Completely lost in the sensations she was feeling, Mara was incapable of saying anything else intelligible, but then Duncan moved his other hand down, and sent Mara careening over the edge.

"Duncan!" Mara shouted, flinging her head back. She tightened around him, the orgasm dominating her, shaking her to the very core. As he withdrew his hands, she flinched—supremely sensitive—and gulped in deep breaths of air. Still in her heels, her legs trembling slightly, Mara twisted to face Duncan and gave him a slow, lingering kiss.

"That was amazing," she said as she threaded her fingers through his, her body still twitching as the final waves of the orgasm subsided. She tugged at his hand.

"Where are we going?" Duncan asked innocently.

"We're going to the bedroom," she answered, knowing that Duncan damn well knew where they were headed. They were both enjoying the back-and-forth too much to ruin it.

"And what are we going to do there?"

"Do you want the angel-answer or the devil-answer?

"Devil," he said as he reached out and gave her backside a squeeze.

Mara responded by reaching out and wrapping one hand around his cock. "Here's your answer, then. As delicious as it's been, no more foreplay. When we get in there, I'm going to push you onto the bed, slide down on this incredible shaft of yours, and ride you until you scream my name while you come."

Duncan's smile was wolfish. "I like the sound of that."

Mara led him to the bedroom and went to one of the nightstands. She pulled a maroon scarf out of the nightstand drawer and draped it over the lamp, making the light diffused and subtle. Mara kicked off her heels. He backed up toward the bed and she gave him a sly smile.

"On the bed," she ordered as she put both hands on his chest and pushed him backward. Duncan didn't resist. Mara followed, climbing onto the bed and putting one knee on either side of him. Hovering above him, she ran her fingers over his shoulders and chest and rubbed his nipples. Duncan closed his eyes and bit his lip.

"You like that," she purred.

He nodded vigorously and his hips bucked when she rubbed him again. She lowered herself until the very tip of Duncan's cock touched her.

"I know what you need," she said seductively, "and you know how ready I am for you, don't you?"

"Yes . . ." His response was more of an exhale than actual words.

With excruciating slowness, Mara lowered herself onto him, savoring every moment that Duncan slid deeper inside her. Duncan's fingers gripped her thighs, and Mara moved his hands from her legs and put them on her naked breasts. While Duncan massaged them, she moved up and down, squeezing her muscles each time to heighten the sensation.

"Mara . . ." Duncan whispered her name and she smiled, understanding why he loved to hear her say his name.

"What?"

"Keep fucking me. Don't stop," he said hoarsely. It was a plea.

"Don't worry, I'll take good care of you." Mara laced her fingers through his and used Duncan's arms to support a little of her weight as she started to move faster. Both of their bodies were covered with a slight sheen of sweat as Mara kept riding her angel, increasing the pace and then pausing before he lost control. As she intensified her tempo again, she could tell by the way Duncan tightened his grip and locked eyes with hers that he couldn't contain himself much longer—and neither could she. The sensation of Duncan deep inside her brought Mara to a second climax. She threw back her head and shouted as she came, and as she tightened around him, Duncan was consumed by his own orgasm.

"Mara!" he shouted as he surged upward. He pulled his hands away from hers and grabbed her waist, keeping her body close against his while his hips bucked and jerked.

Mara had lived for thousands of years, and she'd had her share of lovers, but not one compared to Duncan, to the way he made her feel when he touched her. Not only did he make every molecule in her body feel alive, but she also trusted him. He'd never pushed her, never asked for anything she wasn't willing to share, and there was something deep inside her, a crystal pinpoint of light, that resonated when she touched him. As they'd made love, Mara had given herself over to Duncan more than once, something she'd never done before. It thrilled her and it scared her. She struggled not to let a few tears escape.

As the rampant power of their interlude subsided, Mara rolled to the side and pressed herself along Duncan's body, resting her head on his shoulder and enjoying the feel of his fingers toying with strands of her hair.

"Holy shit," Duncan finally said.

"Amen to that," Mara answered with a cheeky smile.

"I would do anything to make sure we can do that every night." Duncan pulled her closer, kissing the top of Mara's head.

"You'd want me every night?"

"That much and more. But we have to be careful. The powers that be won't like this. Still, not being with you? That would be so much worse." Duncan frowned at the thought.

"I don't care what they think," Mara announced. "I'm not ashamed of you and I've never felt this way with anyone before. I won't give you up for anything . . ."

"I hear a 'but' in there. What's wrong?"

Mara raised herself up on an elbow and ran a finger down his cheek. "I'm a devil, you know that. But there are things you don't know about me, about my family, about who and what I am . . ."

"I've told you before: I don't care. It doesn't matter. We'll deal with whatever comes next. I'm no choirboy myself."

Mara settled back onto the bed and snuggled closer to him, sighing as Duncan wrapped his arms around her. She absently bit her lip, worried. She wasn't convinced Duncan could deal with the truth about her parents, but she wasn't going to ruin this. Not right now—not when she was happy—*actually* happy. They lay together in silence for a few more minutes, enjoying the warm feel of skin against skin, before Mara ran a finger down the center of Duncan's chest, over his stomach, and down the fine trail of hair that led south from his navel. By the time her finger reached its destination, Duncan was completely hard again.

"Well, look at that," she said with a satisfied smile.

"I only have to think about you to get hard," Duncan told her.

"That is such a turn-on." She ran her fingers back up his body. "Next time I'll tie you to the bedposts and do what I want with you," Mara told him.

"Maybe I'll tie you up."

She put her lips close to his ear again. "I've *never* let anyone tie me up, but you can do whatever you want to me. I'll make every fantasy you ever had come true . . . Duncan."

Duncan nearly came again, just from Mara's words, and he rolled, pinning her underneath his body. He settled between her legs as she pulled them apart and raised them up, feeling his hardness bump against her.

"We can get tied up another time. Right now I just want to be inside you again."

"Then don't keep me waiting."

In an instant Duncan thrust forward, filling Mara's body, and as their gasps of pleasure echoed in the room, every worry, every concern vanished into the night.

CHAPTER 22

FOR THE NEXT week, Mara and Duncan took advantage of every private moment they had, but eventually work rudely inserted itself back into their lives. Duncan was called to handle crises in Altoona and Biloxi, and on his way back to Hollis City got diverted to St. Louis. Knowing Duncan wasn't around, Mara made a few minor stops on her way to her primary appointment in Houston. It had been a while since she'd talked directly to Markus Winston, and the time on his deal was running out. One of the minor stops panned out, and Mara landed one more contract. Now she only had to get four more to beat Kemm.

I'd be so screwed if he was still racking up the contracts, she thought, but the comfort was hollow because the other devils were starting to notice his conspicuous absence.

Dressed in a smart tailored pantsuit with a red jacket, Mara wore her favorite sunglasses so she could look around without anyone knowing what she was looking at. At the gate, she presented her credentials and the stadium security team escorted her down to the practice field. Stepping out onto the sidelines, she admired the stadium and soaked in the reek of ambition that pervaded it.

About twenty yards from Mara, Markus smiled charmingly at a cheerleader who was chatting animatedly with him. There was a strict rule about no fraternization between the players and the cheerleaders, but Markus had never put much value in rules—hence why Mara held the contract for his soul. Mara knew the two of them were sneaking around, and she was just fine with that.

Finally Markus glanced Mara's way, and she gave him a smile and a wave. He finished whatever conversation he was having with the cheerleader and she flounced away. Walking toward Mara, Markus displayed all the swagger of a man who felt invincible. He was a cocky son of a bitch, that was for sure.

"Been a while," Markus said. "Why are you here?"

"I'm just checking in. I like to see how my investments are doing from time to time. Plus, we need to talk about your commentator gig. Time's ticking on our contract." Behind the glasses, Mara narrowed her eyes when the quarterback offered her little more than an ambivalent shrug. Mara pressed on: "There are going to be two retirements soon—one at ESPN and one at NFL Network. Announcements are coming and they'll want to fill the gaps fast. Either works for me, but if you have a preference, I'll make that happen."

"I'm not going to retire at the end of this season. I'm playing great, and we're on track to win the Super Bowl. We win the big one and then I have to go for two to solidify my legacy. I ain't going to be no one-and-done wonder."

Mara's frown was dark. "You know what our deal is. You get to be the best quarterback in the league for four years. Then you announce your retirement, do a nice cushy stint as an NFL commentator, and then your ass is mine."

"Not before I win at least two rings."

"Our deal doesn't say anything about guaranteed Super Bowl wins."

"And remind me why? Oh, that's right, you don't have the juice to do it."

Mara's voice turned glacial. "No, I don't have the juice to do that. Too many variables—too many humans with free will. God might be the only one who could pull off a stunt like that, but you know what, you didn't make a deal with Him. You made it with me. *My* deal says you'll be the best QB in the league for four years—which you have been; no one can touch your stats—and *then* you retire to a commentator job."

"Open your ears. I said I'm not retiring, and you can't force me to. So, I do five years in the league and then a few less as a commentator. What's the problem? And what are you going to do about it?" Markus asked belligerently.

Rip your heart out through your asshole? That's probably first on my list, Mara thought before she said, "You do what you need to, Markus, but if you don't announce you're retiring after the end of this season, then you're in breach of our contract and the penalty clause will kick in."

"'Penalty clause'? What penalty clause?" Markus put his hands on his hips and stared hard at her. Mara pushed her sunglasses up on the top of her head and rolled her eyes in disgust.

"What is it with you mortals? You always assume you can renegotiate the terms of a deal, and you never—*never*—read the fine print."

"Go screw yourself. You're fired." Markus turned his back and walked toward the locker room.

"Fired? That's fucking *hilarious.* Trust me, Markus. You will not like what happens if that clause gets enacted," Mara called after him.

Markus gave her the finger.

Mara's eyes narrowed, red and dangerous. "Playing chicken with me is a stupid idea, Markus. A stupid, stupid idea."

CHAPTER 23

MARA STARED AT her appointment calendar. It was December 15, and she still had to gather four more souls if she was going to come in at number one for the quarter. It seemed like plenty of time, but Mara knew it wasn't. She'd spent the morning tangled up in the sheets with Duncan and had logged in late for the staff meeting. Astaroth's frosty "so nice of you to join us" had told Mara everything she needed to know about her boss's mood, so she kept her head down and her mouth shut during the meeting.

Because they were spending nearly every night together, Mara and Duncan were very careful to overlap at Bruisers, so that one always arrived before or after the other to lessen the chance for speculation and suspicion on the parts of their colleagues. Across the bar tonight, Duncan was sitting with his two friends. Mara had yet to meet them, but she knew the tall one was Raymond and the other was Basil. They were talking with two other angels she hadn't seen before. She deliberately didn't look when they got up, but at the last second, she glanced at the door in time to see Duncan look back over his shoulder. She gave him an impertinent wink that promised all sorts of illicit adventures.

Once they were gone, she picked at her salad, watched a little more television, and then gave the current crop of bar patrons a serious look. It was the usual assortment of the disgruntled and bored, until Mara noticed a young couple with their guitar cases leaning against the wall. They were sharing a burger and fries, and Mara felt that prickle of intuition that told her she should pay attention to these two, that they were on the precipice of a critical decision. But that wasn't uncommon for the prospects she found in Hollis City. That's what crossroads were all about, after all. She strolled casually over to their table.

"Hello. May I interrupt for a moment?"

"Sure," the man said with a slight Southern twang, while the woman gave her a suspicious glance.

"I noticed the guitars. Are you two professional performers, or is it just a fun hobby?" Mara's question was genial, but there was another flash of something—anger?—in the woman's eyes as she sat up a little straighter, clearly offended by the word "hobby." Mara knew she was onto something.

Putting his hand over the woman's, the man answered, "We're professionals. At least we're trying to be. I'm Nate Aubrey, this is Kathy Lowe."

"Well, it's lovely to meet you both. I'm Mara—Mara Dullahan—and it just so happens that I represent a little boutique record agency called Inferno. They're just getting started and I've been looking for new acts." She offered them both a charming smile and pulled a business card out of her little purse.

"You don't even know if we're any good," said Kathy.

"No, I don't. Not yet. But you never know what gems you might find in unlikely places like this, and I like to think I have a sixth sense for potential. Tell me a little about yourselves, about what you really want, and we'll see where the conversation takes us." Mara raised her hand and caught the waiter's attention. "Would you be a dear and bring us a plate of the taquitos, and refills on the drinks? I'll take a glass of merlot—"

Nate opened his mouth, but before he could say anything, Mara added, "And I'll take care of the bill."

Two hours later Mara was pleased. Kathy and Nate had been struggling in no-name bars for many years, and they lamented about how they'd have to return to Omaha if they didn't land a recording contract soon. They'd played her a demo and, in truth, Mara had been moderately impressed. They did have talent.

They also had the right look. Nate was tall and lanky, with intense gray eyes and dark hair, and while he was charming and affable, Mara knew his type. He would slip right into the music scene and sample all the temptations it had to offer, and by the time he realized how deep in he was, it would be far too late. A pang of guilt hit her and she squashed it ruthlessly.

Kathy was very much Nate's opposite—petite, blond, and with a nervous energy about her. She was the one who interested Mara, the one who had drawn Mara over to their table, and she was the jewel in this little crown. Kathy was talented but vain, insecure, and jealous . . . and there was just whiff of violence in her—Mara could smell it and it was intoxicating.

Mara brought herself back and held out her phone to show them an email from her contact at Inferno. It was a list of venues where the Aubrey Lowe Band would get booked if they signed with Mara. Nate scanned the list and handed the phone to Kathy.

"You can seriously get us booked in all these places?" he asked. "No BS?"

"No BS. If you sign with us, my firm can absolutely get you booked. First, we'll want to get you into the studio, make you an album to promote. Then we can schedule the venues easily. Inferno has a network that would boggle your mind."

"And what's this going to cost us?" Kathy asked. "Do we have to give up the publishing rights? Change the name of the band?"

"We'd be willing to offer a clause in your contract for master rights reversion," Mara said. "That means Inferno will own the rights to your music for five years, and after that time all the ownership will revert to you. This five-year period will renew for each new album you produce with us."

"Sounds pretty reasonable." Nate tried to sound casual as he looked at Kathy.

"And what about *your* compensation?" Kathy asked as she tried to keep her hands still in her lap.

"Part of the contract will stipulate that when your first album goes platinum—and I'm sure it will—that's when my compensation will kick in. But it won't be money. I'll come for something you possess."

"That sounds a little creepy," said Kathy. "But what do you mean? Like a car, a house, or a diamond?"

"Something like that."

"How do you make any money, then?" Nate asked.

"Aside from a token from each artist that I help sign— the thing I just mentioned—I have a separate compensation agreement with Inferno. I can't discuss details, however. Nondisclosures and all that." Mara shifted in her chair. They were on the edge, and she didn't want to spook them by looking overeager.

Kathy leaned over and whispered something to Nate. He whispered back and finally said to Mara, "I don't know. Without some parameters—I mean, who's to say you wouldn't show up and say that as your part of the deal you demand the publishing rights after Inferno reverts them?"

Mara tapped on her phone while he talked.

"You are a smart man, Nate. That is an excellent question. Without any qualifiers, yes, I could ask for that, but I won't. I'll write into the contract that whatever I take as my token, it specifically will *not* be your publishing rights, and it will fit in the palm of my hand."

"The palm of your hand?" Nate chuckled. "Shit, that could be the key to my mansion, but you know what, if we have a platinum album, I can buy a different house. You put that in writing—that whatever your share is, it will be no bigger than the palm of your hand—and we have a deal."

"Outstanding. I'll have all the paperwork couriered over to the Griffin Hotel," Mara said with a big smile. She could have easily pulled the contract out of her bag then and there, but Bruisers was crowded and she couldn't risk either one of her prospects making a scene. This deal needed a little more finesse before she completely closed it.

"The Griffin?" Kathy said. "We can't afford the Griffin. We're at the Corner Inn . . ."

"Not anymore. My two new stars don't sleep in cheap hotels anymore. I've already made a reservation for you." She held out her phone to show them the reservation confirmation. "Why don't we grab a cab and head over?"

Without even thinking, Nate and Kathy stood up with her, eager and buzzing with adrenaline.

"This is crazy," Nate exclaimed.

"Oh, sweetie, you don't know the half of it," Mara said. "The crazy is just getting started."

At the Griffin, Kathy and Nate were stunned to find themselves booked into the hotel's most lavish suite, and with a little champagne they were soon punch-drunk on dreams and fantasies of Grammy awards and the Grand Ole Opry. After a suitable amount of time had passed, Mara sent a discreet text. Ten minutes later there was a knock at the door and Mara retrieved the contract—in an official-looking Inferno folder—from the imp who delivered it.

"Here we go," Mara said. She put the contract in front of Kathy and Nate. "Before you sign, this section details the terms of our deal." Mara flipped a few pages. "This section details areas of compensation. How Inferno will compensate you and any reciprocal arrangements, and then in this last section, we have our standard noncompliance clauses."

Nate picked up a pen, but Kathy shook her head. "No, just hang on a second."

Mara folded her hands in her lap and forced an earnestly concerned expression onto her face. "What's got you worried, Kathy?"

"This 'reciprocal compensation' idea. Seems a little vague, doesn't it?" asked Kathy.

"Come on, Kath. This is a good deal. Don't blow this for us."

"I'm not blowing anything—I'm just being careful. My daddy said that—"

"I wouldn't cross the street to piss on your daddy if he was on fire," interrupted Nate. "Miss Dullahan's given us a great opportunity. We've seen the kind of other contracts new bands get and this one's pretty darn fair." He grabbed the pen and signed his name.

Mara forced herself to sit very still. Neither had the talent to be a big success individually, but together they were special. This deal wouldn't work unless both signed on the dotted line.

"I'm going out on the terrace. Why don't you two wrap up and we can celebrate." Nate got up, ignoring Kathy's angry glare. After he left the room, Mara let her eyes slide to Kathy, who was sitting with her arms folded, a stubborn frown pinching her face.

"Doesn't seem like Nate's a big fan of your father."

"Nate says my daddy's a drunk, but he's wrong," Kathy snapped. "He just has a few beers every now and again."

Glee colored Mara's thoughts. *Fabulous. Once Daddy sees you've got cash, I bet he's on your doorstep in an instant.*

"But my daddy's not dumb. And he told me to be suspicious if something seemed too good to be true."

"Sounds like a very smart man to me," Mara said.

"And this piece, here, this 'reciprocal' thing. I don't understand what it is. I mean, I get how you explained it, but I'd feel better knowing what it really is. Specifics."

Mara swallowed her aggravated sigh before she said, "These are really minor details in the long run, Kathy. You and Nate have a huge future in front of you, and I'm sure it won't be long before you've moved into arenas and the biggest venues in the country—in the world—where your music will be heard by generations of fans. What's that worth to you?"

"That's everything I've ever wanted . . ."

"Then seize the day, Kathy. Fifty years from now, when the up-and-coming star says you're the reason she got into music—what's that worth to you?"

Kathy almost looked like she was going to cry. How much she wanted to sign was plain on her face, and Mara changed her tactic slightly. "Going back to the mean girls who always told you you'd be nothing but white trash in a trailer with a drunkard for a daddy, returning to them as a famous singer. What wouldn't you pay for that chance?"

Kathy broke. "I'd pay anything for that. *Anything.* Just tell me what I have to give you."

Mara took Kathy's hands in hers and squeezed hard. "Give me you."

Kathy looked up sharply the instant Mara's grip tightened, and gasped when Mara let her eyes shine crimson.

"What *are* you?"

"You know the answer to that."

Kathy's voice trembled. "You're the Devil and you want us to sell our souls."

"Close enough. You'll never get another chance like this, Kathy. Without me, you can look forward to life as a waitress in Omaha, singing at old honky-tonks on weekends, and living in that run-down trailer with the leaky roof. I can take all that away. I can open doors for you that will give you everything you want, everything you deserve."

"Will I even get to enjoy it?" whispered Kathy.

"Enjoy your famous life? Of course! I can show you the part in the contract, but I've guaranteed that I won't come for you for at least twenty-five years—unless, of course, you do something stupid like throw yourself off a bridge. Twenty-five years of the life you've always wanted. The bright lights, the gold records, the world tours . . ." Mara let her voice trail away, allowing Kathy to imagine what the future could be.

"I'll sign." Kathy picked up the pen, hesitated for a fraction of a second, then signed. As soon as Kathy took the pen away from the paper, the ink flamed and the paper crackled as both signatures were burned permanently into the document.

"Excellent," Mara said.

Kathy's face screwed up with worry and she jumped to her feet. "Excuse me, I need a minute." She hurried toward the bedroom.

"Take all the time you need, sweetie."

Chasing her was a bad idea, so Mara joined Nate on the terrace looking out over Hollis City. The signatures were on the paper, but Mara knew she needed to officially seal the deal with them. She looked at Nate, and the guilt she thought she'd crushed earlier stirred up again. He wasn't a bad person, just prone to bad decisions. Mara steeled herself. She had to finish the job. If she didn't, she was screwed—she needed these souls, and Astaroth was asking too many questions as it was.

"You two were talking for a while," Nate said.

"Everything's fine. Kathy just signed."

His shoulders visibly relaxed. He was still looking out at the cityscape. "We're gonna be famous."

"Yes, you are. Hey, come here," Mara said.

Nate turned and to his utter surprise, Mara kissed him, deep and soft. When they finished, he looked away, a blend of sheepish and thrilled, missing the flash of red in Mara's eyes.

"Whoa," he said. "What was that for?"

"Just for luck." Another time, another place, Mara might have considered taking Nate to bed to seal his deal, but she had a whole new perspective now that she'd slept with her angel.

"Don't let Kathy see you do that. She'd be mighty ticked off. She's a little firecracker."

"Oh, I won't forget that. I'm going to leave in a sec—let you and Kathy celebrate. One of the producers from Inferno will be in touch in a few days. Until then, you can stay here, on us."

"Thanks, Mara."

"No, don't thank me."

"Before you go, one more thing?" Nate asked.

"Whatever you want," Mara said amiably.

"Half of me wants to ask you to stay the night with me." Nate's cheeks colored. "But I'd settle for one more kiss."

"Of course." Mara slid her arms around Nate's neck and pressed her lips against his, yielding a little when he pressed for more. When she stepped away, there was a longing in his eyes that was unmistakable.

"That's just a taste of the future," Mara said. "There are going to be a lot of girls all lining up to kiss you."

That thought made Nate turn even more scarlet. "Wouldn't that be something?"

"You take care—I'll be in touch to check in on how you're both doing, and you have my card if you need to reach me for anything."

"Maybe we can pick up again next time," said Nate, clearly referring to the kiss.

"We'll see about that."

Mara went back inside, winding through the large suite toward the bedroom.

"Kathy, I was just coming to find you," Mara said. "I just wanted to say again before I go that I'm very happy you've signed with Inferno. I hope you get everything you deserve. There's one last thing—kind of a tradition I have. A kiss for luck."

"A kiss? Well, I guess . . ." Kathy turned her head, expecting a peck on the cheek, and was utterly flabbergasted when Mara planted a solid smooch right on her lips.

"Hey! Get off me! I'm no lesbian!" she cried.

"Oh please. For the right reasons you would be, and you know it." Crimson lit Mara's irises and Kathy blanched, the kiss all but forgotten.

"Now, you take care of yourself, and of your partner out there. There's a lot of fame and fortune headed your way. Enjoy it while you can, because you can't take it with you."

Kathy crossed her arms in front of her as if a cold wind had washed across the room. "I'm not going to like it when you come for your piece of the pie, am I?"

Mara's smile morphed from friendly to feral. "Probably not."

It was midnight when Mara returned to Bruisers for a cele-
bratory drink, and she settled into her seat with a self-satisfied
smile. She ordered her traditional beer and a shot from Joanie,
but Joe delivered it. As he put the goblet down in front of her,
he said, "Where did you disappear to?"

"I went to sign some paperwork with the two musicians I
met. They're clients now." She swirled the wine and inhaled the
subtle aroma of black cherries and plums.

"But you just met them," said Joe, surprised. "Goddamn,
you work fast."

"I can be very, very persuasive."

"Well, they're lucky they met you, huh? They might have
hooked up with some manager who was going to screw them
over."

The glass stopped halfway to Mara's mouth. Lucky? She
could think of a long list of souls who would disagree with
that statement. "I don't know about that. I do have a ruthless
streak."

Mara glanced toward where Duncan often sat across the
bar, wishing he were there, and feeling a little lost and alone
knowing he wasn't.

"Your blond friend might not be here for a couple of days,"
said Joe.

"My what? Oh." Mara blushed just a little.

"Nothing wrong with liking the dude," Joe told her. "He
seems like a good guy. Gave me some good advice a while back.
Anyway, heard him say the other day that one of his big bosses
had a stick up his backside, so he and his buddies were up to
their necks at work."

"Holidays are always a busy time of year."

"You should go out on a date with him."

"Joe, are you trying to play matchmaker?"

He shrugged. "You never know. Take a chance."

"We work for competing firms. It would be ... complicated." Mara stuck with the standard cover story. Telling Joe that she and Duncan worked for the same company would lead to more questions about Immortal Planes Inc. than she cared to answer.

"Sometimes those are the best relationships." Joe grinned at her. "That's what it was like for me and Donna. Complicated. We'd fight like cats and dogs, but I've never loved anyone the way I loved her."

Joe got a faraway look in his eye when he mentioned his late wife. They'd married in their early twenties and had three children. The whole family had been devastated when Donna was diagnosed with stage-four breast cancer. Mara looked up at the picture of Donna that Joe kept over the bar. It was the two of them in Key West for their fifteenth wedding anniversary.

"You guys look really happy in that picture."

"We were," he said. "One of the few vacations we ever took without the kids. She's my angel. I know she's keeping an eye on me from Heaven."

"I'd like to have that someday." The statement slipped out before Mara could stop herself.

"What are you getting all red for?" asked Joe. "Nothing wrong with wanting someone special in your life. Nice to know that there's someone waiting at home for you."

Mara sighed. If only it were that easy.

CHAPTER 24

MARA STALKED INTO the treasurers' office. It was a week before Christmas, and she'd just gotten back from Boston. She'd been looking forward to an evening with Duncan, but the summons by Astaroth had dashed those plans. Her angel was leaving for Atlanta in the morning, so she hadn't taken Astaroth's demand well. Now she was spoiling for a fight, even one with a Grand Duke.

"What do you want?" Mara's tone was as curt as the pre-emptory email that had summoned her to Hell.

"Sit down," Astaroth said, pointing at the guest chair next to his desk.

Mara raised an eyebrow. Astaroth never invited anyone to sit down. She did as he asked and waited.

"We discussed the incident with Gideon Miller," he said.

"We did."

"I've been looking at your ledger." He tapped his bony fingers on the keyboard and scanned some lines. "You have an impressive pipeline, Mara. Your volume isn't as high as some of the others, but the quality is superior. But I've noticed a trend recently."

"A trend?" She kept her voice neutral. *What kind of fucking trend?*

"Yes. Often your contracts come with some, shall we say, collateral damage. Damage that's good for some of the less experienced demons to practice on. But since you deliberately hastened the demise of Reverend Miller, which is unlike you, there won't nearly be as much." He peered at her with his cold jet-black eyes.

Mara stared back at him, defiant. "You continue to use words like 'deliberate' when it comes to the Miller deal. Do you have any proof of that? I handled his deal the way I saw fit. I have my reasons, and he was still a stellar catch."

"But the young women he fornicated with. It just so happens that shortly after the good reverend's demise, a couple of angels swept in and helped them come to terms with what happened. Almost as if they knew ahead of time what was going to happen. We had dozens of opportunities to gather more tarnished souls with those girls. Now we may only be lucky to get two, maybe three."

Mara offered a nonchalant answer: "I didn't pay much attention to them. Small potatoes. Like you said, I have my sights set on quality, not quantity."

"Well then, keep your eye on that but leave some leftovers for the others," Astaroth ordered. "Not sharing would be a bad habit to develop, and I'd hate to have to break you of it."

Mara's head snapped up and her eyes flared. Had Astaroth just threatened her?

Astaroth stared at her for a long time with his dead eyes like he was trying to pry her thoughts out of her head. Finally he offered a pinched frown. "And then there's the matter of your newest acquisitions. Who were they? Ah yes, the singers. Nate and Kathy. I looked through the details of your contract with them."

"I beg your pardon?" Mara didn't know whether to be terrified or offended.

"Yes. Normally I wouldn't, but given the incidents lately, I thought it best. The language around Kathy's portion of the deal is deliciously detailed, as are the dozen or so clauses you put in there."

"You know I'm a rock star." Mara buried her apprehension under bravado and arrogance.

"But then, when you look at Nate's portion, it is much vaguer. Perhaps deliberately so."

"Kathy was the more promising acquisition. She's got the anger, the jealousy, the driving ambition. Nate will follow where she goes. So, I cut a corner. Year-end is coming up and I wanted the twofer—I spent my time on the valuable soul and less on the add-on, and it worked out. I've hit my required hundred contracts for the quarter. These two brought me one step closer to beating Kemm for the number one spot, and I'll get the last two I need to beat him before the end of the year." She slung an arm over the back of her chair and looked bored.

"I know very well what your numbers are. What I'm concerned with here is sloppy work on your part. With a little encouragement, this Nate could be worth practically as much as his partner someday. You can still make it happen, but he has too many ways out of his deal, if he really wants them. You know I abhor sloppy work and I detest when someone in my organization loses a soul because of it!"

Mara sat back when Astaroth shouted, the gaunt Grand Duke's voice a medley of nails on a chalkboard and shattered bones.

"And just so you know, Kemm still appears to be missing," Astaroth said.

Mara shrugged and let a mask of indifference slide over her face to hide the churn in her gut. "Idiot is probably celebrating his win prematurely. Even more reason to beat him."

"Could be, but people are starting to wonder. Even his brother doesn't know where he is, and he's been asking a lot of questions. Including a few about you."

"Me?"

Astaroth's black eyes stared right through her. "I think he wants to ask you about Kemm. Is there anything I ought to know?"

Her lie was blatant and done with aplomb: "Absolutely not."

"Hmph. You can go," snapped Astaroth. "Get out."

Normally, Mara would have taken offense at such a brusque dismissal, but the mention of Kemm and Kal had unnerved her, and she was just as happy to get out from under the angry Grand Duke's cold glower as soon as possible. She did offer him a challenging stare as she stood, but left the office without saying anything else.

CHAPTER 25

DESPITE THE SEASONAL emphasis of being and doing good, Christmas was a remarkably busy time. Duncan and other angels had their hands full comforting those who were alone for the holidays and fell into despair. They also had to contend with parents who felt they couldn't afford to give their children the holiday they wanted and—unfortunately—with families facing tragic accidents. There was an upside, though. They helped people reconnect with their faith, with the idea of being generous, and with renewed efforts to help the unfortunate. But it was also a season filled with lust, gluttony, covetousness, and jealousy—in other words, the most wonderful time of the year for Mara and her devilish brethren.

Work hours had been long and unpredictable since the start of the month. Mara wanted one evening of quiet, with her only distraction being Duncan. She'd given him a key to her place, but he wasn't at the apartment when she got home. She was disappointed, but knew he'd be along once he wrapped up with whatever soul he was soothing or saving. Outside the apartment, Joyal Street's lamps were decorated with garland and white holiday lights, and there was bustling foot traffic. From what she could see, Bruisers was full, and she liked knowing business was good for Joe. This weekend would be his annual Horrible Holiday Sweater Event, with a generous cash prize for the most heinous holiday sweater.

She pulled the shades shut and dragged her own not-very-horrible sweater up over her head, tossing it carelessly into the laundry hamper. The rest of her clothes followed quickly, and she grabbed a clean towel. She loved the feel of scalding-hot shower water—it would likely burn a human but was just right for her. After washing her hair, Mara used her new almond-orange sugar scrub and went over every inch of her skin. She inhaled deeply, letting the sharp, bright aroma fill her nose and lungs.

She leaned one hand against the wall of the shower and let the steamy water roll off her back, then rotated her head, trying to loosen her shoulders. She should be over at Bruisers looking for the last two souls she needed. If she didn't get them, all her hard work to beat Baliel's record was going to get flushed right down the toilet. But she didn't want to run into Kal in public—he could cause way too much trouble over Kemm. She had no problem going up against Kal, but she couldn't do it in front of everyone. How would she explain that to Duncan? Or anyone else, for that matter? Mara's shoulders tightened.

Once she was out of the shower, Mara threw on her short robe and tied it loosely. She looked at herself in the mirror and smiled. Maybe it was time for Angel-Boy to get an early Christmas present.

Grabbing the blow dryer, she made short work of her damp hair and brushed it out. Then she went through the apartment and turned out all the lights except for the freestanding lamp in the living room and the light over the stove in the kitchen. She grabbed a book to entertain herself and went into the bedroom to wait.

Thirty minutes later, after carefully scouting the street for any signs of angels or devils, Duncan let himself in the front foyer of Mara's building and headed up the stairs. He tossed his hat and gloves on the counter and draped his coat over the back of a kitchen chair as he rolled his shoulders, shedding the stress of his day. Hardly any lights were on and he assumed Mara wasn't home yet, but as he reached for the refrigerator handle to get a beer, that wonderful faint tang of cinnamon reached his nose, followed by a subtle trace of sweet birch smoke.

"Mara? Where are you?"

"In here, Angel-Boy." Her voice drifted out of the bedroom.

The weariness in his bones melted away, and Duncan loosened his tie and slid it out from around his neck as he walked through the apartment, following the sound of her voice. When he reached the bedroom door, Duncan stopped short, letting the tie fall from his hand. He tried to say something, but he had no breath, no voice.

Mara was on the bed, leaning back against a mountain of pillows with her short silk robe barely belted around her waist. Strips of red cloth were coiled around her wrists and each led to a different bedpost. Slowly, she moved one leg and the robe fell away slightly. He let his eyes travel up from the pointed toe, over the curve of her calf and thigh to where it disappeared under the edge of the black silk.

"Speechless, I see," she said.

Duncan's smile widened when he saw the desire in her eyes. His gaze moved to the ties wrapped around her wrists, and he felt himself get warmer. Duncan couldn't shed his clothes fast enough, only unbuttoning his shirt partway before hastily yanking it over his head. He wadded it up and tossed it at the hamper. It missed, bouncing off the wall and onto the floor where it remained, ignored. He came and sat on the edge of the bed and ran a hand up Mara's leg. She shifted under his touch and leaned forward a little.

"Not yet, impatient thing. I want to look at you first." He reached over and tugged one end of her robe's belt, gently pulling it out from around her waist. When it had been discarded, Duncan slowly peeled the sides of the robe apart. Mara was completely naked underneath the silk. He put an arm on either side of her and leaned closer, pulling back slightly as she moved to kiss him. He let his lips hover near hers for a tantalizing moment before he kissed her. When he finally drew back, Mara's eyes were bright, and he could see her fingers flexing with frustrated desire as she held on to the ties.

"You promised." He laughed.

"I won't make that mistake again. Where are you going?"

Duncan got up from the edge of the bed and backed a few steps away. He very slowly and deliberately unbuckled his belt and threw it to the side before undoing the buttons and zipper on his pants. Watching him intensely, Mara moved as far as the restraints would allow. Duncan kicked off his shoes and socks, and then let the pants fell away.

"Christ on a raft." Mara gasped. "Commando? In the winter?"

"Sometimes I like to live dangerously."

Duncan pulled Mara by the ankles so she slid down on the pillows to recline rather than sit. She sighed as he leisurely ran his fingers up her body, letting them wander over her thighs, her waist, her breasts, and up to her neck before drifting back down. He watched Mara close her eyes as she shifted under his touch, and he felt the heat flood through him. Three times he brought her to the very edge and then retreated, letting her passion cool just enough before he started again.

She laughed when he kissed near her navel. "I'm ticklish there . . ."

"We'll see how ticklish you are." He pushed her thighs apart.

Her eyes lit up. "What are you up to?"

"You know exactly what I'm up to."

As he went down on her, Duncan felt her entire body tense and strain. He could picture the taut red straps around her wrists, and tightened his grip on her hips. He flicked his tongue over her once, twice, and that was all it took. Mara cried out as she arched her back while Duncan kept his mouth on her, drawing the sensation out until she collapsed back against the bed and the pillows.

As the heat of her orgasm subsided, Mara's entire body trembled beneath Duncan and he kissed her softly, waiting for her breathing to become less frantic and intense. Rather than wait, however, Mara pulled her legs up and closed them around Duncan's middle, opening herself to him even more. A soft cry escaped her lips as Duncan pressed against her, started to enter, and then stopped.

She stared up at him. "Yes . . ." It was a question and a demand all wrapped up together, and with one thrust of his hips, Duncan put an end to the wait and filled her.

"You feel so good around me," he said between kisses. His words made her strain again against the ties, but true to her promise, Mara didn't let go. Fully seated inside her, Duncan paused, leaned his weight on his left arm and reached up with his right. He covered Mara's fist with his hand.

"Let go. Relax your fingers," he said quietly. She relaxed her hand and he slowly unwound the material, freeing that hand before shifting his weight and freeing the other. Mara immediately tangled her hands in his hair and pulled him in for another deep kiss, and then she ran them over his shoulders and back. Duncan gasped as he felt her tighten and close around him. He would never—never—get enough of that sensation. He moved faster, stronger, and Mara tensed her legs around him, digging her fingers into his back.

"Finish it! I want to feel you come inside me. I want to hear you . . ."

Duncan knew, deep down inside, as his own release rose up like a wave to drown him, that nothing in the universe had ever—could ever—make him feel like this. He slowed his pace, wanting to make it last. Mara put her lips to his ear and nibbled his earlobe.

Say it, Mara. Please, please say it.

He got his wish.

"Duncan," she whispered in his ear, "I love it when you fuck me."

That finished him, and he bellowed her name as he came.

CHAPTER 26

THE MALL PRETTY much looked like it had puked Christmas spirit all over itself. Giant ornaments hung from the ceiling; every pole was wrapped with paper or tinsel—sometimes both—and most shopworkers wore Santa hats as they competed for shoppers' attention and money. In the middle of the food court, Duncan nodded encouragingly to the young man across the table.

"I thought I knew everything," Jake said. "I didn't think I needed anyone else's help."

"We all make mistakes," Duncan said.

"After the things I said? She doesn't want to hear from me."

"I think hearing from her son would be the best present your mother could get, if you want my opinion."

Jake fussed with the coffee stir stick. "I told her I was better off without her, that I hated her for holding me back."

"Were you right?" Duncan asked.

"Shit, no. I've never been so wrong." Shame and self-loathing rolled off Jake in waves.

"Then call her and tell her that. Tell her you made a huge mistake and you're sorry. It won't be easy, but . . ."

"What if she doesn't want to talk to me? What if she hates me?"

Duncan took a deep breath before he answered. "She might be pretty angry. I can't promise she'll want to talk to you, but I know she doesn't hate you. You're her son."

"I don't know," Jake waffled.

"Ultimately it's your call, Jake, but I think it's a chance you're going to have to take."

Jake fiddled with his phone. His eyes, filled with questions and doubts, slid over to Duncan. Looking for permission.

"It's up to you," Duncan said again.

Jake tapped the phone's screen a few times with a trembling finger, and he left it on speaker. While it rang, Duncan let his power drift out to cloak them and block out some of the tumult from the people around them, as well as to give Jake some reassurance. While he couldn't tell the young man what to do, Duncan could, temporarily, muffle external distractions, giving Jake the chance to hear what he really needed.

"Hello?" said a woman's voice.

Jake was silent, a tear leaking down his cheek.

"Hello?" she said again.

"Mom? It's me, Jake."

There was a moment of silence on the other end of the phone, followed by a choked sob. "Honey, is that really you? Are you okay? I'm so glad you called!"

"I'm so sorry, Mom. So sorry. All of those awful things I said . . ."

"It's okay. It's okay. I said some stuff too. Things I wish every day I could take back. Are you all right? We all miss you."

Jake sagged in his chair. "I'm mostly all right. I miss you too." He hesitated. "Mom?"

"What, honey?"

"Can I come home?"

On the other end of the phone, Jake's mom burst into tears. "Of course, you can! You can always come home, Jake. We love you."

That was all Duncan needed to hear. He pushed back quietly from the table, his heart glad, and strolled through the mall. Although he was happy that Jake had reconnected with his mother, he wasn't in the greatest mood. He'd been assigned to the Christmas Eve on-call pool, and had been stuck wandering the Midwest, catching any last-minute crises of faith that cropped up.

If he was being honest, he really didn't like Christmas all that much. He understood it was a sacred time of year, but there were so many lonely souls out there, so many who were filled with sadness and despair during what should be a joyful time. So many who started down bad roads because they felt there was no other choice. And he couldn't save all of them. He almost desperately wanted to be back in Hollis City with Mara, but he had another twenty minutes before he was officially off duty.

He let his mind wander as he walked, and his imagination immediately went to Mara and those sinful red straps around her wrists. That rendezvous had happened almost a week ago and he still couldn't get it out of his mind. Not that he wanted to—he'd be perfectly content to daydream about it every single day. Duncan tugged at the collar of his shirt and shook his head, as if that would clear the thoughts away, and found himself staring at a pair of ruby and pearl earrings in a jeweler's window. They were perfect. Soon a very satisfied Duncan left the mall with a velvet jeweler's box in his pocket, and headed back to Hollis City.

Duncan took the long way to Mara's apartment, just to avoid prying eyes. He didn't like avoiding his friends, but Basil had started asking questions that Duncan wasn't quite prepared to answer. It was a cold night and Joyal Street was empty, save for an elderly man with a cane moving slowly down the sidewalk. The wind caught the old man's plaid scarf and blew it out of his reach. Duncan chased it down and brought it back.

"Here you go," Duncan said with a smile.

The old man, bent with age, tilted his head to the side so Duncan could see part of his crooked smile, the rest of his face obscured by his warm hat. "Thank you, young man. That was very kind of you."

Duncan paused for a second.

"Is something wrong?" the old man said.

"No, I'm sorry," Duncan said. "I thought I smelled something, but it's gone now. Do you need help getting somewhere?" He wasn't about to leave an old man alone on a cold street.

"No, no. My granddaughter and her children live a few doors down. I just needed some fresh air. Love the great-grands, but they're a little loud." The old man chuckled. "But thank you for asking."

"All right then, be careful walking. And Merry Christmas," Duncan said.

"Merry Christmas to you too, son."

Duncan watched the old man hobble away for a moment and then hurried up the steps to the outer door of Mara's building. He disappeared inside, never noticing that the old man turned to watch him—with intense coal-black eyes.

Mara nearly threw the door open when Duncan knocked, and kissed him before he even got through the door.

"You're early," she said happily. "How was your trip?"

"Really good, actually. Ended on a high note."

"Awesome. Are you hungry?" she asked. "I was just making some pasta, if you want some."

"Definitely. How's everything been for you the past few days?"

"Eh" was Mara's noncommittal answer.

"That good, huh?"

"Well, I hit my quota back in November—a banker, a gangbanger, and one ruthlessly ambitious perfume diva—so I don't have to worry about being on anyone's naughty list." She chuckled at her own joke.

"And?" Duncan prompted.

"All well and good to make quota, but I'm still trailing on the leaderboard for the top spot. If I'm not ahead of Kemm at the end of the year, I don't beat Baliel's record, and I've worked too hard to miss out on that. I hit my base quota, but I've got to close a few more deals to beat Kemm, and lately, Astaroth seems to have an unhealthy fascination with my work. I had another private dressing-down from him earlier." Mara frowned.

"Is there a reason he's so interested in you right now?" Duncan asked as he leaned against the island.

"We have a difference in opinion about how some of my contracts are structured, that's all." Mara knew she was glossing over the real reasons, but she didn't want to upset Duncan.

"And what about Kemm? He must know you're breathing down his neck for that top spot." Duncan stood and stretched as he talked.

Mara stopped stirring the pasta for a second. "Kemm and I kinda had it out a few weeks back. He's stayed out of the spotlight since then, but his brother is a little pissed off about it."

"I'm sure it isn't anything you can't handle." Duncan came up behind Mara and slid his arms around her waist. He kissed her neck. "I'm glad I'm back."

"I am too." She relaxed against him.

When the pasta was done, she and Duncan watched some silly sitcom reruns while they ate curled up next to each other on the sofa. During a commercial, Mara brought the dirty dishes to the kitchen, and when she came back, a velvet box was waiting on the coffee table. She eyed it curiously, flicked her eyes to Duncan and then back to the box.

"What's this?" she asked, her finger sliding across the plush velvet, unable to dim her excited smile.

"Just a little something for the holiday."

"Do I get to open it now?"

"Sure."

Mara pried open the top of the container and her mouth formed an "O" as she looked at the earrings. The soft luminescence of the pearls served to make the ruby's color look even deeper and more regal. She took them out of the box and immediately put them in her ears.

"I love them! They're gorgeous. How do they look?" Mara held her hair back so Duncan could see them.

"They pale in comparison to you."

"Oh, we are the sweet-talker tonight, aren't we?"

"Is it working?" His grin was cheeky.

"You'll have to wait and see. Go look on the kitchen chair."

Duncan did as she asked and found a little red bag decorated with a bow. He brought it back to the sofa.

"What could this possibly be?"

"Open it and find out."

Duncan pulled the bow off and lifted out the crumpled tissue paper. Inside was a navy tie. When he looked closer, he realized the pattern on it was little hearts—little hearts with devil horns sticking out of them, crowned by halos. He roared with laughter.

"This is perfect! I love it! Michael insists on the tie as part of his dress code, but there's nothing in there about patterns. You're as brilliant as you are beautiful."

"Yes, I am, and now I think it's time for dessert—and maybe you can model that sexy new tie for me. It should coordinate brilliantly with your birthday suit."

CHAPTER 27

THE WEEK BETWEEN Christmas and New Year's was typically quiet. At Bruisers, Basil looked at his watch and shook his head. This was the third time in the last month Duncan had blown them off after promising to get drinks after work, and he was starting to get pissed.

"He's not going to show up, is he?" asked Raymond.

"I don't think so."

"Do you know what's going on with him?"

Basil shook his head. "No, I don't."

"But you have your suspicions?"

"I think he's hung up on that devil. The one from Bruisers," Basil answered.

"It's got to be just a crush, right? I mean, if he was trying to save a devil, Duncan would tell us, and he hasn't said anything to me about it," said Raymond.

"I hope it's just a crush. I mean, it's one thing to hook up with a devil. I've heard a few stories here and there about angels who did, but to get, like, really involved with one? A relationship? That would make Michael's head explode."

"Maybe we need to distract him? Help him get laid? That might take his mind off it."

Basil snorted. "Have you taken a good look at Duncan? He's never had an issue getting laid when he wants to. You and me? We're another story. Last time I looked we weren't typically at the top of the panty-dropper list."

"I drop plenty of panties, thank you."

"We're going to *make* him go out with us. We'll round up some folks and just grab him on the way out the door. He won't have any choice but to have a night out on the town with us," Basil said.

The next day, it took Basil and Raymond less time than they expected to round up a group of angels with whom to hit the bar after work to celebrate surviving Christmas and to have a little fun before the workload spiked again on New Year's Eve. On the way out of the office they pounced on Duncan, refusing to take no for an answer.

Mara was surprised when the entire lot of angels tumbled into Bruisers, and she caught Duncan's attention. He gave her an aggravated eye roll, and she flashed him a smile and a nod. She understood. They couldn't exactly hang all over each other, not in front of this crowd. As she covertly watched the angels, Mara's smile faded as one with curly brown hair and a smattering of freckles across her nose flirted relentlessly with Duncan. Mara flinched when Joe put another beer down in front of her.

"Not going to meet Duncan's friends?" asked Joe.

"No. I only know a few of them, and like I said before, competing companies. Hanging out with a crowd of them? Someone's bound to get in trouble with the boss."

"The cute one seems to have taken a shine to him."

"She's wasting her time. She's not his type." Mara took a drink. She knew Joe was fishing to see how she felt.

"And what is his type?" Joe smiled at her knowingly and Mara made a face.

"Well, it's not *that*. If you think she's so cute, Joe, why don't you go scoop her up?"

"Too young for me. Does have kind of a nice butt, though." He chuckled while he finished pouring four draft beers. "Joanie, cover the bar for a minute? I have to run back to the kitchen."

"You got it, sugar," Joanie answered, her eyes following Joe through the door. It wasn't the first time Mara had noticed the waitress watching Joe. Joanie was totally into him, but Joe was just oblivious.

The meal, although delicious, was not enough to distract Mara from the rather raucous group of angels. Every time she looked over, the one with curly hair was too close to Duncan for her liking, and every time she touched his arm or brushed against him, Mara's mood got darker and darker. Finally, after a ringing peal of laughter, which Curly followed up by hugging Duncan and announcing how brilliantly funny he was, Mara couldn't take it anymore. She angrily slapped some money on the bar, grabbed her coat, and headed for the door.

As she opened it, she felt eyes on her and looked back over her shoulder, the sensation of being watched suddenly suffocating her. It wasn't Duncan. He had turned away to talk to a tall, lanky angel with ginger hair. There were a few devils around, but they were busy with prospects. She wondered for a moment if it was Kal—three times in the past week, Mara thought she'd seen Kemm's brother watching her. Another glance around the room told her that Kal wasn't there. Then her eyes fell on an elderly man at the bar, a plaid scarf hanging across his shoulders, but he was focused on his soup, not on her. Scowling, Mara turned and left. The old man looked up from his chorizo, rice, and bean soup, watching her with his dead black eyes.

Two hours later the angels left the bar.

"Let's go somewhere else," said Cecilia, the curly-haired angel. "I'm not ready to call it a night yet. What do you think? Anything you want to do, Duncan?" She gave him a coy look, a clear invitation to spend much more of the evening with her. Behind Cecilia, Basil gave him a knowing and encouraging smile.

"I can't," Duncan said. "I've got some things to take care of."

Cecilia's face fell and Basil gave him a disgusted look. A look that said Duncan was an utter moron for not taking advantage of the offer.

"Duncan, hang on a sec. I need to talk to you—" Basil started to say.

"Can't right now, Basil. Sorry. It was fun tonight."

With that, Duncan vanished from the Mortal Plane, taking great care to go in the exact opposite direction of Mara's apartment. When an angel—or a devil—moved among the Planes, their departure was shown by the faintest wisps of clouds or smoke that swirled in the direction they'd gone.

Duncan rematerialized in Los Angeles, walked two blocks, and then disappeared again. Just to be certain Basil wasn't following him, he hit Vancouver, Minneapolis, Charlotte, Madrid, Jacksonville, and finally went back to Hollis City. He waited in the shadows and then disappeared one last time, only to rematerialize outside Mara's apartment door.

He knocked. "Mara?"

There was no answer.

"Mara?"

He had a key, but didn't bother trying to use it since Mara had probably used the chain lock as well. He heard the floor creak behind the door and knew she was inside.

"Please let me in, Mara. I need to see you."

Finally he heard the chain and the lock in the doorknob release, and the door opened partway to reveal Mara's angry, sulky face.

"I'm sorry about all that," he said. "They grabbed me before I left the office and I couldn't say no. You looked so angry when you left—you know I'm not interested in her."

"Well, she's clearly interested in you."

"I don't care. What I'm interested in is behind this door, and only this door."

Mara sighed and let him in. "I know we can't exactly hang out together—shit would hit the fan—but that doesn't make it easier."

"I know." He reached out and hooked his fingers into the belt loop of her jeans and pulled her closer.

"Every time Curly touched you, I wanted to slap the smile right off her face."

Duncan laughed. "'Curly'?"

"Don't ask me to repeat the other things I called her in my head."

Sliding his arms around her waist, Duncan pulled Mara close to him. "All I could think about was being with you."

"Then less thinking and more doing."

Mara slipped out of his arms and walked backward toward the bedroom, beckoning Duncan with her finger. He followed, starting to undress as he walked. By the time he reached the bedroom, his shirt was discarded in the hallway and he was unbuckling his belt. Mara stripped off her pants and sweater, and a moment later they were both naked. Mara kissed him, catching Duncan's lower lip in her teeth, and slid her hands around to squeeze his behind.

"You have a totally tight ass," she said, grinning.

"Glad you like it," he said. "Now turn around so I can see yours."

Instead of just turning around, Mara curved and leaned over the bed. She looked back over her shoulder at Duncan and offered a come-hither smile. Duncan ran his hands up her back, and Mara caught her breath when Duncan pushed inside her. She leaned back, making sure he was as deep as he could go, and dug her nails into the down comforter. Two hours later they dozed off in each other's arms, sweaty, sated, and exhausted.

CHAPTER 28

THE VERANDA WAS spacious and open, and looked out over a massive, manicured expanse of lawn dotted with a few small ponds and several large weeping willow trees. The man sitting in the fan-backed padded wicker chair sipped his bourbon and listened to the birds in the trees. There was no other noise, and he soaked in the serenity of the moment, something rare and precious in his world. With a relaxed and contented sigh, his gaze wandered across the green grass until he came to rest on one particular small pond. Old pain—pain that he knew would never go away—creased the corners of his eyes. By the pond, the branches of two large willows with gold-hued leaves sheltered a white-marble sarcophagus. His eyes lingered, and the stone seemed to glow even in the shade of the trees.

Warm memories, their edges soft and familiar, touched him: her smile, her laugh, the golden glow that always seemed to be around her. *I miss you still, my love. Even your wrath, when you were furious with me, made me love you more. There are so very few brave enough to chide me for a misdeed. You were—you are—everything I have ever wanted.*

Small claws clicked on the patio stone, the steps hesitant, driving the memories from his mind. He didn't turn. He just waited until a nervous voice finally said, "Excuse me, sir? I hate to interrupt your repose."

"Far too late for that."

The serving imp quailed but didn't retreat. "Grand Duke Astaroth is here, sir. He's says it is an important matter you'll wish to discuss."

Lucifer sighed. He knew Astaroth wouldn't bother him unless it was important, especially not when he was here. "Very well, show him in. And bring the rest of the bourbon, and an extra glass."

"Right away, sir."

The old plantation mansion was large, and Lucifer knew that it would take a few minutes for Astaroth to be brought out, so he stood and stretched leisurely. He loved running Hell, but it was a laborious task, plus every now and then everyone—even the King of Hell—needed a few moments of solitude and quiet. Once each month he spent two days here at his country estate and listened to nothing but the water and the wind, perhaps indulging in a good book. The breeze made the ends of his loose linen shirt flutter.

Behind him, the click of nails on stone returned. This time it was accompanied by a second set of soft, nearly silent footsteps. Lucifer turned.

"Lucifer. Thank you for seeing me. I know that you come here to escape the barrage of demands that always accost you. And with you delivering the opening keynote speech at the Annual Employee Conference in a few weeks, I'm sure that hasn't helped." Outside of Hell, and exposed to the bright sunlight, Astaroth looked even paler and more cadaverous than usual.

"Astaroth, my old friend. You're pretty much the only one who'd dare to come here, so I know it must be important. Come, sit." Lucifer gestured to a patio set with an umbrella, so that Astaroth could at least sit in the shade and be a little more comfortable. The imp who had shown him in appeared with the bottle of bourbon and a glass. He put both on the table and looked at Lucifer expectantly.

"That will be all," said the Devil. "You may go—but make sure no one disturbs us for *any* reason. Is that clear?"

"Yes, sir. I'll see to it myself." The imp couldn't get away from the table fast enough. When Lucifer was certain he was gone, he poured himself a double bourbon and did the same for Astaroth. The treasurer picked the glass up and swirled the dark liquid before taking a sip of the smooth, smoky liquor.

"Now, tell me, my old friend, what is so urgent that you were compelled to leave your comfy office?" Lucifer got straight to the point. "Is she hurt?"

"No, no, Mara is fine. Very fit."

"Is her performance lacking?"

"She normally brings in some excellent candidates," Astaroth said after a moment's hesitation.

"Normally?" Lucifer sipped his bourbon.

"As I mentioned on the phone, I've noticed lately that she's had a few anomalies. Showing a little compassion for the usual collateral damage, having a few issues with how her contracts are behaving . . ."

The word "compassion" jabbed Lucifer in the gut, but he remained silent.

"And I've gotten attitude from her on some recent visits. Quite a bit of attitude actually," Astaroth told him.

"Hmmm" was only commentary the King of Hell provided. He gestured for Astaroth to continue, but thought, *If he's here only because Mara is being slightly insubordinate, I'm going to light his jacket on fire and watch him run around the yard.*

"That made me pay a little more attention to her comings and goings, and I think it is simply a matter of her being distracted."

There was a subtle undertone to Astaroth's words that Lucifer didn't miss.

"Distracted by what?"

Now Astaroth hesitated.

"Distracted by *what*?" Lucifer repeated, his voice a little lower, a little darker.

"I think she's distracted by a who, not a what."

"That's why you're bothering me here? *Here?* Because Mara might have found someone to have jolly good romp in the sheets with, and it's got her a little distracted? Astaroth, when was the last time that you got a little?"

Astaroth's expression soured before he said, "Last night, if you must know."

"Really?" Lucifer's eyebrows went up, genuinely surprised. "Good for you."

Astaroth frowned, unamused by the banter, and finally dropped the bomb he'd been holding. "I think Mara's having that jolly good romp with an angel."

The glass of bourbon stopped halfway to Lucifer's lips, and then he slowly put it back down as unease curled in his gut. "An angel, you say?"

"I don't know for sure, but I have a strong suspicion." Astaroth finished his own bourbon and put down the empty glass.

"What's brought you to this conclusion?"

"I've kept a careful eye on her. In fact, as her manager, I took it upon myself to follow her on the Mortal Plane. While I was observing her, I saw an angel go into her building, but I cannot say for certain he was visiting her, as there are three apartments there. And the other thing is her behavior. She likes to hang out at the bar across the street from where she lives on the Mortal Plane, a place called Bruisers. There was a group of angels there, having a rather raucous time—"

Lucifer chuckled. "Nothing like raucous angels. Best hide the good china."

"I noticed she was watching one of the angels. The same one who went into her building. She's very subtle, but she definitely kept an eye on him. And the more flirtatious a female angel got with him, the fouler Mara's mood got. She was jealous."

Lucifer frowned. "Who else knows about this?"

"No one in Hell that I'm aware of. If nothing else, Mara is discreet. She's spent her entire life trying to avoid unwanted attention. I don't expect she'd change that now. Whether or not any angels have noticed, I can't say."

"Could she be trying to make the angel fall?" That would certainly be an annoyance, but far less worrisome than the alternative.

Astaroth shook his head. "My instinct says no. She didn't have that predatory look—you know the one I mean. Lucifer, this could go sideways very quickly."

"She's kept her secrets close all these years, ignored all the contempt and ridicule hurled at her," said Lucifer in tone tinged with regret. "But she can't hide them forever."

He leaned back in his seat, thinking, and Astaroth waited in silence.

Finally the King of Hell leaned forward again and put his arms on the edge of the table. "See what else you can observe, but don't be intrusive. If there's any more substance to this, let me know—preferably before it gets out of hand."

"Yes, sir." Astaroth stood. "Thank you for seeing me."

"I'm glad you came. This is important for me to know. It could raise a lot of questions."

Astaroth started to leave, but stopped when Lucifer held up a hand. He waited while the King of Hell gathered his thoughts.

"Thank you, Astaroth. You've been a loyal friend for a very long time. I don't think I would have trusted anyone else in Hell with keeping an eye on Mara."

"You're welcome. Just because we're devils doesn't mean we shouldn't hold ourselves to certain standards."

Once Astaroth left, Lucifer poured himself one more glass of bourbon and returned to his fan-backed chair. The sun had shifted and with a snap of his fingers, sunglasses appeared on his face. Settling back into the cushions, he shut his eyes and listened to the birds.

Mara, Mara, Mara, my lovely little nightmare. What trouble are you getting yourself into?

CHAPTER 29

IT WAS NEW Year's Eve and Mara wanted to cry as she wandered through the teeming crowds in Times Square. She could smell snow on the air, but the storm wasn't due to reach New York for a few more hours, and the revelers were getting in as much partying as they could before they had to head home. Two days ago she'd managed to land another contract—a down-and-out cabdriver who wanted revenge on the drunkard who'd run down his son in a crosswalk. Mara would have preferred the drunk driver as a mark, but she needed the cabbie's soul to tie Kemm's number for the quarter. Now she needed just one more, and she was starting to feel the pressure.

Her thoughts whirled . . . *Nearly nine million mortals and I can't find one needy, insecure soul. I just need one more—one!— and I'm ahead of Kemm's total. If he wasn't more than a pile of toxic waste, I'd be okay with the tie. I'll still beat Baliel even if I have to share year-end honors, but if Kemm wins and doesn't show? Valafar is already foaming at the mouth. If Kemm's a no-show, things are going to go sideways pretty damn fast.*

For a minute Mara regretted going to New York. Her logic, of a larger crowd equating to a larger pool of prospects, wasn't working the way she'd planned. There were so many people in

Times Square, it was hard to filter out which soul to focus on. To clear her head a little, Mara walked a short distance down Seventh Avenue, away from the teeming mass of revelers, when something caught her eye.

"You need some help?" she asked.

A young man, skinny and dressed in a worn jacket that didn't look very warm, glanced at her. "Why would you want to help me?"

"New Year's Eve is supposed to be fun. You don't look like you're enjoying yourself very much."

"I wanted my first kiss with Alyssa to be tonight, but she blew me off." Dull anger flushed his cheeks. "Told me she'd be here and then canceled."

"Funny, I was going to meet my cousin Alyssa tonight . . ."

"Her name's Murray. Alyssa Murray."

"Seriously? No shit? That's my cousin," Mara lied. "She probably canceled on you to meet me. I'm in unexpectedly from out of town. What's your name?"

"Eddie. Why aren't you with Alyssa, then?" He took a drink out of the champagne bottle he was holding. It looked to be about three-quarters empty.

"We got separated and my phone died," Mara said. "And now I'm not sure how to get back to her place. Maybe you could show me the way after the ball drops? I could put in a good word for you."

"You would?"

"Sure, if you help me out. You really like her, huh?"

"Like her? I love her. I've loved her for years. We're perfect together, but she just doesn't see it. She would have seen it tonight. I should have known she wouldn't come—she only said yes so I'd stop calling her."

Mara could hear the obsession, smell the neediness, feel the desperation. *Oh thank God I've found one*, she thought, ignoring the irony.

"Oh, I'm sure that's not the case." Mara slipped her arm through Eddie's and steered him toward a slightly shadowy area while he poured out his love for Alyssa, his voice slurred from the alcohol. He told Mara about the first time he'd seen the love of his life, when they were six years old. From there he had pursued her, left her secret gifts and poems, watched her.

Mara shuddered a little. This guy had psycho-stalker written all over him. She glanced at the clock: Five minutes to midnight. She was running out of time.

"I'm sure Alyssa just doesn't understand how much you care. What would you do, Eddie, for a date with her?"

That caught Eddie's attention and he tried to stand still but couldn't completely stop his drunken sway. "A date? An honest-to-God date? Oh, I'd do anything." His eyes lit up hungrily.

Mara reached inside her jacket and a few sheets of paper appeared. "You sign on the dotted line, Eddie, and I'll get you that date with Alyssa, and then in ten years I get your soul. What do you think?" Mara let her eyes turn crimson.

"Cool contacts." Eddie laughed.

Fucking idiot, she thought.

Three minutes to midnight.

Mara held out a pen. "Imagine it: Dinner with Alyssa at a nice romantic restaurant. I'm sure she'd wear a very sexy dress . . ."

"You said you were her cousin? You don't look much like her."

"I'm adopted. Stay with me, Eddie. I can see the two of you walking back to her place, and then on the steps . . ."

Two minutes to midnight. Mara started to sweat.

"We could kiss . . . She'd see that I'm a real man, someone who could take care of her, keep her safe." Eddie's eyes nearly rolled up in his head as he fantasized about kissing Alyssa. Meanwhile, Mara counted the seconds.

One minute to midnight.

"Sign the contract and I can open the door for all of that," urged Mara.

Eddie took another swig of champagne, draining the bottle, and carelessly tossed it away. He looked out over the crowd and Mara bit her lip, trying to rein in her impatience.

"Tonight would have been the perfect night for us," muttered Eddie.

"Don't put too much emphasis on the day." Mara put her hand gently on his arm. "There's nothing you can do about tonight. Don't waste all the days coming up because this one didn't go quite the way you planned."

"Huh," Eddie paused, considering what Mara had said.

The crowd chanted, "FIVE . . . FOUR . . . THREE . . ."

"You've got a point." Eddie took the pen and paper. He pressed it against the wall as he signed. The ink flamed.

"TWO . . ."

"Cool trick with the magic ink . . ."

"ONE . . ."

Mara grabbed Eddie and kissed him for all she was worth as the eleven-thousand-pound crystal ball finished its descent to mark the start of the New Year.

"HAPPY NEW YEAR!" the crowd roared as one.

"Whoa, jumped the gun on that New Year's kiss."

"You caught me. I just wanted a little taste of what Alyssa has to look forward to." Regret hammered Mara, nearly taking her breath away. Alyssa had no idea what she was in for. One date was going to turn into a nightmare for her. Mara frowned, trying to shake the guilt off her shoulders, and turned to walk away.

"Hey, aren't we going to Alyssa's?" Eddie demanded.

"Not tonight, no. You'll get your date, but not tonight."

"What do you mean, 'not tonight'?"

Eddie grabbed Mara's elbow roughly and she turned on him, her eyes crimson and furious. She slammed her palm into his chest, knocking him back a step.

"I mean, *not tonight*. You'll get everything coming to you, Eddie. Don't you worry about that."

"What's wrong with your eyes? What are you?" Eddie's voice was shaking. The fear had finally broken through his champagne haze.

"Eddie, I'm going to let you noodle that one out yourself. Now go home. I'll be in touch."

Cowed, Eddie walked away, listing a little to the left as he went. Mara watched until he disappeared around a corner, wishing she could wash the taste of him out of her mouth. She spat on the sidewalk and when she looked up, time stopped.

Staring daggers at her across the street was Kal. He pointed at Mara and dragged his finger across his throat before melting back into the throng. Mara's heart hammered in her chest.

Kal was coming for her.

CHAPTER 30

AFTER NEW YEAR'S, Mara kept her anxiety over Kal close to the vest, always having an excuse for why she was distracted whenever Duncan asked her. She felt like shit keeping things from him, but the whole situation with Kemm's annihilation wasn't something she was willing to share with anyone. It had been a quiet night, and Mara was curled up on the sofa with Duncan's arms around her, watching the football game. It was the playoffs. During the halftime break, the commentators threw it to the reporters on the field, and when Markus Winston appeared on the screen, Mara perked up.

"Go ahead, Markus. Flap your gums. You'd better say the right thing . . ."

"Since when do you care what he has to say?" Duncan asked.

"The next words out of his mouth are probably going to have a pretty profound influence on the rest of his life." She leaned forward, her elbows on her knees.

"That's right," Markus said to the reporter, all his swagger on display. "We are going all the way to the Super Bowl this year. With me handling the ball, there's no stopping us."

"Do you have anything to say about the rumors we're hearing about your retirement?" the reporter asked.

For a fraction of a second, Markus hesitated.

"Don't be stupid," Mara said to the TV as she sat up straighter.

"Since when do you believe rumors?" Markus asked the reporter.

"You've got your hooks in Markus, don't you?" Duncan asked.

"You know it," Mara said as she waited for Markus's answer.

"Are they true?" the reporter pressed.

"No way, man." Markus puffed out his chest. "I'm playing the best football of my life. We're going all the way to the big game, and then next year, we're going to go again. I guarantee it!"

"Back to you, Clint," the reporter said as Markus headed for the locker room. "And you heard it right from the source: Markus Winston is not retiring at the end of the season. Texas fans will certainly be happy about that!"

Mara shook her head. "Oh, Markus. Markus, Markus. You're so screwed."

After the game, Markus left the stadium and stopped at a gourmet wine shop to get a few bottles to take home. The main parking lot was full, so he pulled his tricked-out SUV into the lower lot and hustled up the stairs. Amber, the cheerleader he was banging, was going to sneak out and meet him. He didn't notice the loose lace on his shoe. After he was done shopping, Markus was two steps down the stairs, a bag in each hand, when he tripped on the lace and plummeted headfirst to the bottom of the steps. He landed in a limp, bleeding heap.

Four days later, much to the surprise of the doctors, Markus regained consciousness in a private room in Houston Methodist

Hospital. Over the next twenty-four hours, some memories came back, and the doctors informed him about the extent of his injuries. Not only did he have a brain injury, Markus had shattered his ankle, broken his wrist and several ribs, gotten pins in his hip and knee, and severely dislocated the shoulder on his throwing arm. When he realized that not only was he going to miss the games that would bring his team to the Super Bowl, he was going to miss the big game itself—the doctors had to sedate him.

Markus was still hospitalized the day of the championship game, and he told his family that he didn't want any visitors on game day; he didn't even want to watch the game. As he lay in bed, the TV flickered to life. He grunted angrily, and with his good arm he reached for the remote. Nothing happened when he pushed the power button.

"What, don't want to watch the game?" Mara leaned in his doorway wearing a Green Bay shirt. "C'mon. *Everybody* wants to watch this game. They're on the edge of their seats to see if your team can rally in the face of adversity."

"Go a'y. I don' wan' teh see game, don' wan' see you."

"Make me. And I *do* want to watch the game."

"Nuz," he growled, pressing the call button. "NUZ!"

"The nurse ain't coming, Sweet Cheeks. She owes me a favor, so it is just you and me for the duration of the game."

"Bitch."

"Well, I see the brain injury has only impaired your regular speech and not your capacity to swear. But I don't want to listen to you slur your words for the next few hours, so . . ." Mara snapped her fingers.

"What? What's that going to do?"

"Unbunch your panties. Although you still hear your voice the way it is, you sound normal to me."

Markus's attention was unwillingly drawn to the screen. The crowd had done a moment of silence to pray for his swift recovery. When the game started, it was a knife in the gut to watch Deion Boyle, the backup QB, trying to marshal the team. They didn't look good, and Green Bay scored early.

"Did you do this to me?" Markus asked.

"No. I warned you at the start of the season that if you broke our deal, then that nasty little penalty clause would come into play."

Mara put a folder that was a good two inches thick on the little table next to Markus. "That penalty clause, which I have flagged if you'd like me to read you the exact wording, stipulates that if you deliberately broke our deal, then you would *never* win a Super Bowl. Ever. Not even if you manage to recover from this mess. The instant you announced you weren't retiring, you opened the door for all this shit to happen."

"This isn't fair . . ."

"Fair?" Mara was indignant. "Your deal was more than fair. You did this to yourself."

"I want the commentator job," he whispered.

"No can do. I told you that the other day too. There were two openings, but they've both been filled—plus, who would hire you to be on TV now? Your speech is totally fucked up. And you'll never play ball again. There are pins in your hip and your knee. Your shoulder was so badly dislocated that it's going to take months for the torn ligaments and tendons to heal, and that was your throwing arm. Not to mention the broken ribs and the fractured skull."

A tear ran down Markus's face and he angrily wiped it away with his working hand. Mara was unimpressed with the tiny show of emotion, knowing it came from self-pity and not any true sense of remorse.

"You're still going to have a nice, long life. But no more celebrity. You're just going to be one of those sad what-coulda-been stories on late-night cable as you fade into obscurity. Hope you enjoyed blowing all your millions on gambling and women, because it won't be long until the hospital bills and therapy sessions—even with insurance—ruin you. You can kiss the fancy house and the Escalade goodbye, and if you think Amber is going to stay with you now? Think again."

"What about Coach? My team?"

"Coach Givens will probably come see you. I'm not sure why, but he does like you. Your teammates are another story. You've been a giant dickhead your whole career and most of them don't give a shit what happens to you."

Markus looked at her, angry. "I inspired them!"

"You bullied them, so shut your piehole. The only one who is going to stick by you is your mom, and as far as I'm concerned, that guarantees her a first-class one-way ticket to Heaven someday."

The bleakness of his future was a crushing weight on Markus's chest. "Then why don't you kill me now?"

Mara was indignant. "Please. I'm a devil, but I do have *some* standards. I'm not a murderer. Oh, look. Green Bay just scored again." She put her feet up on the edge of the bed. "This is going to be an *awesome* game."

CHAPTER 31

MARA TAPPED A nail on the bar and scanned the crowd for the fourth time. She was still on edge from her encounter with Kal on New Year's Eve and even though she was fairly confident he wasn't at the bar, it was crowded, and there was no way to be 100 percent certain. She felt Duncan next to her before she saw him, and when he bent—ostensibly to pick up the jacket he'd dropped—she couldn't contain the gasp of pleasure that followed as his fingers trailed up her leg when he stood up.

"You're a wicked thing," she whispered, not looking at him.

"I'll take that as a supreme compliment. Is everything okay? You're wired for sound tonight."

"Had an incident with a coworker the other week, and it's going to get ugly when I do run into him. I just don't want it to be here."

"Then let's go someplace that's not here," Duncan suggested.

Mara glanced over at him, her eyes flashing with all the carnal ideas running through her mind, and she licked her lips.

On the far side of the bar, Kal watched Mara. She'd been on high alert from the moment she'd walked in, and it had been hard for him to stay hidden. Twice he thought she'd spotted him, and now he smirked as he watched Mara stand up and whisper something in the blond angel's ear, her body grazing his. The lust in the angel's eyes was unmistakable as he watched Mara leave the bar, his gaze lingering on her bottom as she walked. Five minutes later the angel left Bruisers too.

Things had just become so much more interesting. Kal left a five-dollar bill on the bar, pulled up the collar of his jacket, and strolled out into the night. Outside, he nearly walked straight into the devil with the gold-ringed eyes whom Mara had embarrassed at the start of the training class.

"You were here yesterday," said Kal. "You got a hard-on for that little bitch too?"

"Mara? No fucking way," Seth spat.

Kal thought about punching him just out of spite, but decided it wasn't worth the hassle. "I didn't mean that you wanted to bone her, jackass. I saw you nearly get your balls sliced off in the training session. If she embarrassed me like that in front of Baliel, I'd want some major payback too. What's your name again?"

"Seth. And you're Kemm's brother, Kal. What did she do to you?"

"Rank bitch killed my brother. Didn't just kill him, annihilated him, and I'll have her head for that."

Seth's eyes bulged. "Seriously? She must have had help, right? I mean, she's got no flames, no wings. What do you think Lucifer will do to her?"

"I don't know. Might depend on who judges her. She destroyed Kemm, so I'm partial to complete annihilation, but I would be satisfied to see her stretched naked on a rack until her joints pop and then let me have my fun with her. It is amazing how many creative things you can do with a blade."

"I know what blade I'd like to use on her," he said as he grabbed himself.

"Tell you what," said Kal. "If I get any say in what happens to her, I'll ask them to give you first crack at her . . . if you help me drag her in. I've been stalking her for weeks—she lives just across the street."

"Deal," hissed Seth, the gold rim of his eyes glittering in the dark. "Do we grab her now?"

"No, I want to—" But Kal suddenly stopped himself and grabbed Seth, shoving him back into a canopied alcove.

"Whoa, I didn't think you were into dudes."

"I'm not. Shut up. Look!" Kal pointed.

Walking casually down the street was Duncan, seemingly not paying attention to where he was going. He browsed a few shop windows, walked past Justa Cuppa, and then stopped. The angel looked around and then slipped into Mara's building. Mara appeared at the living room window and drew the shades closed, and a minute later the lights went out.

"I was right!" Kal's voice was gleeful. "She's hooking up with the angel. This just gets better and better."

"So, what do we do now?"

His mouth nearly watering with anticipation, Kal said, "Meet me here tomorrow night. We'll take her then. I know exactly where we can stash her."

"Stash her?" Seth asked.

"Just until the Annual Employee Conference. It's only a few days away. No way she can weasel out of anything if she gets outed for destroying another devil and fucking an angel in front of the entire company," said Kal. "I'll get to see her ruined, humiliated, and quite possibly vaporized."

They shook hands and went their separate ways.

The following day was a long one for Duncan. He started in Los Angeles, then bounced to Chicago, and then got diverted back to Vancouver, but it had been worth it. He'd saved a couple of souls and brought comfort to several who had lost those dear to them. But he was longing for a cheeseburger at Bruisers and to feel Mara's warm body next to his. Satisfied his manager would be at least marginally pleased with his report, and hoping that the good results would mean a pass on his most recent cursing infractions, Duncan hit save, and said a silent prayer that the network wouldn't crash. He sighed gratefully when it didn't, and shut down his tablet. Vancouver was nice, but he was ready to go home.

He took a risk and materialized right behind Justa Cuppa. Hurrying to the front, he let himself into the building, his steps light with anticipation. He'd been looking forward to coming home all day, and as his key clicked in the lock, he wondered when he'd started thinking of Mara's apartment as home.

"Mara, are you home?" he asked, his key skipping on the island.

Then Duncan's entire world unraveled. In the living room, books and magazines were scattered, one chair was completely overturned, and Mara was prone and unconscious on the floor, a devil with gold-rimmed eyes leaning over her.

"*Mara!*" Fear filled his voice and all of Duncan's angelic power surged, but he felt one moment of searing pain in his head and then nothing.

CHAPTER 32

WITH A GROAN, Duncan came to on the cold, hard tile floor. He curled up in a ball, his head screaming, and gritted his teeth while he tried to remember what had happened. He dragged himself up using the kitchen chair and pressed his hand to the back of his head. It was a little sticky. He stared at the semidry blood on his hand. Then it all came back to him.

Mara! In a flash he remembered seeing her—unconscious— with another devil standing over her. Then—nothing. He touched the tacky blood on the back of his head again. Someone must have hit him with something; that much was obvious. He eyed the cast-iron frying pan on the floor. Despite his fear, he looked over to the living room, and a wave of relief crashed over him when he didn't see her body—or worse, some awful pile of ash and bones. That meant they'd taken her somewhere. For the moment he could believe she was still alive.

Righteous anger coursed through him. *When I find that son of a bitch, he's going to figure out what a real smiting feels like.*

He racked his brain trying to figure out where they might have taken her. It was doubtful they'd taken her back down to Hell. If whoever it was had just wanted to expose their affair, they would have simply ratted Duncan and Mara out to HR and been done with it. But they'd taken her, and that meant it was personal. He tried to stem the rising tide of panic that he felt, but he knew he couldn't figure this out alone. He grabbed his phone and tapped his way to Heaven's intranet. The magic circle of doom appeared on the screen.

"Do not crash on me!" he shouted at the phone. *"Not today!"* The wheel spun for a few more seconds and then opened the division schedule for him. He flicked through the screens until he found what he wanted. Basil and Raymond were working on the Null Plane today.

The Null Plane was the part of the Universe where the Immortal Planes and the Mortal Plane all intersected. Mostly, the angels and devils managed to keep living humans out of it, although there had been some rare exceptions over the years. Uncommitted souls—like those of atheists or ones with a nearly perfect balance of sin and grace—wound up in the Null Plane when they died, and were later sorted out, going either to Heaven, Hell, or in rare cases, Oblivion. From time to time, most angels and devils got stuck on a rotation in the Null sorting out these sometimes thorny situations. But there was one other purpose of the Null Plane: immortals who broke the rules beyond what HR was willing to handle were often brought there to be processed, judged, and punished. And that was what Duncan was most afraid of.

"Basil!" Duncan tried to keep his voice down, but several angels glanced at him, and he knew by their expressions that he looked terrible.

"Holy crap, Duncan. What happened to you?"

"Long story. We need to talk. Privately." Duncan's eyes scanned the area.

"Yeah, we were just going on break."

"What's going on?" Raymond asked, ambling up to them with two large coffees. "I'd have gotten you some if I knew you were stopping by, Duncan. Shoot, you're bleeding, you know."

"I know. I'll heal that up later. Come on."

Duncan found an out-of-the way area, partially concealed by several tall file cabinets. His friends watched while he paced, his mouth set in a hard, grim line, and they both flinched when Duncan slammed his open palm against one of the file cabinets.

"Dude, what's wrong?" Raymond asked.

Duncan stopped. If he was going to ask for their help, he would have to tell them everything. His sigh was deep, nearly defeated. "I know I've been ditching you guys lately, and I'm sorry for that. I am," he said sincerely.

There was a long, yawning moment of silence before Basil finally said, "Come on, out with it, brother. What's going on?"

"I've been seeing someone."

"A girlfriend? Dude, that's great!" Raymond replied.

Basil narrowed his eyes shrewdly, and said, "No, not just a girlfriend." He paused, his expression morphing to incredulousness. "No way, man! Not her? I wondered, but I didn't think . . ."

"Not who?" said Raymond. "I'm missing something, aren't I?"

"It's that pretty devil from Bruisers, isn't it?" Basil asked.

"Yes. And her name's Mara."

Raymond's eyes nearly popped out of their sockets. "You've got a devil for a girlfriend? For real? Whoa . . ."

"Keep your voice down!" Duncan snapped.

"Sorry, dude, got carried away," said Raymond.

"Hang on." Basil gasped. "Did you say Mara? I only know of one devil by the name of Mara."

Raymond nodded, brightening. "Oh, you're right. I heard she's, like, some kick-butt acquisitions ninja. Going to break some big record this quarter, I think."

"That would be her," Duncan confessed.

Fear tinged Basil's voice. "Are you insane? Do you have any idea what Michael will do if he finds out? 'Go berserk' doesn't even begin to cover it. Talk about sleeping with the enemy—"

"No, I'm not insane, and yeah, I have a pretty good idea of what will happen. And if you're going to judge me, then I'm outta here," Duncan snapped.

"Okay, okay!" Basil raised his hands as a peace offering. "But just tell me this: Has she asked you for anything?"

Duncan struggled not to lose his temper. He knew the questions were out of concern and friendship, but they irritated him anyway. "No, and I appreciate the concern, but she hasn't asked for promises, favors, or proposed any deals, and she hasn't tried to make me shirk any of my angelic requirements. She is not trying to make me fall. I promise you that."

"Okay, so you've got yourself a bad girl. What's this got to do with why you're all knotted up—and bleeding like you got mugged?" asked Basil.

"Because she's missing. A couple of other devils took her."

"Oh man. That's not good," Raymond said.

"This has got to be personal," Duncan continued. "If whoever took her just wanted to screw with us, we both would have gotten reported to HR. But instead he kidnapped her, and whoever was working with him gave me this."

Duncan touched the back of his head, and this time he used an iota of his angelic power to heal the cut and remove the blood from his hair.

"I haven't seen or heard anything," said Basil. "But I've gotten to know a couple of the devils we're stuck with down here. I'll see if I can find anything out."

"Great. Try to keep Mara's name out of it if you can, at least for now."

"Sure thing."

Raymond rubbed his chin. "I haven't heard anything either. Most everyone is trying to get all their stuff done down here. With the Annual Employee Conference happening in a couple of days, everyone's focused on that. But I'll keep an ear out too."

"Thanks, guys. I need to go. I have a few other places to search."

"Hey, Duncan," Raymond said as his friend turned to leave. "Be careful, will you? This could get ugly for you, too."

Duncan nodded in acknowledgment, but he really didn't care what happened to him. He only cared that Mara was safe.

Mara's head felt like someone had hit it with a sledgehammer, and the excruciating pounding didn't fade when she finally opened her eyes. She groaned and pushed herself to her knees before she realized there were chains around her wrists, etched with runes and symbols that would bind a devil's powers.

Mara's eyes turned crimson for a moment as she directed her attention to the manacles, ignoring the chafe, and sent a miniscule bit of power down her arm as she physically pulled at the chain. The restraints rebuffed the effort and her second effort made the magical symbols tremble. That was all Mara really needed to know: the spell wasn't particularly powerful—it was only meant to restrain a demon with average power, at best. When the time was right, it would be easy to break them.

The snigger behind her went right up Mara's spine.

"Welcome back, Mara. I wasn't sure you'd be awake." Kal laughed, a mocking smile dancing across his face. Next to him was Seth, his gold-ringed eyes gleaming, staring like she was the star attraction in a carnival freak show.

"Your brass ones aren't big enough to take me on yourself, Kal? Had to team up with this imbecile?" She jerked her chin toward Seth, careful not to let her surprise at his presence show.

"I am so looking forward to your ass-kicking," said Seth.

"The only kicked ass will be yours, you little . . ." Mara stood up straight and let her eyes shine crimson.

"Behave yourself," Kal admonished. "You somehow managed to destroy my brother, although I don't see how."

"Kemm? Even if I had the juice, why would I waste my efforts on him?" snorted Mara. "Second-rate shyster."

"Don't you talk about him like that!" roared Kal.

"What? You mean tell the truth about him?" Mara continued to bait Kal. *Come on, be stupid enough to open the cage. I took care of Kemm—I have no problem getting rid of the two of you if I have to.*

Kal's hands balled into fists, and he spit at her. "Freak. I don't know how you did it, but you did. His ash reeks of you—I wasn't certain at first, but now I know for sure—and that's all I'll need to show Lucifer and the Grand Dukes. You didn't just bend a couple of HR rules, Mara; you *broke* one of the big ones, and you're going to get what's coming to you."

"Oh, we'll see who gets what," she said, throwing up a wall of bravado.

"You're right, we will. And if you don't play nice, maybe we let the cat out of the bag about your angel," sneered Seth.

"What are you blithering about?" Mara wasn't going to admit to anything that might jeopardize Duncan.

"Your little slice of angel food cake came home before we got you out of the apartment," Kal told her.

Mara grew very still, her heart smashing against her ribs. If Kal had hurt Duncan, there wasn't anywhere in the universe that he'd be able to hide from her.

"Suddenly so quiet. Cat got your tongue? You know I'm telling the truth. I thought about shredding him once I knocked him out, but I figured it was so much better to leave him alive. Hold his future over your head."

Mara hid behind a wall of indifference. "Whatever. Wreck his career if you want. I was just in it for the sex." It was probably the most profound lie she'd ever told, but she wasn't going to give Kal an inch.

"We'll see how much you're willing to spill when Lucifer questions you." Kal leveled one more hateful stare at her and sauntered away, Seth trailing in his wake. The door's boom had an ominous echo. Mara slowly sank to her knees. Everything was falling apart, and the abject fear of what Kal and Seth might try to do to Duncan swamped her. Mara's stomach roiled and she heaved, yet nothing but bile burned up her throat. She spit as she tried to rid her mouth of the vile taste, and sank back against her heels.

She closed her eyes and focused her thoughts. *God? I know you probably don't get too many prayers from devils, but Duncan's special. Don't let them hurt him because of me. Please. They can do anything they want to me, I don't care, but leave him out of this. Keep him safe.*

"You look constipated," Melchom told Astaroth.

Nothing on Astaroth's face moved, save for his eyes sliding to the side as his fellow treasurer waited for a response. "A bit crass, don't you think?" he finally said, annoyed.

"Woman trouble?" Melchom raised his eyebrows expectantly.

"Not the kind you're implying, but yes, you could say that. Have you seen Miss Dullahan lately?"

Now Melchom frowned. "No. Why?"

"She has two souls now overdue to be collected, and that is very unlike her. She's always punctual, sometimes even early, but she is never, ever late."

Astaroth's phone buzzed, making the whole desktop vibrate. He looked down sourly. He hated that wretched phone, always buzzing and never giving him a moment to himself. It was his own little hell within Hell.

"What?" he barked.

A whispered voice slithered out of the speaker: "I heard a rumor. You said to call if I heard a rumor. Some questions are being asked on the Null Plane about your girl."

"What kind of questions?" Astaroth's voice was humorless and impatient. He had spies everywhere, devils and even a few angels. Every single one of them owed him a favor, including the demon on the other end of the phone.

There was silence for a moment. "Questions that spell a lot of trouble."

"Be more specific, you little worm. What about her?"

There was a banging noise in the background. "I have to go. I've answered enough questions. This makes us even. It makes us even, Astaroth." The phone line went dead.

The Grand Duke's eyebrows knit together as he hung up the phone and slipped it into his jacket pocket. He hated to admit it, but things were going to go to hell in a handbasket and he wasn't sure he could do anything about it—not before the Annual Employee Conference started.

"Trouble?" asked Melchom.

"Perhaps. I'm not certain yet. I'll be back soon."

"Trouble for Mara?" the burly demon asked.

"Possibly. I need to go ask a few questions."

Melchom sat up straighter, his face morphing into a savage display of anger. His chair skittered back and tipped with a crash, and he lumbered across the room to follow Astaroth out the door.

"I will come too. If they will not talk to you, I promise— they *will* talk to me."

CHAPTER 33

EVERY YEAR, IMMORTAL Planes Inc. held an enormous all-employee conference. Three days of meetings, strategic planning, networking, and a healthy dose of partying in the evenings. Every angel and every devil—from the very top of the organization to the bottom—was expected to attend. The amphitheater in the Null Plane was the only venue big enough to host both divisions at the same time. In the greenroom behind the amphitheater's main stage, waiting to be called for his opening remarks, Lucifer paced, rehearsing his speech in his head. Astaroth, after a quick knock on the door, slipped inside.

"Is it time?" Lucifer asked, adjusting his tie.

"Just about. I'm sure Jophiel will be here in a moment to send you out."

"Then why are you here?" Lucifer asked, making a note of Astaroth's minute hesitation.

"I'm not sure where Mara is."

Lucifer's voice simmered: "Not sure where she is? What—exactly—does that mean?"

"She's overdue."

"You're starting to piss me off, Astaroth. Explain. Quickly."

Astaroth huffed out a sigh. "Mara is always very prompt with her collections. Of all the staff, I've never had to chase her for a soul who's come due. As of today, she's late turning in two of her contracts."

Lucifer leaned his hands on the back of the sofa, making every effort to not shred the material with his nails.

"And she is never—ever—late. Nor have I seen her in the audience. She's officially beating Baliel today. You know she wouldn't miss that."

"No, no, she wouldn't," Lucifer said, a deep frown creasing his face.

I know this isn't the best timing," added Astaroth. "I just wanted you to be aware in case there were any . . . surprises . . . today."

"Well, it wouldn't be the Annual Employee Conference if someone didn't run naked across the stage, right?" The smile on Lucifer's face didn't reach his eyes.

"Michael wouldn't be delaying her just to try embarrassing you, would he?" asked Astaroth. "He still hasn't forgiven you for the incident."

"The incident . . . ? Oh. Is he still upset over that? It was four hundred years ago." The Devil sniffed.

"'Still upset'? Sir, you . . . pantsed him during his keynote address."

"He has no sense of humor."

Jophiel hurried in. Heaven was on the hook for this year's conference, and no one was a better event organizer than Jophiel. Wearing a headset and flying through screens on her tablet, the angel sighed sourly at something she read and then snapped her attention to Lucifer.

"Good afternoon, sir. We're nearly ready for the opening remarks, so if you'd like to make your way to the stage? Baliel will bring the meeting to order, cover the agenda, and then introduce you. We've got you set for a twenty-minute session, and we have a full agenda."

"I'll do my best, but I have a few unscripted comments I'd like to add."

The color drained out of Jophiel's face, but she plastered on a forced smile. "Of course, sir. We'll adapt to whatever the day brings."

"Liar," Lucifer teased.

Jophiel looked horrified.

Out in the main meeting room, often called the gallery, Duncan—Raymond and Basil with him—pushed past several other angels to get seats in the front. The gallery was built like a huge amphitheater, with seats in a semicircle that rose in tiers around the stage. On one side, angels filed in to fill the seats, and on the other side, their devilish comrades piled into their own spaces. Duncan leaned forward and strained to look, searching vainly for any glimpse of Mara or the devil he'd seen standing over her in the moments before he'd been knocked unconscious. He slapped his palms on the railing.

"Damn it," he cursed. "Where is she? She can't simply have vanished."

"Have you considered that someone might have . . . ?"

"Don't you even think it!" Duncan jammed his finger into a startled Basil's chest.

"Hey!" Basil knocked his hand away.

"Something wrong?" They turned to see Archangel Gabriel in the seat next to them, and both Duncan and Basil had the good sense to look embarrassed.

"A disagreement," Duncan said quickly.

"Are you sure?" Gabriel asked. "You look really upset about something. If I can help . . ."

"DeMarco!"

Duncan felt his spine stiffen when Michael shouted his last name, the Archangel's deep voice commanding attention. Everyone's attention.

"Michael," he said, doing his best to sound pleasant. "How can I help you?"

"'Help' me?" Michael asked with a roll of his eyes. "Sit down and stop making a spectacle of yourself."

Give me a fucking break, Duncan thought, resenting being scolded like a wayward child. He paused, considered ignoring his boss, but then sat down instead. Michael gave him one last dirty look before he walked away.

"He's such a . . ." Duncan's whispered voice trailed away, remembering who was on his other side, and he glanced at the Archangel.

"I think the phrase you're looking for is 'uptight ass,'" whispered Gabriel with a conspiratorial grin.

Duncan did his best not to laugh, but before he could say anything to Gabriel, the lights in the amphitheater dimmed, and a spotlight illuminated the stage—and Baliel's sleek presence. Everything about the Grand Duke was polished and precise, from his suit to his perfect hair to his abnormally white teeth. He was, as Basil might say, a real panty-dropper.

"Welcome to IPI's Annual Employee Conference." Baliel's voice was deep, smooth, and as polished as the rest of his image—unlike the foul-mouthed bully he could be in Hell. "You all received an agenda for the next three days in your welcome packet. Today we start with opening remarks from Lucifer, executive vice president and managing director of Hell. Lucifer's comments will be followed by a high-level overview of company results from Archangel Uriel, SVP, Heaven. Tomorrow, God will be joining us with an overview of the state of the Mortal Plane before we move to our breakout sessions.

Details for those are outlined in the agenda. Day three has additional workshops and team-building activities that I'm sure we're all looking forward to. We'll conclude that evening with closing remarks from Archangel Michael, executive vice president and managing director of Heaven, and then our usual bacchanal—ah, celebration."

Baliel paused and let his glittering dark eyes roam over the crowd. "Now, before we kick things off, does anyone have any issue that needs attention beyond our normal channels? This is your chance to speak up and be heard!"

In the thousands of years that these meetings had taken place, only twice had issues been brought forward. Once, it had been collusion between an angel and a devil to cook the books, and the other time had been about a human who'd found his way to the Null Plane and had the audacity to apply for a job. So, when Kal stepped forward and onto the main floor, Baliel's mouth opened in shock, and at the side of the stage Jophiel nearly hyperventilated as she watched her detailed timetable implode.

"Oh, I have some business!" Kal shouted, his voice carrying easily throughout the cavernous room. "I have proof that my brother, Kemm, was annihilated by another devil! I have the evidence of that right here." He patted his jacket pocket.

"You fool, that's a matter for Hell's HR team and for Lucifer, not for the entire company," Baliel said.

Kal walked over to a shadowed corner where another demon was holding a chained figure, the face concealed beneath a dark hood. He tore the cloth off. Duncan gasped when he realized who it was. Kal shoved her hard, sending Mara sprawling onto the floor.

"It matters to both when she's also having an affair with an angel!" he yelled.

"*Mara!*" Duncan's voice rang in the gaping silence.

Mara heard the fear in his voice and knew it wasn't because Kal had outed them, but for what might happen to her. Her head snapped up, her eyes filled with hope and that very same fear, and she locked eyes with Duncan. If the angel calling her name hadn't confirmed their affair, the expression on her face surely did.

"Look at them," Kal crowed. "Could it be any more obvious? There hasn't been a more egregious attempt to corrupt our system since Mammon and Edaiel were caught cooking the books and colluding. And honestly, I really don't care about this disgusting, sordid little affair. But what Mara did to my brother . . ."

"DeMarco! What is the meaning of all of this?" Furious, Archangel Michael strode onto the open floor in front of the stage, blazing with righteous wrath and pushing Kal out of the way without so much as a glance.

"Hey! I was talking!"

Michael looked back over his shoulder at Kal. "We'll get back to your issues in a minute. I have something to handle here," he said, arrogantly dismissing Kal. Without another look at the pissed-off devil, Michael made a sharp gesture with his hand, and Duncan shouted as Michael used his power to grab him, yank him from his seat in the front row, and toss him to the floor. He landed in a heap at the Archangel's feet. A collective gasp at Michael's audacity erupted from the angelic side of the gallery.

"What do you have to say for yourself?" the Archangel barked.

Duncan scrambled up, but rather than answer Michael, he looked to Mara. His boss inserted himself between them.

"Don't look at her! This kind of behavior is unacceptable, DeMarco. Totally outside the pale." Michael went on to lecture Duncan, using words like *disgusting, disappointing, perversion, disrespect, embarrassment,* and *fornication*.

Kal fumed as Michael commandeered the floor, for the moment focusing all the attention on Duncan. Seth nudged him from behind.

"He's going to ruin it," whispered Seth.

Kal assessed the room. A little drama might not be a bad thing. He had a sealed bag with Kemm's grainy gray ash tucked safely in his pocket. He had everything he needed—all he had to do was give the bag to Astaroth or one of the other Grand Dukes, and they'd smell Mara's scent in it as easily as he did.

"No," he said to Seth. "This is way better. Watching Michael beat the piss out of her little boy toy will hurt Mara in ways we never could. And then she'll still get what's coming to her." He patted his pocket. "Come on, we'll have a front-row seat to the show."

CHAPTER 34

"WHAT IS MICHAEL thinking?"

Lucifer, still hidden by the curtain at the side of the stage, was incredulous. He could see the looks of outrage and shock on all the other Archangels' faces, and the anger in the rank and file. Even if Mara and Duncan were having an affair, even if Mara had annihilated Kemm, as the other devil was accusing, publicly humiliating Duncan was not the way to handle it.

"Thinking? He's not. He's a terrible people person," huffed Astaroth. "He really shouldn't have anyone reporting to him. All he cares about is how the situation will reflect on him."

The Devil turned his eyes to Mara. Seemingly rooted to her spot on the floor, she was shaking, clearly growing angrier with every word that tumbled out of Michael's mouth. Her fists were clenched and Lucifer could see blood dripping from where her nails had cut into her palms.

"Mara's not going to put up with this foolishness much longer," Lucifer said, his eyes glittering with anticipation and delight. "We'd best be ready for the storm."

"Are you ready, sir? If she loses her temper, this will blow back on you. There will be . . . questions."

"I don't have much choice, and I've been waiting for this day for a long time." The Devil clapped a hand on Astaroth's shoulder. "I think it is safe to say that no one is *ever* going to forget this employee conference!"

Duncan, tired of the verbal abuse, squared himself up to face the Archangel. Michael looked like he was out for blood, and Duncan knew he was screwed six ways to Sunday, so it didn't really matter what he did or said. That realization was liberating. If Michael wanted a fight, Duncan would give him a fight.

With his salt-and-pepper hair and piercing blue eyes, Michael cut quite the striking figure in his tailored suit. He looked at his tablet and then looked back at Duncan, shaking his head in disappointment.

"Not the most stellar career, DeMarco. Mediocre, actually, and quite unsatisfactory."

"Calling people out in front of a group is poor management," Duncan replied, refusing to be bullied by his boss.

Michael's eyes flared. "Silence! You don't get to lecture me on management. I've had enough of your attitude and insubordination!" he shouted, and the gallery of angels stirred again, increasingly uncomfortable with the unfolding display.

"Then why have you put up with it?" asked Duncan. "I've wanted a transfer out of your division for ages. If I'm such a problem, I think you'd want me out of your hair."

"And pass my problems on to someone else? That's not how I work. If something's broken, I fix it."

"I'm not broken!" Duncan shouted.

Michael heaved a disgusted sigh. "You know I try my very best to hold all of our angels to the highest standards of integrity so that we can truly engage with and inspire the souls most in need of our help—"

Duncan interrupted before the Archangel could continue on to Heaven's visions-and-values statement. "I'm done with this, Michael. I'm done with you."

"You'll show me some respect!"

"Respect?" Duncan just shook his head. "You know what, Michael? Blow me."

There was a perfect moment of silence as every devil and angel present wondered if they'd heard Duncan correctly, if he had really just said that to an Archangel.

And then Michael erupted in fury. Golden wings exploded out of his back and an aura of white light surrounded him as his eyes took on a golden hue. In an instant he hurled a ball of shimmering energy—angel-fire—at Duncan, who cried out in agony as it enveloped him.

"Duncan!" Mara screamed.

"I'm going to love watching him burn, Mara!" Kal shouted from his seat. "He'll only be able to take so much of Michael's fury before he's incinerated for eternity. Just like my brother. Then it will be your turn to burn, you bitch!"

On the main floor, the angel-fire disappeared, leaving Duncan on his hands and knees, grimacing in pain. He dragged himself to one knee. With some effort, his breath raw and ragged, he managed to stand and open his own wings, a clear gesture of defiance. A gasp rippled through the angels, although it was hard for him to tell if they were shocked or thrilled by his resistance. The Archangel smothered Duncan in another ball of angel-fire.

The white-hot flames dug into every pore on Duncan's body, eating into him and leaving a trail of bright knife-sharp pain in its wake. Duncan screamed in agony. Through the haze, he managed to focus on Mara, and stretched out a hand before collapsing again, blinded by the mind-numbing pain.

"I'll not tolerate such insolence and insubordination," Michael thundered before his voice languished into a sneer. "You've debased yourself in sin."

Duncan tried to pull himself off the ground again, every fiber of his body in anguish. He knew there was no going back, but no matter what, he wasn't going to meet his fate on his knees.

"*I've* sinned? So has nearly everyone in this room," Duncan said, his chest heaving.

"You're sleeping with . . . that?" Michael offered Mara a snide, dismissive glance. "How is fornicating with a devil anything other than a blatant sin? Please, educate me."

Duncan looked over at the devil who had so completely enamored him, hating the terrified expression on her face, hating the chains he saw at her wrists. He smiled at her, every moment of their time together warming him, strengthening him. He never took his eyes off Mara as he answered:

"Because I love her, and I'm sorry I didn't tell her sooner," Duncan said as loudly as he could so everyone could hear. He knew the answer would be unacceptable to Michael, but it was the truth.

Michael trembled with wrath. "You have one chance to recant, Duncan DeMarco. Take it."

"No. I won't recant something that's true. I love Mara."

"*Recant!* Condemn this devil for trying to corrupt you, and you—*even you*—will find forgiveness. Repent now!" Michael commanded.

"Forgiveness? Who's telling lies now, Michael? I can see it in your eyes—there's no forgiveness there. I love Mara, and if you don't like it, you can go to hell."

Time stood still for Mara when Duncan said he loved her, but the joy that flooded through her body was followed by pure, unadulterated horror when she saw the murderous look in Michael's eyes.

"No!" The scream tore out of her, lacerating the air and nearly shattering her voice, and Mara felt a deep tremor inside her, a power aching—demanding—to be unleashed. The fetters and chains around her wrists exploded, turning into nothing more than shards, dust, and debris that clustered at her feet. Free from them, Mara shredded her own self-imposed bonds, letting every true fiber of her being loose for the first time. Ever.

And she roared.

Go to hell! The words echoed in Duncan's head. Calmness settled over him after he flung the defiant words in Michael's face. This would be the last straw for the Archangel, and he knew it. He took some small comfort in the fact that if he was going to be extinguished from existence, at least everyone would talk about him for a long, long time. He looked over at Mara, wanting to see her once more Michael's fire consumed him. Her eyes were blazing, and she was screaming something, but all the noise seemed very far away.

"I love you, Mara. I truly do. Forgive me," he whispered, unsure if she could hear him.

Livid, Michael raised his arms, gathering the angel-fire he'd need to obliterate Duncan from all existence. Above the din of the audience, a roar—not unlike the roar of a lion but far more terrifying—filled the gallery as a ball of black devil-fire slammed into Michael's chest. The Archangel flew backward and skidded along the polished floor for at least fifty feet, stunning everyone in the room.

Michael leaped up, furious—his hair disheveled and his suit torn. The edges of his wings were singed and black. Mara had put herself between him and Duncan, her true demonic nature on full display before the assembled crowd. Free of her shackles, her glossy black-feathered wings fanned out on either side of her body. And instead of scarlet irises, Mara's had turned blue. Flames danced around her eyes, painting her face, fanning out to cloak her in an aura of flaming-blue power. She pointed at Michael.

"You will not touch him again!" she thundered.

CHAPTER 35

CHAOS RULED IN the Null Plane. Every eye was riveted on Mara . . . and her wings. Her gorgeous, black, glossy, *feathered* wings.

Like death and taxes, the fact that only angels had feathered wings—and white ones at that—had held true for all the eons since God had created the universe and incorporated the Immortal Planes shortly thereafter. Angels had white feathered wings; devils had black leathery ones. And the fact that Mara not only was the exception to that rule, but also had the juice to challenge an Archangel, sent a massive shock wave through the entire gallery.

Behind Mara, Duncan moved slowly, getting to his feet as he tried to recover from Michael's attack. Hearing him, and the muffled curse he muttered as he stood, gave Mara some reassurance that while he might be battered, Michael had not broken him. The Archangel was staring at her, slack-jawed, and she returned the look with blatant hostility. Realizing there was no imminent attack from Michael, Mara turned to the gallery and, amid the demonic throng, saw Kal sitting in his front-row seat.

The sight of him focused her whirling, angry thoughts: *If you'd just gone to Lucifer with your evidence, I would have taken whatever punishment he doled out. If you'd just annihilated me when you had the chance . . . But no, you had to turn this into a complete circus. Put a spotlight on my affair with Duncan as your little cherry on top. We could have done this quietly, but you put Duncan in Michael's crosshairs.* The sound of Duncan screaming in agony rang in her head. Mara's blue flames intensified as she took a few steps toward him and pointed.

"You."

The blood drained from Kal's face.

"My affairs are my business, Kal. You shouldn't poke your nose where it doesn't belong." Her voice was flat, calm, but soaked with the promise of revenge, and those seated around Kal leaped away to avoid being in the path of Mara's wrath. But instead of the black demon-fire everyone expected, Mara's blue eyes flamed and she reached out a hand toward Kal, closing her fist on empty air.

Her smile turned cold as Kal whimpered. He twisted and moaned, his agony increasing. Thrashing, Kal tried to grab onto Seth, but his partner in crime backed away a few steps before he fled from the room. Mara tightened her fist and narrowed her eyes, and Kal's agonized squeals reached a new octave as his skin began to bubble. Pustules erupted on his face as the skin blistered and cracked, and blood leaked out of his ears. Finally, with a sickening, audible snap, Kal's body exploded into a charnel-house shower of ash, bone bits, gore, and entrails. Grand Duke Paimon, the only devil near Kal to have remained seated, laughed approvingly and picked up one of Kal's rib bones. She sucked out the marrow and then used the jagged end to pick her teeth.

Behind her, Mara felt Michael draw his power in and she spun to face him, ready to counter whatever strike he was planning. Both fanned their wings, ready to close for another round, but before they could, Lucifer stepped between them.

"I think we all need to just calm down for a moment." The Devil smiled charmingly at Michael, but the Archangel returned the gesture with an icy look of contempt.

"Lucifer."

"Michael," Lucifer responded, grinning even harder at the aggravation in Michael's voice before he turned to Mara. He gave her an affectionate look.

"Mara," he said.

"Daddy," she responded.

"Wait . . . ? *Daddy?*" said Duncan, who'd finally regained his feet.

"I told you. My family's a little complicated," Mara said, still looking at her father.

"Well, there's a fucking understatement," Duncan muttered under his breath.

CHAPTER 36

DADDY.

As if her feathered wings hadn't been shocking enough, with one single word, Mara had dropped a megaton bomb on Heaven and Hell. Utterly flabbergasted, Michael stared at Lucifer. He opened his mouth once and closed it, and then he opened it again.

Finally Michael managed to sputter, "Your *daughter?*"

"Yes, my daughter. Isn't she lovely?" Lucifer grinned, still relishing Michael's discomfort.

"Her wings!" the Archangel shouted. "They have feathers! How?"

"Ah, her exquisite wings. Fortunately, she takes after her mother in that regard."

"She has feathered wings," Michael repeated, but this time the disbelief in his voice was replaced with anger.

"Master of the obvious," snorted Mara, but her snigger subsided when Lucifer raised a warning finger in her direction.

"As my daughter so eloquently noted, you've said that already. You're repeating yourself, brother. And all this is hardly appropriate subject matter for a corporate meeting."

From high up in the gallery on the demonic side of the room, a raucous voice shouted out, "This is the best fucking mandatory meeting *ever!*"

Lucifer didn't look over but he pointed, snapped his fingers, and a demon in the top row exploded, showering his companions with gore. While it was not a complete annihilation, it would still take centuries for the fool to piece himself back together.

Completely ignoring what Lucifer had said, and what he'd just done to the impertinent demon, Michael said, "You just said . . . she takes after her mother?"

"That I did, but we can get to that in a moment. Before we resolve this delightfully delicious affair, I have to deal with something first," Lucifer said.

"Yes! Mara must be punished! She's annihilated *two* devils from my team without your permission!" Valafar roared from his seat. He banged on the arm of his chair for emphasis, and a chorus of cheers and catcalls erupted from the demon horde. Lucifer narrowed his eyes, displeased by the Grand Duke's boisterous call for swift judgment and slightly disturbed by the bloodlust in the crowd. As devils, it was part of their nature, but knowing their hunger was directed at his daughter made Lucifer bristle.

"Enough!" Lucifer raised his voice and all the others subsided, even the rampant whispering in the audience. "The Grand Duke raises a valid point. Mara, you clearly broke the rules just now when you obliterated Kal."

"He started it," Mara said.

"'He started it'? You're going to lead with that?" Lucifer gave her a look, and Mara shrugged.

"What about Kal's accusation? What about what she did to Kemm? She has two heads to answer for." Valafar's voice rolled through the room again.

"I heard you the first time, Valafar." Lucifer glared at the Grand Duke before he turned to his daughter and asked, "What do you have to say about all of this, Mara?"

"I had my differences with Kemm, everyone knows that, but it would be against the rules to snuff him out."

Lucifer studied her for a moment as he thought, *You're probably lying about Kemm. In your shoes, I certainly would.* He was pleased, however, that she didn't flinch or look away.

"What happened to Kemm will remain a mystery," Lucifer proclaimed. "Kal stated he had evidence with him, but now it is mixed in with whatever scraps are left of him. If it was physical evidence, it will have Mara's mark on it no matter what. And if it was knowledge Kal held, it has been obliterated with him—"

"—I demand—"

"SILENCE!" Lucifer roared. "You will not interrupt me again, Valafar."

The entire gallery hushed.

"Now, as I was saying, this squabble cannot go without some sort of censure. Unlike my angelic counterpart, I would normally handle this privately." Lucifer leveled a disapproving stare at Michael.

"But Daddy's little girl gets away with murder." Baliel's whispered comment was loud enough to hear, and Lucifer's eyes flared. He didn't want to, but Mara had to be punished. If he didn't, a dangerous precedent would be set.

Lucifer looked at his daughter and he silently mouthed the words, *I'm sorry.* Mara almost breathed a sigh of relief, thinking that Lucifer might not lose his cool over what she'd done to Kal. But when she heard Baliel's snide taunt, her heart sank. Then suddenly, with a flick of Lucifer's wrist, Lucifer sent

Mara flying. She flew up into the air and rocketed across the room—pulled by an invisible force—until she slammed into the stone wall so hard, the granite cracked. The impact made every bone scream and she only had a moment before she was yanked back down and slammed into the floor just as hard.

Shaken, Mara pushed herself up to her hands and knees, managing one ragged, labored breath before she hurtled straight up and into the ceiling. Granite chips and shards rained down and Lucifer let her stay in the divot she'd created in the stone for a few seconds before smashing her back into the floor. Spiderweb cracks radiated out from beneath her prone form. It felt like every bone in her body was pulverized, and she gasped for air.

A cloak of white feathers enveloped her as Duncan knelt and grabbed her shoulders, his white wings mantling over her protectively. Mara was covered with dust, and the feathers of her wings were ruffled and askew. She leaned against him, trying to orient herself, while Duncan glared up at Lucifer. Golden-white light intensified as he gathered whatever angelic power he had to stop the Devil from touching Mara again.

Lucifer smiled at Duncan, secretly pleased that the angel had leaped to Mara's defense. "Settle down, son. Settle down. I admire that you're even thinking about going up against me, but you don't have the juice to do it. I can guarantee you that."

After staring at Duncan for a long heartbeat or two, Lucifer looked over and let his angry gaze rake the assembled demons and devils, the red flames writhing around his eyes, the smallest flicker of blue appearing here and there. "Let that be a reminder. No one is annihilated like Kal was without my approval. That had best be clear to everyone." He looked back at Mara, who had just gotten shakily to her feet with Duncan's help. "While

I appreciate your decisive approach to being challenged, Mara, you overstepped. Don't let it happen again."

Mara was shaking so badly from her battering that she could barely stand. In fact, Lucifer guessed that if Duncan weren't holding her, she probably would have fallen back down. He ground his teeth, conflicted, knowing he had to dole out discipline but hating that he'd just roughed up his only child. He could feel the eyes of the Grand Dukes resting on him, waiting, judging, looking for any weakness they could exploit. Some of them wanted blood and he knew they wouldn't be satisfied with such a lenient punishment.

As much as it upset him, Lucifer had to do more. He couldn't treat his daughter differently—a double standard would bring chaos to Hell. He also knew that, short of demon-fire, Mara would be able to withstand any physical punishment he could dole out. So, he was going to have to hit her where it really hurt.

"Additionally, you will forfeit credit for any contracts that you closed after you met your basic quota for the quarter."

The pack of devils murmured and gasped as Mara's head snapped up. "What?"

"You forfeit your number one position—no one-thousand-soul coin, and no extra bonus for beating Grand Duke Baliel's record. As of today, you start over if you want that record. Plus, you'll do weekly status meetings with Astaroth for the next two quarters—which will be reported to me—so we can be sure you're back on track."

"Hey! But I—" Even as battered as she was, Mara was indignant, but she stepped back when Lucifer let the anger show on his face and intensified his flames.

"Don't push me, Mara, or would you like me to add more to your punishment?" he growled, deliberately glancing at Duncan and then back at Mara.

"No. No, I don't," she said, subdued. Her flames faded a little, but Mara left her wings out and on display.

"I thought not," Lucifer said quietly before he turned to the gallery and projected his voice. "The coin and the win for the year will go to Unkurra."

Lucifer nodded to a she-devil from Baliel's team who had been a distant third in the year-end competition, and she squealed in disbelief. Valafar opened his mouth, but Lucifer cut him off. "And because you've lost two very capable earners from your organization, Valafar, I will have Astaroth and Melchom withdraw three five-hundred-soul coins that you can award to anyone in your organization—other than yourself—as you see fit. I trust that will be satisfactory compensation for your inconvenience."

Valafar made a show of considering the offer, but was smart enough to agree before Lucifer's patience ran out. "That's acceptable," grunted the Grand Duke.

"Enough!" roared Michael. "You need to answer for . . . this." Michael made a dismissive gesture at Mara that angered both Lucifer and Mara, but it was Duncan who spoke.

"Her name's Mara, and you'll treat her with some respect," he ordered the Archangel.

"Stay out of this, DeMarco. Lucifer, who is her mother?" Michael demanded.

Lucifer folded his arms across his chest. "Nuriel."

"You're *lying*!" The accusation in Michael's voice was nearly overwhelmed by the pain that clawed through his words.

In the gallery, there was a murmur and a rustle of feathers as Lucifer's words sank in. Nuriel hadn't just been an angel. She'd been an Archangel, and had disappeared eons ago.

Lucifer smiled as Mara fanned her wings, and he glanced at the demonic side of the audience. Now they all knew: not only was Mara his daughter, but she was the daughter of an

Archangel. And he knew that every devil who had ever called her "freak" or any other derisive name was suddenly realizing just how screwed they might be.

CHAPTER 37

"SO, NOW YOU know all the family secrets," Mara whispered to Duncan as she did her best to ignore the gawking looks and shocked stares. "Well, at least the really juicy ones."

"I guessed your mother was an angel when I first saw your wings," Duncan whispered back. "I don't care about that, you know."

"I didn't think you'd care about my wings. I thought you'd care more when you saw my eyes like this." She gestured at the blue flames dancing around her eyes, identical to Lucifer's red ones. "Because I do have my father's eyes. And who wants to be with the Devil's daughter?"

"I do. I love you," Duncan told her, and he locked his fingers with hers.

Mara leaned in against him, her head on his shoulder. "I love you too."

"Ah, blossoming romance," said Lucifer with a satisfied smile. He ignored the swirling whispers that churned through the room. He even tore himself away from his daughter and her angel to focus his attention on Michael. Lucifer knew this whole affair was far from over.

"I want to hear this from your lips," snapped Michael tersely.

"If you must, although you'll just accuse me of lying too."

"Tell. Me. Everything." Michael bit each word out, nearly choking on the acrimony. This was too personal, too bitter, to be aired in public, but he'd started the avalanche that he was now being swept up in.

"Nuriel was the most fascinating, beautiful, alluring angel I'd ever met," Lucifer said. He paused for a second, debating whether to be the bigger man, but elected to throw a little salt on Michael's wounds. After all, he was the Devil. "But you already know that, don't you, Michael? It must be hard for you, brother, to have loved her the way you did for all those eons, knowing she didn't feel the same. Knowing now that Nuriel chose me, and not you."

Michael's face twisted in pain. "You made her fall," the Archangel accused.

"I did nothing of the sort. I fell in love with her, and for some reason—which I've never been able to fathom—Nuriel loved me, too. Loved me enough that she chose to leave Heaven of her own accord to be with me," said Lucifer. There was a touch of amazement and wonder in his voice, as if he still, after all these years, couldn't believe she'd chosen him.

"I don't believe your lies."

Sanctimonious prick, thought Lucifer just before he challenged Michael: "If you're so bloody smart, tell me this—if Nuriel had truly fallen, she would have left a blazing trail of angel-fire across the heavens when she fell, correct?"

"I don't—"

"It is a yes-or-no question, Michael. Answer it," Lucifer demanded.

Michael fumed. "Yes, she would have."

"And the rest of you"—Lucifer looked at the gallery, to Raphael, Uriel, and the other Archangels—"did *any* of you see Nuriel fall?"

To a one, they shook their heads. A falling angel was a spectacular and terrifying sight, and not something that would be missed.

"Impossible! She would have never gone with you. You are the Prince of Lies, Lucifer. You must have forced her . . . forced yourself on her!" Michael thundered with self-righteous rage.

Lucifer laughed out loud. A big, rolling guffaw. "'Forced'? Surely you're delusional, Michael. You knew Nuriel. You worked next to her for eons, loved her from afar for eons. Do you really think that anyone—even you or I—could have forced her to do anything she didn't want to do?"

Michael had no answer for that. He trembled with impotent rage.

Lucifer paused for a moment, his expression growing surprisingly wistful. "Nuriel dampened her angel energy so we could be together with no one being the wiser. And imagine our utter surprise when we realized we were having a baby." He looked over at Mara, his face a mixture of pride and sadness before he continued. "It was a hard pregnancy, and once Mara was born, Nuriel was somehow . . . less." He frowned.

"So, this creature, this abomination," said Michael, gesturing at Mara, "she weakened Nuriel? She diminished her? And you did nothing?"

Mara's head snapped up, her face such a mix of sorrow and guilt and pain that Lucifer nearly lost his mind. "If you ever call our daughter an abomination again, Michael, so help me God, I will end you."

The entire gallery caught its breath. Among the gasps, Lucifer heard one throat clear, and he glanced at Astaroth, who shook his head. His friend was right. If he and Michael fought, it would devastate the realms. Lucifer took a deep breath and continued, his voice as calm and moderate as ever.

"Nuriel suspected that a portion of her own grace was gifted to our daughter, and once we saw her wings, we were convinced of it."

"What happened to Nuriel? Where is she now?" demanded Michael. "You're right, I do know her, and if this *is* her daughter, then she'd be here to defend her. You must have her imprisoned. Where are you keeping her?"

Mara interrupted, the indignation and pain in her voice palpable to everyone. "My father doesn't have her imprisoned or enslaved, you ass. You want to know what happened to my mother? She died. Every year she faded a little more, no matter what my father tried to do for her—and he tried everything. By the time I was six, she was little more than a ghost, and she was so sad."

"Nuriel and I knew what was happening," added Lucifer, his voice also ripe with sadness. "The loss of her grace—whether it was given to Mara or was the price she paid for falling in love with the Devil, we never knew—but she refused to give up and let herself return to God. She refused to leave Mara."

"I hated seeing her like that," Mara said, her voice barely audible.

Again, Lucifer paused, the pain in Mara's voice stabbing at him. "I remember, at the end, Mara sat on the bed with her mother and told her she didn't want her to be in pain. That she would understand if her mother had to leave, that she would forgive her. And I remember how proud Nuriel was. Forgiveness was so important to her. I know. I needed her forgiveness more than once."

"And that was when I promised her I'd never try to make an angel fall," Mara added.

The Devil and his daughter shared a look, a common memory, and Lucifer waited for Mara's unspoken permission, continuing only when he saw her nod: "Three days later we watched Nuriel go to sleep and the energy that was left inside her drifted up, a thousand tiny beautiful pieces of glittering light. They swirled around our heads before they vanished up into the sky."

Every angel seemed touched by the story, and every devil utterly baffled. Lucifer used the moment of silence to glance at the devils in his division. The ones who weren't confused looked resentful. He wasn't worried, though. Those were personnel issues that he could work out later. In private, if necessary.

"Where is she?" demanded Michael, his tone nasty as he dragged Lucifer's attention away from the devilish rank and file.

"I entombed her remains. She is in a beautiful space, safe and honored. There may not be much I can honestly say I love in this universe, but I loved Nuriel—by God, she was the love of my life. And I love my daughter."

"Funny way of showing it," muttered Mara as she smoothed the feathers on one of her wings, still disheveled from being slammed around. Duncan tried not to smile. Lucifer gave her a look that was perfectly balanced between parental annoyance and pride.

"You might be my child, but you are also an employee of Hell and aren't going to get special privilege when you screw up," Lucifer said testily, knowing annoyance was the emotion he needed to show, and then he glanced at Michael. "After all, what would we be without rules and order?"

"I've had enough," snapped Michael. "I won't tolerate this unholy—"

A deep voice, soft but firm, interrupted him: "Yes, Michael, you will. You'll tolerate it and you'll be quiet."

Michael's eyes flared but he said nothing as an elderly angel slowly walked out onto the floor, a collective intake of breath following him.

Mara heard Duncan whisper in awe, "Metatron?"

"*That's* Metatron?" Mara's voice filled with astonishment, and a little fear. If Metatron's here, that means God had something to say about all of this. She and Duncan might be screwed after all.

Metatron was the most senior of all the Archangels. He had served God and IPI since the dawn of time, and was now God's chief of staff. As such, he often served as God's proxy, bringing business decisions and strategy changes directly to the leadership teams in both Heaven and Hell. He was a legend throughout the Immortal Planes.

"Metatron. It has been far too long. You look well," said the King of Hell, inclining his head in a rare show of deference.

"It has been a very long time, Lucifer. I see you've been busy."

Lucifer shrugged. "It is important to make the most of your time."

"Indeed." Metatron gave Lucifer an amused look before he turned to look at Michael. "Michael, allow your wrath to subside while I—"

"But they are fornicating! An angel and a devil . . . And what about Nuriel!"

"Michael." There was a warning in Metatron's voice.

The Archangel didn't heed it. "This is unacceptable. Anything less than a full reprimand with—"

Metatron waved his hand gently and there was a sudden silence as Michael's voice, and the revulsion in it, disappeared.

The Archangel reddened, looking utterly apoplectic when the words ceased to come out of his mouth.

"*There's* a divine miracle," Mara muttered under her breath. Duncan shushed her and she jostled him a little in response.

"Do not interrupt me again, Michael. It's unprofessional and rude. This entire situation has been handled poorly," Metatron said, his voice stern.

There was silence for a long, lingering moment. While the words "handled poorly" were relatively benign, coming from Metatron they were a stinging rebuke for everyone in management, especially Michael and Lucifer. The Devil managed to look sheepish, but the silence that followed only increased Mara's anxiety.

"What if God sides with Michael?" she asked Duncan, her voice little more than a whisper. He shook his head, not able to answer her.

"May I ask a question?" asked Archangel Gabriel from the gallery.

"You may," Metatron responded.

"I will, of course, bow to God's will, whatever that may be in this situation, but it seems to me we have a conundrum. By giving in to his baser nature with a devil, Duncan has—to an extent—set himself on the road to becoming a fallen angel. Yet, it seems that Mara feels genuine love. That's evident in what we've seen today. Perhaps that is thanks to her parentage, but perhaps it has to do with Duncan. So, has the devil started to corrupt the angel, or has the angel started to redeem the devil? And how does one pass judgment on such a complicated situation?"

Metatron smiled. "Excellent and perceptive questions, Gabriel. Allow me to elaborate on—" Before Metatron could say anything else, however, yet another voice chimed in.

"How you angels handle this is your business, but we have rules in Hell," said Baliel.

Mara ground her teeth, knowing in her gut that Baliel was going to bring up Lucifer's fraternization policy. She stiffened, ready to speak out against him, until Duncan leaned closer and said in a low, soft voice, "I know you want to, but don't. If Metatron's here, it's out of our control."

"I hate feeling this way," she whispered back. There was anger and resentment in her voice.

"I suppose suggesting that we just submit to God's will wouldn't go over so well?"

Mara gave Duncan a blistering stare but fell silent, understanding the point he was making.

Metatron raised his eyebrows at Baliel's implication that there were rules in Hell but not in Heaven.

"With all due respect," added the Grand Duke when he noticed the look—Metatron did, after all, outrank him. "But it must be addressed. Lucifer, you've made it clear how you've handled the situation regarding Kal. But what about your rule about no relationships between angels and devils, lest your wrath be invoked? We just covered this in a training recently, and this situation seems like a clear transgression to me."

Mara held her breath.

"There's no rule." Lucifer's answer was mild, as if as if he were making an observation about the weather.

Everyone on the Hell side of the amphitheater stirred, and Mara's mouth sagged open when she heard her father's statement.

"What do you mean, there's no rule? What about you stripping the skin from devils who broke it? Cutting their wings off? Those punishments are legend," pressed Baliel.

"'Cutting their wings off'? What's this about, Lucifer? God would never have condoned something so extreme," Metatron demanded.

"Before everyone's knickers get more twisted, let me explain," Lucifer said. "After Nuriel passed, I was bereft, inconsolable. And a few weeks later I was approached by a devil who discovered he had feelings for an angel. I did not, perhaps, handle it as well as I should have. I raged at him, telling him it was a foolish idea that would only lead to his turning soft. I told him that if I found out he was having a love affair with an angel, I would remove his skin with a carrot peeler and cut his wings from his back with my bare hands." Lucifer paused and shrugged. "If I remember correctly, I went on in quite graphic detail about what I'd do. Some of the staff overheard me. Stories spread, grew, transformed, and soon everyone thought this rule existed. I elected to not clarify the misunderstanding."

"Are you kidding me? Why would you do that?" Mara asked, her voice sharp. Myriad emotions flooded through her: anger, bewilderment, relief, and a few she couldn't even name.

"Why? I did it for you. Because I was afraid that someday this would happen. No devil and angel had been together before your mother and I. If you and Duncan stay together, perhaps have a child, one of you might diminish the way your mother did. I never wanted you to feel that kind of pain, that helplessness."

Mara bit her lip. Even though she'd seen the pain her parents had gone through, it had never occurred to her that there was a reason for Lucifer to oppose a devil-angel relationship other than his own sorrow and grief. Meanwhile, the gallery was blanketed in an uncomfortable silence, unsure how to respond to such raw honesty from Lucifer.

The Devil faced Metatron. "And that's why I hid the fact that Mara is my daughter. I know what Hell's like—I rose through the ranks until God split the immortal realm into Heaven and Hell and promoted me. Every single devil in here would have tried to use Mara as a pawn, either to cut me down or to cozy up to me. So, I made my own deal with Astaroth—that he would mentor her, look after her. Make sure she was safe—and tell me if she ever looked like she was having feelings for an angel."

Every Grand Duke turned to stare at Astaroth, who remained where he was, looking haughty and satisfied.

"So, there's no rule about angels and devils having . . . ?" said Baliel, his voice a mixture of anger and admiration.

"No," said Lucifer. "I'd hoped that anyone who felt strongly enough about an angel would have thought to dig into the bylaws and find out for themselves. I never cleared the air because no one ever asked me about it." He tossed his daughter a fleeting glance.

Mara dropped her head, completely disgusted with herself and her own lack of resourcefulness. *The answers were right in front of me. I'm an idiot.*

"Well," said Metatron, "now that we've cleared all that up, shall we get back to what I was going to say?"

No one was unwise enough to disagree.

"This entire debacle has been brought to God's attention," the senior Archangel said. "And after careful consideration, He has determined that no laws of Heaven or Hell have been broken, and therefore no punishment should be meted out to Mara Dullahan or Duncan DeMarco. The codes for both realms say that angels and devils cannot and will not have long-term romantic entanglements with *humans*, especially with the intent of procreation. It says nothing about romantic entanglements with each other."

Mara's shoulders dropped and her breath came out in a rush. She hadn't even realized she'd been holding it in. The instant Metatron said he'd brought word directly from God, she'd been terrified. The Archangels ran the daily business of Heaven, and—aside from Metatron—Michael was the senior Archangel. The Grand Dukes ran the daily business of Hell, with Lucifer presiding over all of them. But presiding over both Michael and Lucifer was God—chairman and CEO of Immortal Planes Inc. Whatever God decided, there would be no appeals.

Metatron continued, "And because our laws have not been broken, Duncan and Mara may continue their relationship as they so choose, so long as neither directly or overtly interferes with the work of the other. If either does, then I will be the only one to review the situation and, if warranted, judgment will not come from Michael or Lucifer, or even me. It will come directly from God."

After his pronouncement, Metatron snapped his fingers, removing the invisible gag from Michael's mouth before he walked over to Duncan and Mara, sizing them up. The white-gold glow of angel-fire in his wizened eyes made them shrink back a little, despite the fact that Metatron was several inches shorter than both of them.

"You have both caused quite a ruckus," he said in a gentle voice.

"That was never the intent. I'm sorry God had to be troubled by all of this," Duncan said respectfully.

Metatron nodded. "He figured something like this might eventually happen, especially after Nuriel resigned to be with Lucifer. Now, do you both—"

"God *knew* about that?" Michael sputtered. "He knew Nuriel left Heaven to be with Lucifer? And He said nothing to me about it? *Nothing?*"

A resonant, crystalline chime sounded in the room, echoing through the chamber as a diamond-shaped point of light appeared in the middle of the floor. The chime reached its crescendo as the light—silvery white and blindingly intense—winked out. Left in its wake was a very short older woman in a pinstripe pantsuit and her hair done up in a French twist.

"Michael, I most certainly do *not* answer to you," the Almighty said sternly as She pursed Her lips and looked over Her glasses.

The sudden appearance of God left Michael speechless, but not so much Lucifer, who grinned and said, "I like the pantsuit. It's a good look for you."

"Don't start with me, Lucifer. I was in the middle of something. Do you have any idea how long it will take to get my schedule sorted out now?"

Wisely, Lucifer declined to say anything else.

God looked up at Mara and Duncan—both of whom were afraid to meet the Almighty's eyes—and waited. When neither of them spoke, God finally said, "Would you both look at me, please?"

"My Lord . . . ah, Lady . . ." Duncan couldn't get the words out right.

"Either is fine, son. Remember, I can appear in any form needed for any situation. I can be man or woman, young or old, pristine or filthy, large or small, and any color of the rainbow. I once went with purple skin to Burning Man. Fit right in, no one even guessed it was me."

"Burning Man?" Metatron asked.

"Always wanted to go. Anyway, I can be whatever is required at any given time. Just now I was at a meeting of the Homeowners Association for Evergreen Acres, a Boca Raton retirement community. They put a lovely spread out for the luncheon."

"A Boca Raton luncheon?" Michael asked.

"I won't warn either of you again," God said, cutting off any commentary from Lucifer.

"Yes, Father," Michael said with respect.

"As you wish . . . Mother."

God rolled Her eyes at Lucifer and turned Her attention away. "Now, back to the two of you: Duncan, Mara, I believe Metatron has shared my perspective on your relationship?"

Both froze.

"Cat got your tongues? I *did* just ask a question," God said, but it wasn't unkind.

"Yes," blurted Mara. "Yes, he did."

"And do you both understand it?" asked the Almighty.

"We do," Duncan said, and Mara nodded.

"Very good." God nodded. "I think my business here is concluded. Metatron, a moment?"

While God and Metatron conferred, Michael strode toward Mara and Duncan, his eyes riveted on the impudent angel. Mara's wings spread, ready to meet whatever Michael was willing to throw at them. *You take a swing at him and it will take God to separate us*, she thought.

"DeMarco," Michael barked. "On Monday morning, you'll report to my office *promptly* at seven—"

God stepped in. "No, he won't, Michael. Duncan, as of right now, you report to Archangel Gabriel."

"I have to approve any transfers—" Michael started to say.

"Oh, really? Even the ones I directly authorize?" God peered over Her glasses at Her obstinate Archangel.

"I . . ." Michael's voice trailed away.

"You'll have the chance to discuss all of your concerns on Monday, Michael. Be in my office at eight a.m., and if you have other meetings already on the books, move them. Don't be late."

"Yes, ma'am." Michael nearly choked on his words.

Lucifer, who had been silently enjoying Michael's upbraiding and discomfort, asked, "Will we be continuing with the conference?"

"No, not today," said Metatron. "I'll have Jophiel reschedule it."

In the back of the room, a brief stressed-out whimper escaped Jophiel.

The words "transferred to Gabriel's division" were music to Duncan's ears, and he shut his eyes and folded his hands. *Dear God, thank you for that favor. Thank you, thank you, thank you.* Duncan's prayer was sincere and earnest. Suddenly, and shockingly, he heard God's voice inside his head: *You're very welcome.*

CHAPTER 38

AFTER GOD'S FINAL pronouncement, Michael gave Duncan one last icy stare and stalked out of the chamber. Jophiel hurried to dismiss the crowd, even though no one was really paying attention to her. There was shuffling and whispering as the angels began to disperse, and on the other side there was just as much whispering as the devils tried to figure how to process what had happened. Mara watched as Gabriel found his way down the stairs and onto the floor. Trailing behind him were Basil and Raymond. The archangel came over to them and held his hand out to the angel.

"Duncan. Welcome to the team."

"Thank you. Appreciate the opportunity to keep working."

"Well, I admire my brother for his results, but he does have a very rigid way of looking at the world. I think you'll find I'm more flexible."

Mara stuck her hand out to Gabriel. "Hi. I'm Mara."

Gabriel smiled and shook her hand. "And so you are. Pleasure to meet you."

"Thank you."

"Since the conference is postponed, when do I need to be in the office tomorrow?" Duncan asked.

Gabriel laughed. "After today, I think you've earned a day or two off, Duncan. Go take a break, decompress, and then meet me in my office on Monday morning. Let's say nine o'clock. We'll talk about your assignments and what new numbers you have for this year. And by then I'll have received your files from HR."

"Monday, then." Duncan shook Gabriel's hand again and the Archangel left, only to be replaced by Basil and Raymond, their faces incredulous.

"Duuude . . . " was all Raymond said, drawing the word out several syllables while staring at Mara.

"I don't bite," she said, but Raymond looked like he didn't believe her.

"I'm sorry I didn't tell you guys earlier about all of this," Duncan said.

"We get it, Duncan," said Basil. "Well, no, we really don't, but you can make it up to us and tell us the whole damn story later, when we go out for a beer and you actually show up!" Duncan and Raymond gasped in surprise when Basil swore, and Mara couldn't resist a soft laugh.

"No, no more ditching either of you," Duncan promised.

Behind Mara, Melchom lumbered up, his jutting tusks menacing and sharp. Basil and Raymond took one look at him and excused themselves, assuring Duncan they'd catch up with him at Bruisers.

"Maybe now you'll wear your flames more? You are pretty, Mara, but you are much prettier with the flames. I always tell you that." Melchom's voice was a deep rumble.

"I'll wear them in Hell more, just for you. No reason to hide them now that the cat's out of the bag."

Melchom, who was a good foot taller than Duncan and probably three times as wide, looked down at the angel and frowned a little.

"Be nice to him, Melchom. He's important to me," Mara warned.

"Harrumph. You. Angel. You will be nice to my Mara or I will squeeze your head until it pops like a melon." Melchom reached out and poked Duncan squarely in the chest with one meaty finger, pushing him back a step despite the angel's best efforts to hold his ground. Melchom didn't say anything else. He just gave Duncan one last stern look and lumbered off to return to his office.

To Mara's dismay, their solitude was short-lived, as Grand Duke Valafar loomed large over both them. His lip was pulled back in a sneer over his skeletal teeth. Mara gave him a disdainful look as her eyes went from his small piggish eyes down to his portly waist and sloppily tucked shirt.

"Have something to say, Valafar?" Mara challenged, quietly gathering some of her power in case the volatile Grand Duke did anything stupid.

"Kemm and Kal were two of my best employees. I won't forget what you did to them, you little bitch," he snarled, spittle foaming on his lips.

"Well, if those two fools were your best, you're kinda screwed, you—"

"No need for name calling." Lucifer appeared on Mara's other side.

"Ah, of course, Daddy's got to fight your battles," Valafar scoffed, making sure his voice was loud enough that the other Grand Dukes who were still there could hear. Furious, Mara bristled, but her father just laughed heartily.

"Oh, she doesn't need me to fight for her, that's for damn sure. If the two of you want to throw down right now, I'll give my permission and I'll stay out of it. Is that what you want, Valafar? To try to take your own pound of flesh? To see how you fare one-on-one against my little girl in front of everyone?

Before you do, you may want to ask Michael how he felt after they tangled. Don't forget, blue flames burn the hottest."

Mara fanned her wings out as her blue flames flared and Valafar hesitated.

"I thought not," Lucifer said, his voice smug with fatherly pride.

"She should be punished—"

Mara's eyes narrowed.

"And she *has been*, or weren't you paying attention a little earlier? I consider the matter over, but if you'd like to continue the conversation privately, I would be happy to do that."

Valafar backed down, but not without a final comment to Mara. "The Devil's daughter and you spread your legs for an angel? Disgusting. If I were your sire, I'd be ashamed." He spit at Duncan.

Mara's fiery aura flared and she slapped Valafar across the face, leaving a red palm print on his cheek. "Watch your mouth," she snapped.

The Grand Duke hissed in shock. To be struck by a lower-ranking devil was embarrassing, and all the other Grand Dukes had seen it. Valafar glowered at her but retreated, and Mara knew he wouldn't soon forget the slap, or his own reluctance to fight her.

"So, you're the angel sleeping with my daughter."

Duncan flinched as Lucifer slowly looked him up and down, assessing him, waiting.

He elected not to dissemble. "I am, and I assure you, she's more than a booty call to me."

The colloquial phrase made Lucifer's mouth quirk into a smile before he turned to look at Mara. "I've watched you.

Your talents are impressive. I've been a hands-off father, and I know you understand why."

"I do. If anyone had figured out who I was, they would have seen a tool to be used against you. I still could be, you know," Mara replied.

Lucifer laughed. "Just as I said about your mother, I dare anyone in either realm to try forcing you to do something you don't want. You know I'm proud of you, don't you?"

Mara smiled but looked away, clearly trying to hide the tears that sprang into her eyes. There was silence among the three for a moment, and then with one fluid motion, Lucifer stepped right up to Duncan and stared him in the eye. Now that the Devil had allowed his inner flames to subside, his expressive eyes were once again dark brown, and Duncan realized that they were the same shape and shade as Mara's. She really did have her father's eyes.

Lucifer said, "I understand that relationships have their rocky moments, believe me. So, if the two of you argue or fight, that's your issue to work out. But let me make something perfectly clear to you, Duncan: if you try to use her, if you do anything to deliberately hurt her—*anything*—I will peel the skin from your body using a spork and pluck every last feather from your wings with my teeth, and even God won't be able to stop me. I just want to make sure that we are crystal clear on that point."

Without waiting for an answer, Lucifer reached out and straightened the collar of Duncan's shirt, and then the King of Hell gave his daughter a kiss on the cheek. "Dinner sometime soon, then. Just the three of us."

"I'll call you," Mara said.

"Excellent. You take care of yourself." He waved over at Astaroth. "Astaroth! It has been a bitch of a day, hasn't it? I think it's time for a couple of drinks, old friend!"

CHAPTER 39

AS SOON AS they were able to escape from the Null Plane, Mara and Duncan retreated to her apartment, where Mara threw herself into his arms. Her heart was pounding as the reality of what had just happened really settled over her.

"I thought Michael was going to destroy you. When he covered you in angel-fire . . . I've never been really terrified before. It's a horrible feeling."

He ran a hand down his hair. "I know. I felt the same way when Lucifer was throwing you around the room. I thought that was only the start. There were plenty of devils who were looking for your blood."

"Nature of the game in Hell. Devils tend to be a hair more cutthroat."

"Will this make your life more complicated?"

Mara thought for a minute. "Yes, but nothing I can't handle. I don't have any reason to hide now. Lucifer's going to have a hard time too. Some of the Grand Dukes are going to be a handful." She paused and sighed. "I'm sorry I didn't tell you about who my parents were, or let you see my wings. I hated feeling like I was keeping secrets from you, but in Hell, secrets are the coin of the realm. If you know someone's secrets, you own them."

"I don't care about that. I'll confess, it was a bit much to process in the moment, but I love you for you, and I don't care who your father is or who your mother was. I am sorry you lost Nuriel so young. I never knew her."

"Thank you." Her voice was shaded with sadness. For a moment, Mara just allowed herself to feel safe and protected in Duncan's arms. He'd said he loved her. Those were words she'd never believed she would ever receive—at least not with sincerity.

"You really love me?"

"I really love you, Mara Dullahan. All of you. Black wings, King of Hell father, Archangel mother. Every last bit." With a finger, Duncan tilted her head up, and Mara allowed herself to melt into him as they kissed.

"I just realized something," she said, nodding toward the living room window. "We don't have to close the curtains ever again if we don't want to."

"Won't everyone over at Bruisers appreciate that?" Duncan laughed.

Hours later, curled up in bed, Mara stared at the ceiling, thinking. She knew Duncan was curious but that he was giving her time for her own thoughts. Finally she rolled to her side and ran a finger down his chest.

"Monday's going to be . . . Damned if I know what Monday's going to be," she said.

"That's about how I feel. I'm looking forward to my meeting with Gabriel. It is such a relief to know I don't have to report to Michael anymore. But I'm a little worried about what extra notes Michael might have put in my HR files."

"If he starts any shit with you, I'll kick his ass."

Duncan laughed and then kissed her. "If I need you to rough him up, I'll let you know."

"Are you going to see Basil and Raymond after work?"

"Basil wants to. He's texted at least a dozen times about it."

"You have to go. They're your friends, and you promised them. We can catch up later. Plus, I have no idea how late I'll be. Monday is going to be interesting for both of us."

Duncan pulled Mara closer. "What are you going to do when you go in?"

She sighed. "Get back to the grind. I have a reputation to build back up, and 625 quarters of being number one until I officially break Baliel's record. I'm going in wings out and guns blazing. If anyone wants to start something, good luck to them."

"I'd expect no less. Are you hungry?" Duncan asked.

"Famished."

They ordered an extra-large pizza and opened a bottle of wine while they waited. Neither said much as they thought through everything that had happened, but it wasn't an uncomfortable silence. Mara tucked her legs up under her and swirled the wine in her glass before finishing it. Duncan poured another half glass for her.

"What would you have done if God had said something different?" Duncan asked.

"Probably gotten my inner bitch involved."

"Oh, would you? With God?" Duncan poured himself some more wine.

"I didn't say I would have won." She frowned. "I hated having our fate in someone else's hands—I don't like feeling helpless."

"Neither do I," Duncan admitted.

"What would you have done?"

"I probably wouldn't have started with my inner bitch," he said with a laugh. "But I wouldn't have been too proud to beg."

Mara tilted her head. "You would have begged?"

Duncan reached out and took her hand. "If it meant keeping you safe, and being with you, there's nothing I wouldn't do. I would have no problem throwing myself at God's feet and begging. And if that didn't work . . ."

"Inner bitch?" she asked.

"Inner bitch." Duncan clinked his glass against hers.

About ten minutes later the pizza arrived and they devoured it in no time, along with a second bottle of wine. After that, Mara stood. She started to unbutton her shirt and then reached out a hand to Duncan.

"Again?"

"Again," she said, her smile seductive. "And again, and again, and again. Until you can't stand up."

Duncan let her lead him down the hall and into the bedroom, where they spent the rest of the night in each other's arms—not falling asleep until sunrise.

CHAPTER 40

ON MONDAY, DUNCAN made sure he was early for his meeting with Gabriel. He wore his best suit and shoes and his favorite tie, the one Mara had given him at Christmas. The reception area outside the office was open and inviting, with modern furniture and brushed aluminum details. An expansive set of windows let light in, and there were so many plants, it nearly felt like Eden. He took a seat to wait and the Archangel strolled in a few minutes later, a large coffee in hand. He was wearing jeans and a button-down chambray shirt with the sleeves rolled up.

"Good morning, Duncan. Come on in."

They went into his office and the Archangel gestured for him to sit at the small round table in the corner. After Duncan sat, his new boss sat in the other chair.

"Do you want some coffee? I can have someone get you a cup."

"No, thank you. Already had two this morning."

"Fair enough." Gabriel sat easily in the chair and ran a hand through his hair as he looked at a folder in his free hand. His light brown hair had blond highlights.

He'd be right at home on the beach in Santa Monica, thought Duncan.

Gabriel put the folder down. "I just got your file from Michael's assistant this morning. You'd think it was one of the original Ten Commandment tablets, with all the fuss it took to get it. But before we get into this, there's one thing you need to do if you're going to work for me."

"What's that?" asked Duncan.

"While I love the tie, you totally need to lose the suit, dude."

Duncan laughed, disarmed by the Archangel's use of the word "dude." "Really? No suits?" he asked.

"Really. Michael loves order and I appreciate that about him, but I find that flexibility drives results that are just as good, if not better. So, as long as you make your numbers, you can show up here in shorts and a tank top for all I care. Of course, when you're working with clients, I expect you're smart enough to know how to dress for any given situation, but for daily business in the Heavenly Plane? The suit's way too formal."

"I can live with that." Inside, Duncan was doing backflips.

Gabriel perused Duncan's file briefly. "Well, all in all you have an excellent record, but I see you consistently get flagged for cursing. And it seems that Michael has held that against you for quite a while, using it as a barrier to block promotions or transfers. Oh, and there's a lovely handwritten note in red ink about insubordination and your predilection for fornicating with devils. Your thoughts?"

"Both are accurate. To be honest, I'm planning to continue fornicating with one particular devil for the foreseeable future. Second, I do have a bad habit of swearing. But I'll do my best to improve in that area."

Gabriel smiled. "I couldn't care less how many times you use the word 'fuck,' or any other curse words, for that matter. There are worse habits you could have. And the insubordination?"

Duncan didn't have an immediate answer and looked at the floor.

"Don't sweat it. You weren't the right fit for Michael's management style. I'm not surprised you rebelled, given you were stuck in an untenable situation. I would have. A word of advice, though: In the future, avoid telling an Archangel to 'blow you,' okay? Generally, that does fall into the career-limiting-move category."

"Fair enough."

"How do you feel about Michael stonewalling your promotion path?"

"I hadn't really thought that much about it," Duncan said. "I figured my demerits always weighed me down. But now that I know? Well . . ." He paused for a minute and thought. "It kinda pisses me off, to be honest, but that's in the past. I'm not going to waste time dwelling on it. And being part of the rank and file has its perks."

"Such as?"

"I wouldn't have met Mara if I'd been riding a desk up here."

Gabriel smiled a surfer-boy smile. "That is very true, and your relationship with her makes you unique among angels. I see a bright future for you, Duncan DeMarco, and I'm very glad you're in my division now. I want you to continue operating in the Mortal Plane, and I've adjusted your quota of saves for this year to reflect my expectations instead of Michael's ridiculous ones. Even Michael couldn't do the number of saves he had you tasked with for the new year."

Duncan looked over the paper quickly: his quota was half what he would have gotten from Michael, and there was a generous bonus for beating expectations for the year.

"I'll get started right away," Duncan said. "Thank you for taking me on under your division. I appreciate the opportunity, Gabriel. I won't disappoint you."

"I know you won't." The Archangel stood up and held out a hand. Duncan stood and shook it.

In the morning, after Duncan had left for his meeting with Gabriel, Mara flared her wings and opened a door to Hell. She marched into the office, wings free and blue flames dancing around her eyes. Devils popped up from behind cube walls to gawk at her as she walked by, but not one tried to stop her, and not a single insult was heard. Mara made sure to cut through Accounting on her way to her office.

"Good morning, Loretta."

"G-G-Good m-morning," Loretta squeaked.

"I have some paperwork due for you, I think?"

"N-no, no rush," shrilled Loretta. "Whenever you have time."

A few more twists and turns through halls brought Mara to her department. Coming around a corner, she ran into Grand Duke Paimon. Her greenish-brown skin glistened under the artificial light.

"Mara. That whole thing with Kal the other day? Well done. Very well done," she said.

"Thank you." Mara was surprised. Up until now, Paimon had never really paid much attention to her. *But I guess things change when they find out you're the boss's daughter*, she thought.

"The only thing that would have made it better would have been Valafar pissing himself." Paimon let out a roaring laugh. "Next time, maybe!"

"Maybe," Mara said, not wanting to hint at any kind of interest in a confrontation with Valafar. At least not yet.

She sat down at her desk—thanks to Kal's interference, she was behind on several collections and needed to get cracking on those, plus there was a whole new quarterly quota looming. Mara was nearly done with the paperwork and had set her schedule for the next two weeks when a knock at her door startled her.

"Frankie?"

"Shhhh!" he hushed her.

She indulged him. "And why am I hushing?"

"I wanted to let you know that Valafar's pretty pissed at you. About all of it, but especially about slapping him in front of everyone. The other Grand Dukes have been riding his ass over that."

"And you're telling me this why?"

The blond pockmarked devil glanced around. "You gave me that guy, Donald, a bunch of months back. The guy who wanted the promotion. After closing him, I kinda went on a hot streak. I beat my goal. Hadn't done that in a couple of quarters and Valafar was up my ass."

That was an image in her mind Mara didn't need. "That can't be fun."

Frankie shook his head. "Well, you did me a solid, so I wanted to return the favor. Like I said, Valafar's still hacked off about you slapping him. He's been kinda talking big about payback. Wanted you to know he was gunning for you."

Mara knew that already, but did appreciate Frankie coming to her. "Good to know. Thanks, Frankie."

"Sure thing. Well, gotta go . . ."

Mara stopped him before he could leave. "Hang on a sec, Frankie. I have a proposition for you."

"You want to make a deal with me?" He sounded baffled.

"Yeah. You work for Valafar, so what do you say: Keep an eye on him for me? When he's ready to come at me, give me a heads-up?" There was no harm in having an early warning system in place.

"In return for what?"

"I'll give you one soul to close per month. A quality mark, not just some junkie stealing his dad's wristwatch to barter. Our deal will go until Valafar makes his move, and I put him in his place once and for all."

Frankie's eyes lit up, but he hesitated.

"What's going on in that little brain of yours?" Mara asked.

"Getting a mark is great, and I appreciate that, but I take on all the risk here. If Valafar finds out, he'll shred me into so many tiny pieces, it will take me a thousand years to piece myself back together."

"Valid point," Mara acquiesced.

"Coach me," Frankie said.

"What?" Mara was surprised. That was the last thing she'd expected him to say.

"I don't want to rely on handouts, Mara. I need to be better at closing deals. The courses they offer in the training department won't teach me shit. But I can learn from you."

"All right," she said slowly. "I can work with that."

"Then I'm in," Frankie said in a gleeful whisper.

"If you tell Valafar—or anyone—about this, our deal is void, and they will never find you. Do you understand? *Never*."

"Agreed!"

"Let's make this official," Mara said. *Sorry, Duncan*, she thought, *but this is business.* She pulled Frankie's face down and kissed him. When she let go, the skinny blond devil staggered back, a stupid grin on his face.

CHAPTER 41

AFTER WORK, MARA was in her usual seat at Bruisers. When they'd left her apartment in the morning, Mara and Duncan had agreed to meet there, although Duncan warned her that he might have a late meeting. She arrived a smidge after five and said hello to Joanie, who was waiting tables. Joe waved when he turned around, and after he finished mixing two margaritas, he came over.

"Where have you been?" he asked. "Big trip?"

"Sort of. A big shake-up at work, so things have been a little crazy."

"They didn't lay you off, did they? Sons of bitches." Joe's face darkened.

"No, I still have my job. I've never told you this—I keep it on the down-low—but one of the big bosses is my dad. I don't talk about it much because I don't want people treating me differently, but I can guarantee you, they won't lay me off. Not unless I burn the whole office down or something like that."

"It can be tough being the boss's kid. Joe Junior used to bus tables here when he was in high school and always said I busted his chops way harder than anyone else."

He brought Mara her beer and she spent a minute looking around the bar. There were two devils at one of the dining tables, and they gawked until she stared right at them and raised her eyebrows. Then they suddenly became very interested in their menus. There was also a cluster of four angels on the opposite end of the bar. They didn't seem to be paying much attention, but Mara did notice a covert glance or two. There was, however, one friendly face. When she looked across to where Duncan usually sat, Basil was there, and he raised his glass of wine in her direction. She smiled and returned the gesture.

At a quarter past five, the front door opened and Duncan came in. He walked directly to her without any hesitation and gave Mara a kiss in front of the entire bar. With his lips pressed on hers, Mara felt like she was going to simply slide out of the chair.

"Hey, baby. Have a good day?"

"After that kiss, I don't remember what happened today and I don't care," she said.

"Well," said Joe. "Look at the two of you. Not trying to keep everything so hush-hush anymore?"

Mara blushed. "No. Some of the crazy changes I mentioned the other day ended up working in our favor. We have to be careful not to overlap our business interests, but as long as we stick to that rule, no one can object to our relationship."

"Excellent. You shouldn't have to hide it when you're in love with someone," Joe said.

They both looked at him.

"What? I'm not blind, you know. I've been watching the two of you make doe eyes at each other since, what? August? September? Please. Give me a little credit."

"I do not make doe eyes," Duncan said, his own cheeks coloring.

"Oh, but you do, son. Great big ones when you look at her." He hooked a thumb at Mara.

"Well, if you're so observant, why is it that you've never noticed Joanie making doe-eyes at you?" Mara asked, her tone a touch self-satisfied.

"What? Bah. No way. She wouldn't be interested in an old fart like me." Nevertheless, Joe glanced toward Joanie, only to catch her looking at him. She glanced away, blushing hotly.

Mara rested her chin in her hand as she leaned on the bar. "Go ahead, tell me I'm wrong."

Joe blustered for a moment, looked over at Joanie again, and headed back to the kitchen, muttering to himself.

Duncan and Mara moved from the bar to one of the dinner tables. They laughed and joked over their salads and meals, and prattled about their day. They both knew that, at some point, both Michael and Valafar would try to make them miserable, but that was a situation to be dealt with later. For tonight, they simply enjoyed not having to hide from the world, and when they left the bar to go back to Mara's apartment, they held hands as they walked.

EPILOGUE

DUNCAN AND YEHUDIAH waited quietly at the back of the small living room, their presence masked for the moment while the old man in the recliner fell asleep watching a rerun of *Jaws*, his favorite movie. Other than the volume from the TV, the house was quiet. His wife and grown daughter were at the store. Duncan moved a little deeper into the room and kept himself hidden from human eyes, just in case the old man woke up.

Joe Louis Jones had lost weight, and a lot of his hair. Duncan hadn't seen Joe in more than twenty-five years, and even though he knew time had passed, it was still shocking to see Joe as an elderly man—especially when Duncan didn't look like he'd aged a day. Because he and Mara didn't age the same way mortals did, they had lived in the apartment across from Bruisers for several years but then moved, claiming a work transfer.

Before that, however, they had the pleasure of seeing Joe and Joanie get married, and Joe Junior start to work for his father, with the goal of taking over Bruisers when Joe finally retired. When the moving van was packed, and Mara and Duncan were ready to leave for the West Coast, Joe had hugged Mara and cried—even though he tried to hide it. And he reminded them that they were welcome anytime at his bar because they were family.

Duncan quietly moved back to Yehudiah's side. "Thank you for this," he said.

"You're welcome. But I cannot delay the inevitable tonight."

Before he finished the thought, there was a ripple in the air, and Mara materialized next to Duncan.

"You promise she isn't here to poach Joe's soul? No deals we don't know about?" Yehudiah asked Duncan.

"I'm right here," Mara said indignantly.

"Then answer my question," the Angel of Death said.

"I'm not here to poach," she replied, rolling her eyes. "We have this conversation every single time. Of all the devils you've dealt with over the eons, Yehudiah, I'll admit I've been a pain in your ass, but have I ever tried to poach a soul you're rightfully entitled to collect?"

"No," Yehudiah admitted, "but you frequently make the transition difficult."

"Okay, guilty as charged," Mara said. "I promise—no shenanigans tonight."

He held up a hand. "Be quiet. It's time."

A strange silence settled over the room and the volume on the TV faded into the background. Mara felt like she was holding her breath. In his recliner, Joe sighed once and his soul separated from his body. It floated for a minute, fuzzy and unformed, and then became more solid. He looked around, confused, and then he noticed Yehudiah.

"Who are you? Why are you in my house?" Joe barked.

"It's your time to go, Joe. I am Yehudiah, and I've come to take your soul to Heaven." The Angel of Death's voice was soothing and deep, and Joe visibly relaxed as his soul instinctively knew the angel was telling him the truth.

"I died?"

"Yes. Your heart was old. It was tired," Yehudiah answered.

Joe turned and looked at himself in the chair. "I look like I'm napping. I'm really dead?"

"You are, and I'm sorry, but it does happen to everyone. You've had a very long life, Joe Louis Jones. But before we go, some friends want to see you."

"Friends?" Joe was clearly puzzled.

As Yehudiah spoke, Duncan and Mara stepped out of their concealment and watched Joe's eyes go wide. Duncan's large white wings were visible, and he had the glow of angelic power around him. Mara elected to stay in her human form. She didn't want to overwhelm Joe's soul.

"Duncan! Why are you here? It's been what, twenty-five, thirty years? You haven't aged a day! Wait, you have wings. Damn, this is one crazy dream."

"You're not dreaming, Joe," Duncan said. "I'm an angel."

"An angel? I'll be damned. Imagine that. An angel used to drink in my bar," said Joe with a shake of his head. Then he asked Yehudiah, "Shouldn't I be more frightened by all of this?"

"If you were still in your mortal form, you would probably be, as they say, 'freaking out,'" answered Yehudiah. "But your soul has an intuitive understanding of the afterlife, so all of these things are not so shocking to you now."

"Because I'm dead. I see." Joe bobbed his head and his gaze went past Duncan's shoulder. His smile brightened. "And Mara! I always loved seeing you at the bar . . . Wait . . ." He frowned. "Are you dead? You're too young to be dead."

"It is so good to see you, Joe. No, I'm not dead." She gave him an affectionate smile.

"Then you're an angel too?"

"Not exactly."

Joe was quiet for a moment, his eyebrows scrunching as he thought through the possibilities before he finally said, "You're a . . . devil?"

"I am." Mara allowed her wings to materialize and some blue flame licked around her eyes, and Joe stared at her, mesmerized.

"But you and Duncan . . . you . . . how?"

"A long and complicated story," Mara said, taking Duncan's hand. "But thanks to you and your bar, I met Duncan and my existence changed forever. Together we've turned Heaven and Hell on its collective ear."

A smile crossed Joe's face. "You're still together?"

"We are. A few epic fights along the way, but you work through things for love," Duncan said.

"I knew the two of you were a good match." Joe nodded with satisfaction.

Glancing at the door, Yehudiah interrupted, "We need to go."

Duncan and Mara knew that Joe's daughter, Rebecca, and Joanie, were on their way home from the store. They didn't want Joe's spirit to be there when the two women discovered that he'd passed on while they were out. When souls witnessed the grief of families, it often made the transition much harder.

"Will Joanie be okay?" asked Joe.

"She will. Your children are fond of her and they'll make sure she's looked after for the rest of her days," Yehudiah told him.

"And my kids?" There was a quaver in Joe's voice as he began to realize he was really leaving them all for good.

"Eddie, Rebecca, and Joe Junior, and your grandchildren and great-grandchild will all be fine as well," reassured Yehudiah.

"Mara and I are fond of your family," Duncan said. "Let's just say that Mara 'encourages' other devils to leave them be, and I look in on them when they have serious moments of doubt. I'll be with them through your funeral and after, so I promise they won't be alone."

Joe looked surprised. "You'd do that for me?"

"Of course we would. You're our friend, Joe. It is the least we can do for you," Mara told him.

"Hmph. Friends with an angel and a devil. No one would ever believe it. Okay, then, I guess I'm ready." Joe took a step toward Yehudiah and stopped. "Wait! Will I see my Donna when I get to Heaven?"

"You will. She's waiting to see you," Yehudiah said.

Concern and worry flooded Joe's eyes. "How do I explain Joanie to her?"

Mara took both of Joe's gnarled hands in hers, raised them up, and gave the knuckles an affectionate kiss. "Joe, you'll be fine. Donna won't mind."

"Donna won't—? If that's what you think, then you don't know my Donna," Joe howled.

"She's known about Joanie from the start, and she's glad you found someone to make you happy. Donna never wanted you to be lonely," Duncan said. "And someday she'll welcome Joanie as well. There is no petty jealousy in Heaven, only love and understanding."

"She's not gonna kick my ass, then?"

"Language," Yehudiah chided.

"No, she's not going to be upset with you," Duncan repeated. "I promise."

Joe's shoulders slumped with relief.

"Come, Joe Louis Jones," said Yehudiah, spreading his wings and letting a soft golden light imbue the room. "Forever awaits you."

As he allowed Yehudiah to enfold him with his wings, Joe looked back at Mara and Duncan with a twinkle in his eye.

"You kids be good," he said, "but not *too* good."

AUTHOR'S NOTE

"If your path demands you walk through Hell,
walk as if you own the place."
—Unknown

Writing is hard. But it is so very worth it. So, if you are thinking about writing a book, my advice is do it. Start writing. It doesn't matter if your first draft is good or not. A first draft's only job is to exist—in fact, I usually call my rough drafts my "piñata" drafts. It may look a bit odd, but if I hit it long enough and hard enough with a big stick, then something really cool will come out. There will be days when you'll be frustrated, and days when you'll doubt yourself and what you're doing. But if you have a story inside you, don't give up on it.

And remember, as much as writing can be a solitary endeavor—just you and a blank page—it is also a team sport. The editor who makes you look long and hard at what you've done with the goal of turning "good" into "great." Fellow authors who encourage and give you advice. Friends and family who offer that shoulder when you feel like you're never going to get anything done. The artist who creates the map of your world, the cover of your book, or the sketches of your characters. So, when you feel alone, don't forget that you're not, not really.

I wouldn't have been able to write this book without the support of so many different people, and I want to take a moment to thank the people who helped make *The Devil Inside* a reality.

First: all of you, the fabulous readers who are still reading this, even though the story is over. THANK YOU. Without readers, a book isn't much more than symbols on a page, and I especially need to thank the two hundred and fifty readers who supported *The Devil Inside* long before they were able to read it (and I really had no idea it would take quite this long!). If you hadn't taken a chance during my campaign with Inkshares, I might not be where I am now—especially since so many of you were willing to support a second book even when *Shadow King* hadn't been released yet. So, I am eternally grateful that you were willing to take that leap of faith.

Second: my husband, Jeff—for the constant support, and for all the times I've been so engrossed in my reading or writing that I haven't realized he's three sentences into a conversation with me and I have no idea what he said. I love you and thank you for being patient in those moments.

Thank you to the many wonderful authors who I've met through the Inkshares platform and through Writing Bloc. The support and friendship you've offered is an amazing and wonderful thing. I wish all of you the very best in your writing adventures. I considered naming everyone and then decided against it because I'm too terrified that I'll leave someone important out. So, please forgive me for not naming names—you know who you are, and you are all rock stars!

However, I do have one exception to the above rule, as I do need to call out my friend Mike X. Welch, who seemed determined to keep my spirits up and see me cross the finish line with my Quill funding—even if he had to drag me over that line all by himself. I am not entirely certain what I did to attract his attention while we were both working on getting our books funded on Inkshares, but I'm glad I did.

To my friend Joe, who wore #45 on our high school football team, and who will smile (I hope) whenever he sees the references to 45 Joyal Street in this book. I'm not sure he took me seriously when I "threatened" to put him in my book. Well, Joe, now you can really tell everyone that you had a character named after you in a novel.

To John Robin and Lizette Clark from Story Perfect Editing Services: I am so appreciative of your insights. I think the advice you provided has really put the polishing touches on this story. And I would be remiss without a huge thank-you to Charlene Maguire from Shapeshifter Studios and Kiss the Sun Creative, the very talented artist behind my cover.

And of course, to the team at Inkshares, especially Avalon and Adam. It has been a wild ride and I am grateful for the opportunity.

Thank you all so very, very much—I will always be grateful and appreciative of your support, friendship, and enthusiasm. I hope you enjoyed *The Devil Inside*! So, until the next time: have many excellent adventures within the pages of your favorite books.

GRAND PATRONS

Jeff DePiero
Harry Hamilton
Kathryn Hamilton
Joel Mason
Charlotte McEnroe
Michelle Morone
Mike X. Welch
Ravin Warnakulasuriya

INKSHARES

INKSHARES is a reader-driven publisher and producer based in Oakland, California. Our books are selected not by a group of editors, but by readers worldwide.

While we've published books by established writers like *Big Fish* author Daniel Wallace and *Star Wars: Rogue One* scribe Gary Whitta, our aim remains surfacing and developing the new author voices of tomorrow.

Previously unknown Inkshares authors have received starred reviews and been featured in the *New York Times*. Their books are on the front tables of Barnes & Noble and hundreds of independents nationwide, and many have been licensed by publishers in other major markets. They are also being adapted by Oscar-winning screenwriters at the biggest studios and networks.

Interested in making your own story a reality? Visit Inkshares.com to start your own project or find other great books.

CPSIA information can be obtained
at www.ICGtesting.com
Printed in the USA
FSHW012122120421
80392FS